The Thuggery Affair

The Thuggery Affair

by

ANTONIA FOREST

FABER
FANFARES

First published in 1965
by Faber and Faber Limited
3 Queen Square, London WC1
First published in Fanfares edition 1979
Printed in Great Britain by
Jarrold and Sons Ltd, Norwich
All rights reserved

British Library Cataloguing in Publication Data
Forest, Antonia
The Thuggery affair.—(Faber fanfares)
I. Title
823'.9'1J   *PZ7.F7585*
ISBN 0–571–11330–3

To
ANTHONY C.
who asked for it
(in more ways than one)

Author's Acknowledgments

The lines and verses quoted in the last three chapters of this book are taken from the untitled poem beginning "I met a man this morning" which is attributed (though without absolute certainty) by the late Monsignor R. A. Knox to Patrick Shaw-Stewart who was killed in France in 1918. Since it has not been possible to trace the late Mr. Shaw-Stewart's executors, I very much regret that I have been unable to obtain the usual permission to make use of these lines and cannot, therefore, offer the customary acknowledgements.

I can however thank J. and E. H. for allowing me to use their car registration number at a critical moment in the story.

Only For Those Who, Like The Author, Prefer Accuracy If They Can Get It

The first story about the Marlows was written in 1947—that is to say (at the moment of writing) seventeen years ago. A good deal has happened since then; for instance, almost everyone who reads this book has been born between then and now; we have a Queen instead of a King; instead of merely being the wilder fancies of science fiction, rockets do now land on the moon. On the other hand, the fictional time which has passed in the six books written about the Marlow family is just on eighteen months. Since it would be a bore, to me as well as everyone else, to keep strictly to period time (who cares that clothes and sweets still had to be rationed in 1947?) each story has been given a background more or less consistent with the year in which it was written. But this creates its own difficulties. In 1947, naval cadets did still enter The Royal Naval College, Dartmouth, at the age of 13. Since then, after various changes of mind, Their Lordships of the Admiralty have settled for 18. Short of expelling Peter Marlow from Dartmouth (something which is unlikely to happen) the only other way of coping with this seems to be to say that the fictional time in which the Marlows exist is in the period called Since The War; and that anything true during that time can be true and happening "now" in the books I write about them.

A.F.

13th September 1964

Contents

CHAPTER ONE

"There's a Hole in your Boatie"

The gusty air, sodden with midnight rain, still smelt of darkness and time out of mind, though the last of the dark had dwindled into daybreak and the reflections of the pollarded willows wavered across the snail-grey surface of the river. Lawrie Marlow sploshed her gumboots gently in the inch or so of water in the bottom of the canoe, wondered a little was it safe for it to be there and decided not to mention it.

She was positively enjoying the excursion, which surprised her, for in the ordinary way her twin Nicola would have occupied her seat while she herself stayed snug-a-bed; moreover, for the past fortnight she had been complaining bitterly that half-term without Nicola, who had gone joyfully off from school the previous afternoon to spend the week-end in London with her friend Miranda West, would be utter scrudge (the Lower Fourth's Word of the Month for all disasters from leaking ball-points to expulsions); and though Nicola had offered such consolation as she could, pointing out that it wasn't as if *all* their half of the family would be away—Lawrie would have Peter—"No, I shan't. Peter'll have Patrick"—*and* Ginty—"Yes, I s'pose so. But that's not the *same*"—it was clear she meant to go however badly Lawrie felt about it, for she'd remarked eventually that if Lawrie had been invited to spend half-term with *her* best friend T. Keith *she* wouldn't have refused simply on Nicola's account: to which Lawrie had replied, "No, I know. But that's diff'rent." And then, to crown all, their grandmother, who lived in Paris, had invited Ginty

to fly over, all expenses paid. Not even Lawrie could suppose
Ginty would be allowed, let alone want, to refuse an invitation
as fab, glam and above all—since their grandmother was well
known to prefer her grandsons to her granddaughters—sur-
prising as that: so that they were all slightly puzzled that Ginty
should have moments of talking as if the whole thing were a
foul bore and she couldn't care less. (Naturally, she told no one
she was suffering from a Premonition that the plane was going
to crash on take-off, have engine failure over the Channel and
burst into flames on landing; or that she had been thinking of
the week-end in terms of the friendship (she half-thought it
more than that) which had developed between herself and
Patrick Merrick during the Christmas holidays. But in fact, the
moment she arrived at London Airport, her Premonition de-
parted, and the week-end itself was such a box of delights that
Patrick lost his place in her thoughts for at least ten days.)

Peter Marlow, sitting well forward to help the trim of his
canoe, dipped his paddle to keep the prow pointing downstream. The lock gates which barred their way were beginning
to open in a succession of reluctant jerks and he was concen-
trating on taking his craft neatly through the exact centre. This
he achieved. They shot through into the chamber and Lawrie,
encouraging a touch of the gruesomes, watched over her
shoulder as the gates closed again behind them. Water began
to trickle through the sluices, and the chamber walls, their
newly uncovered growths of water weed dripping fast and
heavily, rose slowly higher and higher.

"Can't you hurry it?" shouted Peter to his friend Patrick,
who was working the windlasses by the lock gates, anxiously
attended by his spaniel Bucket.

"Niet. The sluices must be blocked. Hardly anyone uses this
stretch nowadays. They don't even have a lock-keeper here in
summer now."

"Disgraceful, hrrmp," said Lawrie, in the manner of any
comic admiral of film, radio or television. "Fellers should have
known I'd be passin' through, what? Want to keep me here for
ever, hrrmp? Mut'ny, that's the ticket, mut'ny."

"There's a Hole in your Boatie"

Patrick sat down, grasping Bucket's collar in case the spaniel took it into his beautiful but self-willed head to canter off on the track of some especially entrancing scent. His long legs dangling over the wall, he said "All River Boards to be hung in chains from the yard-arm suit you?" The chamber's echo hollowed his words, and he and Peter began to hoot experimentally.

Lawrie hooted once or twice too and then gave up, hugging her knees and gazing interestedly about her. "And what will I think about?" thought she, dipping a hand nonchalantly over the side and withdrawing it hastily from the cold inhospitable water, as if thoughts, like horses, could be put through their paces and stabled again at will: and, acting on this principle, trotted out a jet black steed who had his ears back and showed the whites of his eyes: suppose then, the gates before them wouldn't open, would they be bottled up in this derelict lock for ever? *No*, thought Lawrie, all firm common sense, *we would not*. For not only could Patrick, free on the bank, go for help, but she had just seen the staples driven into both walls by which they could climb out. So that was all right. But there were other possibilities: Peter might drop his paddle and in reaching for it overturn the canoe: and then, held fast in mud and weed, they would drown—or no: Peter could do the falling in: *she* would dive instantly to his rescue while Patrick rushed for help. . . . Lawrie's hand went back into the water and flipped to and fro as she composed a front page story for the *Colebridge and District Mail*.

BOATING TRAGEDY IN HOGGART'S LOCK
THREE DEAD IN RIVER DRAMA

Tragedy struck today in Hoggart's Lock. The bodies of Lawrence Marlow (13) and Peter Marlow (14) were recovered from the weeds by frogmen after the discovery of an upturned canoe raised the alarm. It was evident that Lawrence (known to her family and many friends as Lawrie) had met her death in a heroic attempt to save her brother's life after their home-made canoe had overturned. Less than a mile away, the body of Patrick Merrick (15) was found in the field where Mr. Harry Cartwright's prize bull Mayfield Thunderer is at large.

"There's a Hole in your Boatie"

It is thought—Lawrie paused. If Patrick and Peter died too, it wouldn't be half so sad about *her*: besides, dying *not* saving someone was a bit wasteful: so scrub those bits and have Peter be rescued because she'd held him up just long enough, and the bull chase Patrick up a tree he could shout from. Satisfied, she resumed *Lawrie and Peter are the youngest daughter and son of Captain and Mrs. Geoffrey Marlow, D.S.O., R.N. of Trennels Old Farm, Westbridge, and Patrick is the only son of Mr. and Mrs. Anthony Merrick, M.P. of Mariot Chase, Westbridge. Peter Marlow, who is at the Royal Naval College, Dartmouth, is following in the footsteps of his father and elder brother Giles. For Lawrie an even more brilliant future had been predicted. All who have seen her in the Kingscote School plays are convinced that Lawrie had it in her to rival the greatest actresses of the past. When the news reached Captain Marlow on board his cruiser he told our reporter: "My daughter's death was in the best traditions of the Service. I am proud of her." Mrs. Marlow, mother of eight, said with tears in her eyes: "I am prostrated with grief. Lawrie was my favourite child—"*

At this beautifully melancholy thought her own eyes filled with tears; and it then occurred to her, too late, that canoes, unlike beds, lack blankets under which one can sob, luxuriously and unheard, till one falls asleep. So it was fortunate that at this moment she was overtaken by an enormous sneeze needing a handkerchief. Her brother jumped violently and nearly dropped his paddle.

"*Binks* look *out!*"

"'S all right. Panic over," he said, recovering both balance and paddle. "No need for gallant rescues." And added, after a moment, "What's so funny?" But since the joke was plainly not for sharing, Lawrie could only snort and gulp and say she didn't know, he just was.

Almost unnoticed, the water level was now dropping steadily as if the sluices had cleared themselves; presently they guggled in a satisfied way, the sound of trickling water stopped, and Patrick and Bucket got up and began to struggle with the windlass which controlled the second pair of gates. For some moments nothing happened and then, just as Peter was deciding he'd better climb out and give a hand, a vertical band of light appeared directly ahead and widened in rapid jerks: so he drove the canoe through to the open river at great speed instead and drew in to the bank. Patrick closed the gates, scrambled down the bank accompanied by Bucket in a great flurry of paws and ears and sat down in front of Lawrie, Bucket crowding in beside him. The two boys eased the canoe away from the bank and paddled on downstream.

Lawrie sploshed her gumboots again, wondered about it and decided after all not to say nonchalantly *I say—my feet are getting wet* because someone would be sure to tell her not to fuss. All the same, she couldn't help glancing uneasily from the water in the canoe to the water in the river where it belonged: quick, solid-looking stuff, much too nearly level with the gunwale: if she let herself, she'd be thinking in a minute how flimsy the sides of the canoe were. Even Bucket, fore feet planted on the gunwale, back pressed against Patrick's side, seemed unhappy: half-consoled, half-alarmed, wholly deceived by Bucket's whines and shivers at the sight of a water-rat, she went on saying nothing until it suddenly occurred to her that there was another way: she prodded Patrick gently in the middle of his back and, when he looked round, went into an elaborate, comic pantomime of rising water, boat sinking, swim for the shore boys—

Patrick said loudly and instantly "The Titanic's going down! Lifeboats away! Every man for himself! Abandon ship!"

"Not me," said Peter. "It looks much too cold and dangerous. I shall go down with my ship. What's happening, anyway?"

"We're knee-deep back here, that's what. Have we anything we can bail with?"

"Search me," said Peter, determinedly cheerful though inwardly crestfallen that the canoe, constructed last holidays by Patrick and himself according to his own infallible specifications, should do this to him. "Yes, of course we have. Lawrie's gumboots."

"Why mine? *Honestly!*"

"Why not? They're watertight, aren't they?"

"There's a Hole in your Boatie"

Lawrie had two thoughts: one, which made her giggle, was how completely mad it sounded to be using gumboots which ought to keep water out to put water in—when she told about it back at school, she would say *and the water was absolutely gushing in and we all had to take off our gumboots and bail like mad*; the other, which stayed so far down in her mind that she could hardly be said to be thinking it at all was that if they *should* sink, it would undoubtedly be better to be minus gumboots and this way hers would be off without shame or panic; just as it might be as well to discover that her arms were being hampered and so get herself out of Giles's antique mackintosh, a garment she and Nicola held in common and which, with her own jeans and a pullover borrowed from Peter had seemed today's proper costume. So, careful not to rock the canoe, she tugged her boots off and began to bail two-handed. As she did so Patrick began to sing his own river-shanty version of "Georgie and his Dinah".

"*There's a hole in your boatie, dear Peter, dear Peter,*
There's a hole in your boatie, dear Peter,
A hole."

Peter drove his paddle into the water and snorted, a strangled noise, half-exasperation, half-laughter.

"*Then plug it, dear Patrick, dear Patrick, dear Patrick,*
Then plug it, dear Patrick, dear Patrick,
Plug it."

"*But how shall we plug it, dear Peter, dear Peter,*" sang Patrick and Lawrie in chorus. "*But how shall we plug it, dear Peter, with what?*"

"*Put a sock in it, dear Patrick, dear Patrick, dear Patrick, Put a sock in it—*"

This solution, both practical and punning, made first Peter and then the others laugh so that paddling and bailing ceased and the canoe turned gradually broadside to the stream. As it floated sluggishly on, the banks grew steeper, the river narrowed and quickened: the roots of a sapling blown down in the winter gales, its branches held fast on the river bed, lifted above the surface—

"There's a Hole in your Boatie"

Lawrie made a loud and frantic noise of warning.

There was a moment of controlled panic. The paddles clawed at the water, the canoe hesitated, shuddered and came heavily round. Just beyond the swirl of water, the tree roots menaced like the Rackham illustration in Lawrie's copy of *The Wind in the Willows*—

"Gosh," breathed Lawrie, gazing back at it.

"You may well say Gosh. That was nearly us finding a watery grave," said Patrick solemnly.

Lawrie eyed his back. She said uncertainly "You're joking."

"Wot, me? Never. If you hadn't yelled we'd all have been bobbing around crowned with water weed."

"We could have swum," said Lawrie, determined not to let Patrick tease her into being scared-after-the-event, which was something she could manage quite well for herself.

"*You* might. But what would have become of me?"

"*You* can swim! *You* swim better than Peter!"

"Is that so?" said her brother indignantly. "And where d'you get *that* notion from?"

"Last summer," said Lawrie. "The regatta."

"The only thing we did in that, me against Patrick, was the diving, and if you'll excuse my calling your attention to it—"

"He won," said Patrick.

"Yes, well—"

"Yes, well, and if you don't start bailing again, we'll all be swimming for it any minute now," said her brother briskly.

"Wow-oo," said Lawrie and began hurriedly to scoop water over the side. Above the splashing noises she was making she heard Patrick say "No offence meant and none taken *natch*—but d'you think maybe we didn't put the old tub together quite right? Or have we just sprung a leak?"

"Neither," said Peter, observing with some relief that the banks were dwindling again and the river becoming broader and slower as it neared the sea. "Much more likely three are two too many for her. Sorry, but you and Lawrie will have to walk home."

"*Walk?* Us? Why?"

"Because if we nearly foundered coming downstream, what d'you think it'd be like going up?"

"I wouldn't know. No one's ever told me about boats. D'you mean you want us to walk home so that you can be quietly lost without trace?"

"You are a supersonic clot. No. So that I can try to get her home still afloat."

"Then wouldn't it make more sense if we towed her home and no one paddled?"

"It might. Always supposing, of course, that one of us has some rope on him."

"This one hasn't."

"Nor this one, either. But Lawrie has, haven't you, gel?"

"Me? No! Why should I have? You never said—"

"A fine thing," said Peter solemnly. "Why d'you think we let you come at all if it wasn't so that you'd bring the rope?"

"But I tell you, you never—oh, it's a joke. Well, har, har, *har*, then. And in case you haven't noticed, there's no tow-path for towing, either. So sker*wash*" and she ground her right thumb into the palm of her left hand.

"She's right, you know—hey, we've arrived!" as the canoe lifted to a swell that was none of the river's making. "H.M.S. *Amethyst* has rejoined the Fleet! We actually made it!"

He put his hand over his shoulder, Patrick shook it vigorously, and they paddled on between mudflats grooved by fast-running rivulets towards the silver line where the river lost itself in the quietness of slack water and gulls floated, level with their eyes. "But no ducks at all," complained Peter. "Where's this morning flight you keep telling me about?"

"Gone over to the marsh by now. Sorry, but we're hours too late. I'd no idea it would take so long to get this old tub to the estuary when I said start at four."

"So we have to come again tomorrow?"

"Only we can't. Tomorrow's Sunday and there's a bye-law against wild-fowling."

"This is the end! D'you mean we can't come and *look* even?"

"*Look* by all means. I thought you said shoot."

"There's a Hole in your Boatie"

"Only *one* I'd like to shoot, *once*, just to have done it," said Peter, patting the rifle which lay across his knee, tightly wrapped in his mackintosh. "One duck, one goose, one rook, one pigeon—"

"That's terribly restrained of you. Here's to them that shoot and miss."

"Arrh, me ol' darlin', so be yew dü think as I dunno as that's how yew fine falconers dü toast yourselveses over them there glasses of port, ever so gouty yew dü be, me ol' darlin'. Did you ever bring the hawks here when you had them?"

"Not actually here. I flew Regina at duck up on the marsh last summer before she made off but Jon preferred rook-hawking. He thought it made more sense to keep down rooks."

"Rooks rather get me. I know they damage crops and all that caper, but I do dig all that noise and flop when they're being a rookery."

"Me too, likewise. Jon was talking like a farmer."

Peter used his paddle to fend off a mudbank. He said, "I wish we'd known Jon properly. It seems so odd that he should have been our cousin but you knew him so much better."

"Yes," said Patrick aloofly, grasping Bucket as the canoe grounded briefly and then floated off again.

"Sorry. Wouldn't have mentioned him if you hadn't."

"Not to worry," said Patrick, frowning absently at the back of Peter's neck. "I—"

"I say!" said Lawrie, suddenly suspending bailing operations. "Look at those!"

"What? Where?"

"*There!* Out to sea!"

Peter and Patrick looked. A pair of swans, necks rigidly extended, were flying fast across the bay, their wing-beats powerful, audible, visible. The sky was a misted blue, the sea sparkled—

"Shoot those!" cried Lawrie, bouncing excitedly.

"Couldn't," said Peter, watching them.

"Why not?"

"Too far off." Which was true, but not the real reason. This he gave, half-involuntarily, a moment later. "Besides, there's only two of them."

"What's wrong with that?"

"Oh, you," he said, still watching the swans who were certainly too far away now.

"What d'you mean, oh you? I thought that's what we came for, so's you could shoot something."

Peter twitched an embarrassed shoulder. The swans flew into the bank of haze, which clung unseen to the surface of the sea midway between the shore and the horizon, and were gone. "Well, *honestly* !" said Lawrie. "I give up—"

Unfortunately, in the excitement of the moment, she had also given up bailing and the seeping water was suddenly about their knees in a cold triumphant rush: the canoe was foundering—

And then the whole thing turned farcical. As they lurched hurriedly to their feet, the canoe settled quietly on a mudbank two feet below the surface, leaving them splashing and stranded: Bucket, whining loudly, half-swam to the nearest mudflat where he shook himself violently, throwing out spray like a twirled mophead, and then raced to and fro, barking frantically.

"Oh go on, you goon," exclaimed Peter, exasperated, as water lapped over the tops of his gumboots and his sister, mackintosh and gumboots balanced on her head, became so convulsed with laughter that she seemed likely to fall into the deep water channel at any moment. "Wade over to Bucket. You don't need to get more soaked than you are already." Lawrie, still laughing, splashed away in a lurching, drunken fashion: Patrick watched Peter push his sleeves as high as possible and said interestedly, "Tickling for trout?"

"Ha-ruddy-ha. What's the easiest thing? Drag her as she is or raise her here and tip the water out?"

The easiest thing turned out to be a combination of both. Rather wetter than they had been, heavily splashed with sandy mud, they finally beached the canoe keel up. Breathless and hot they stood still, ankle-deep in the buttery smoothness of the mudflat. "Where's Lawrie?" said Peter, looking wildly about him, as if Lawrie couldn't fail to land herself in unnecessary trouble at such a moment: sink to her waist in mud, be swept out to sea—

But Patrick said "There" and Peter, looking where he pointed, saw his sister already off the mudflats, seated on a sandy promontory wiry with marram-grass, her gumboots up-ended beside her. Bucket, also seated on the promontory, his tongue lolling out, cocked his head on one side and barked encouragement.

"Do we leave it here?" said Patrick.

"If we do, the tide'll take it. Help me drag it over where Lawrie is and I'll come back for it this afternoon."

"I suppose," panted Patrick, as they tugged the canoe forward, one either side, leaving a brontosaurus trail, "it is actually going to be *worth* coming back for?"

"Should hope so," panted Peter. "All that work. And expense. Don't think there's anything wrong with her. Just—too—many of us—in her."

They manhandled her to the promontory, turned her keel up again and looked her over. Lawrie, stepping cautiously on the sharp grass, joined them. "*Is* there a hole?"

"Can't find even a pinprick. *Must* be your enormous weight burst the Plimsoll line. Anyway, I'll come back this afternoon and look properly. I'm much too wet and sloshy to do it now." And he sat down, tugged off his gumboots and emptied them. Patrick did the same. Peter, his toes wriggling inside his wet socks, said, "You will tell your ma and pa we didn't actually take you out on purpose to drown you, won't you?"

"I shan't you know. I shall tell them that's exactly what you did. I'll tell how Lawrie rocked the boat—"

"I *didn't*!" exclaimed Lawrie, dismayed and indignant. "I only forgot the bailing, but it wasn't on *purpose*—"

"Take no notice," said her brother. "Old Clothhead'll come to it in time—"

"—*if* they were at home. But they aren't. More or less there's only me and our Nellie—"

"There's a Hole in your Boatie"

"*Really?* Are your ma and pa stuck in London? Can we spend the rest of half-term at your place, then?"

"Pa has some Parliamentary dinner tonight, so it wasn't worth while their coming down. But I thought I would." Since he'd taken it for granted Ginty would be home for half-term, he'd been furious last night at the waste of all that huha to get himself home too: still, he was glad now he'd come anyway. "And actually, if you'd waited five minutes you'd have heard me issuing invitations instead of having to gatecrash in that couthless way."

"Can only say most humble Marlow never noticed any magnificent invitation coming his despicable way until he asked. Well, I suppose we ought to take ourselves home before we all die of rheumatic fever," said Peter, trying to force his feet into his gumboots again. "Ugh, aren't we all fiendishly uncomfortable? Do buck up, Lawrie. Look, we'll stroll on. It's much too chilly to stand around waiting."

Somehow, he and Patrick were ready while Lawrie was still in her socks, her mackintosh lying on the grass. As the boys and Bucket strolled on, Lawrie, thrown into a confusion of haste, stamped her feet into the wrong gumboots, put her left arm into the right armhole of her mackintosh and had to start all over again. But even while she shrieked "Wait for me! Don't be such scrudgey goons! *Wait for me!*" she knew that half-term without Nicola was being infinitely more fun than she'd expected. The thing she'd most dreaded—that Peter and Patrick would make it clear they'd much rather she didn't tag along, which would have meant choosing between the two hatefulnesses of tagging on regardless for company's sake or pretending she preferred half-term on her own—hadn't happened. She was genuinely sorry there was only the rest of today and all day tomorrow and Monday till teatime and then she'd be back at school. . . .

Squelching damply, Lawrie pounded after Peter and Patrick, caught up with them and took her place in the middle.

CHAPTER TWO

"Two Pigeons Flying High"

———————————

They went home over the downs, walking as fast as possible in the hope that this would help to dry out their clothes which clung and flapped like, Lawrie said, wriggling uncomfortably, a whole boatful of old codswallop. Almost everything which could be said about the canoe had already been said for the fourth or fifth time, but Peter, as they reached the crest of a down, was saying it just once more. "So if she *is* all right when I look at her this afternoon—no actual hole or anything, I mean—it's all right with you if we go again tomorrow?"

"Not before breakfast," said Patrick, "because I've said I'll serve early Mass. But after, if you like."

"Niet. *We'll* be at church then."

"Can't you go to your early service?"

"Wot, me in my state of 'ealf?" said Peter, who could rise before dawn to watch the morning flight, but found it impossible to rise as early as two hours later in order to go to church. "Not on your nelly. Make it Monday, then."

"Suits me," said Patrick accommodatingly; and then, indicating the downs to the east, he said, "The Thuggery on the prowl."

That pack of boys the village called them: Patrick, adding one more to the nouns of association listed in *The Boke of St. Albans*, called them in cheerful exaggeration A Thuggery of Teds. Still, they rarely crossed the Rushton; they were seldom seen in Westbridge itself.

They were distrusted rather than disliked, though there had

never been anything tangible against them in the absence of even one unsolved village mystery; but when any unexplained calamity first occurred—a burned rick or a robbed offertory box—suspicion invariably swung and pointed to *that pack of boys* like a compass to the north: and over garden fences and pints of bitter the village had taken to grumbling that they were getting fed up seeing that pack of boys always around: that no one could make out what Miss Culver thought she was up to, having that pack of boys always at her place: and as for helping her with her pigeons—a fine lot of help that pack of boys must be.

The grown-ups vaguely supposed the members of the pack still came and went, new faces and old hands appearing, disappearing and reappearing at irregular intervals: their children knew that, on the contrary, the pack had remained pretty constant for some time now. Apart from the one called Jukie who had been there right from the beginning, they knew the others only by their clothes; and this morning the whole seven were out: Jukie and Purple Streak in front, followed by Red Ted and Black Check, and behind them, Green Stripes, the newish one, with Blue Bobble-cap and Yeller Feller running to catch up. And, unusually, Miss Culver herself made an eighth.

They knew Miss Culver, of course; not only because she was on nodding terms with their parents but also because her appearance (squat striding body and thick red hair worn, as all her life, in what she still thought of as a Dutch bob and everyone else as a Beatle cut, her prominent teeth and different eyes, green and grey, in a face the colour of barley stalks) was so nearly grotesque as to be noticeable. Predictably, she wore tweeds, hard hats and brogues and most people thought of her as in her fifties, though in fact she was ten years older. Peter and Lawrie knew her only at a distance—devotional in her family pew in church, sporting among the foot followers of the local Hunt, lordly on the by-pass in the white bullying monster she drove herself—for she had "called on" their mother during the Christmas term and so far they'd never actually spoken to her. Patrick, who had done so frequently, detested her.

"Two Pigeons Flying High"

"Why?" asked Peter curiously, for though Patrick had the normal average of dislikes and hates, he wasn't often as vehement as that.

"She raises my hackles and my gorge. She's a loathly female."

"Arrh, me ol' darlin'," said Peter, dropping into the bogus dialect which sometimes amused but more often maddened his listeners, "'tes roight she be no oil paintin', that's for shure. But ain't *loathly* a mite strong, now? 'Tes shure's fate us can't none of we do aught but the best us can wi' the 'orrible features the good Lord—"

"Look—if I chose my friends by their faces, most of them I wouldn't have. Even pa can't bear her and you can't say he isn't a tolerant type."

"You mean he puts up with you?"

"I'm the least of his worries. No, it's just—well—he says she stands four-square and looks him straight in the eye and talks to him man to man and it frightens him to death. And ma says she's a natural-born bully. Which is lucky for me or I might have been shanghai'd to help look after her feelthy pigeons too."

"You and The Thuggery all one big happy gang together? Eh, ma puir laddie, what you've missed."

"Like it keeps me awake at night man, regretting. D'you know she had the Nerve Unspeakable to tell Jon he should get rid of the hawks?"

"Did she really?" Since it was self-evident his cousin Jon had not complied, Peter grinned with relish and prepared to hear an account of the battle.

"In case they forgot themselves and knocked off one of her horrible little freaks. And a good thing too. Put them out of their misery. Did you know the Carrier pigeons they breed for show have so much wattle on their bills they can't see to fly?"

"You don't say," said Peter solemnly.

"And I'll tell you something else—"

"No, I'll tell *you* something first. Before this conversation—"

"Two Pigeons Flying High"

"*I* always thought," said Lawrie, sure of her facts, "that Carrier pigeons carried messages. So it can't be true they breed them so that they can't see to fly. Can it?"

"It can, because Carrier pigeons don't—" Patrick began.

The air vibrated. Lawrie shouted, "It's the swans again!" But almost before they could look round, a rushing clatter of wing-beats passed overhead and Peter shouted, "Pigeons!" aiming his rifle and prepared (not quite sportingly perhaps) to bag his one bird by firing into the flock. The other two halted, gazing upwards, waiting to congratulate, jeer or sympathize as his marksmanship deserved. And then Patrick cried out and slammed the rifle barrel downwards with his left hand while his right waved wildly, pointing to a place in the sky high above the pigeons.

"A falcon! Look! Right above them! Can't you *see*?"

Peter and Lawrie gazed and could not: black specks floated, multiplied, dissolved before their staring eyes: and then, almost before they realized what was happening, two birds fell through the mass of pigeons wheeling in a patch of sky to their left. One hit the ground, bounced and fell back. The other flung up into the sky again above the flock, hung for an instant plain even for Peter and Lawrie to see, and stooped again.

They heard, without registering, the angry shouting behind them as they raced towards the spot where the second bird had fallen and where the falcon was now floating down on to the body. As they ran Peter trod on something, stumbled, dropped mackintosh and rifle, grabbed them up again and ran on. "Don't go any closer," panted Patrick, checking suddenly. "We'll scare her off. Bucket! Heel!"

Bucket, never a noticeably obedient dog, hesitated, one paw raised, looking back over his shoulder, his tail moving hope-fully. And then he went forward again, belly to the ground, whining every now and then with pleasure, with—but that would be absurd: recognition it couldn't be.

"What's he doing?" panted Lawrie.

Patrick silenced her with a furious movement. He watched

"Two Pigeons Flying High"

Bucket draw closer and closer still to the falcon where she sat mantling her quarry, and waited for her to rise. Beyond a few wary liftings of her wings she never budged. And at last Bucket collapsed on to the turf only a few feet away, his tongue lolling out, his tail fluttering in ecstatic welcome.

"Stay there," said Patrick to the others.

He still told himself it couldn't be. It was six months since he had freed Jon's falcon Regina from the camouflage net and she had stared at him as if he were an enemy and he had let her fly. This *must* be some other made hawk, used to dogs and humans. Only—someone else's lost falcon would be wearing bells and jesses and he had freed Regina from hers when he let her fly so that she should be neither hampered nor retaken—

All this time he was moving closer, in the leisurely fits and starts which the falconer calls "making in". And still the falcon went on busily depluming her pigeon with no more than a lift of her head and a wary stare before getting back to work. . . .

"Regina?" he said almost inaudibly.

The falcon turned her head and looked at him, her wings half-spread. He said again, coaxingly, "Regina?" and prepared to make the final test: if she jumped to his fist—

"Here—you! Stand aside—quickly!"

He had been so rapt into a world which held nothing but himself and the falcon that every nerve in his body started. Remembering to move gently, he looked over his shoulder and turned slowly round. Miss Culver, breathing hard and making impatient sweeping gestures, was standing ten yards away; behind her lounged The Thuggery, Jukie standing as usual a little apart. Peter and Lawrie, looking a good deal less organized, stood one either side of the ground between Miss Culver and himself.

"I said stand aside! Quickly! I want to get him before he flies off again."

"She," he said automatically. Miss Culver had a shotgun too —an altogether heavier affair than Peter's. Patrick's mind registered this a few seconds before he grasped the full implications.

"What do you mean *she*? And do as I say! Pronto!"

"Two Pigeons Flying High"

"Regina's a falcon," said Patrick, eyeing Miss Culver, he now observed, along the barrel of her shotgun. "Falcons are females."

"He or she, it's been taking my pigeons morning after morning. We've been after him for days. Now—out of my way!"

It was an autocratic voice—one which issued orders rather than put itself to the trouble of saying *Please* and *Thank you*. A small child or an employee with an interest in keeping his job might have been intimidated: but Patrick was neither. He said, "Regina belongs to me."

"What d'you mean? That's a wild hawk."

"And of course," he said, avoiding a direct answer, "you'll expect compensation."

"Naturally. But that can wait. What I want *now* is to be rid of that hawk. I don't breed prize birds to provide free meals for predators."

"Naturally not. I don't expect it'll happen again."

So far, he had kept his eyes on her face. But now anger and frustration made it so much plainer even than usual that he was obliged to look aside: and since Miss Culver invariably interpreted inability to look her straight in the eye as proof of nervousness, this was unfortunate. She raised the shotgun whose muzzle had gradually been dipping towards the ground and aimed it—at Patrick in the first instance but beyond him, presumably, at Regina. The Thuggery swayed instinctively forward.

"I'm counting to ten," stated Miss Culver, her cheeks beginning to glow like dull embers, "and I suggest you jump aside—fast! One. Two. Three.——"

Unalarmed, Patrick thrust his hands into the pockets of his jacket. Out of the corner of his eye he saw Peter shake his rifle free of his mackintosh as if to say that if guns were the argument there was one on their side too.

"—Four. Five.—"

The situation was rapidly becoming stark, staring bonkers. And if one or other idiot fired its gun or The Thuggery rushed him, Regina would fly and almost certainly be shot. Patrick, courteously insolent, said *to* Peter and unmistakably *at* Miss Culver, "Didn't anyone teach you your firearm manners ever? Pa never stops telling me *Never never let your gun Pointed be at anyone.*"

"Seven—" But Miss Culver's rifle barrel had dipped again. "You're the Merrick boy, aren't you?"

"I have that high honour," said Patrick extravagantly, aware he was quoting but unable for the moment to lay his hand on the author.

"Yes. Well. Look here now——" Guns were definitely no part of the argument now. It would have been one thing apparently, thought Patrick hilariously, for Gunslinger Culver to pepper a peasant but quite another to murder a Merrick—"you get my point, don't you?" Good humour and chap-to-chappery were now, apparently, in bloom. "You do see, don't you, that that falcon of yours can't continue to breakfast off my pigeons?"

"Of course," said Patrick aloofly, hunching his shoulders a little.

"When Group-Captain Marlow told me he was taking up falconry again, I told him his birds must be flown on the Crowlands. You recall that, don't you? You were present. I made it perfectly clear that—"

"I remember exactly," said Patrick, a small jet of anger lighting itself. "Jon said he'd do his best to see the hawks didn't fly your pigeons. And he said as he'd be using them as rook hawks there was a fair chance they wouldn't. That was *all*."

"Look here now—there was a clear understanding your hawks would be flown only on the Crowlands. That's an undertaking I expect you to honour."

"Impossible," said Patrick. "No one *could* make that sort of promise about hawks."

"Don't bandy words with me, there's a good lad. I'm giving you this last chance. But any more trouble from that hawk of yours and I shall shoot it without hesitation."

"Here's to them that shoot and miss," said Peter cheerfully, just in case anyone had any doubts whose side he was on: and grinned past Miss Culver at Jukie, inviting him to a brief alliance against a female ancient who was making a nuisance of herself.

He never knew whether Jukie acknowledged the alliance or not, for Miss Culver's pent exasperation exploded in such a volley of rage that he could only stare in astonishment while words which to his mind had been laid away in mothballs before he was born assaulted his ears: words like cad, no gentleman, blackguard, ill-bred, vulgar and the like. He was incredulous; he was fascinated; the hope grew that perhaps she would end her—was *tirade* the word?—by flinging down her glove and challenging him to a duel. But that, of course, was altogether too much to hope; Miss Culver merely turned on her heel, waving The Thuggery "off" with shooing motions of her arms. Jukie, balancing backward and away, seemed to move in his own good time. And then they were all gone over the hump of the down.

"Well!" said Peter, gazing after them. "Eh, me ol' darlin's! Did 'ee ever hear the loike o' that now?"

Lawrie made a double V sign, pleased, naturally, that their side had won. All the same, now the excitement was over, she found the whole episode really very—*odd*. For it wasn't The Thuggery, it was Miss Culver herself who'd almost started a rough-house. And that was most funny-peculiar because grown-ups were there to put a stop to rough-houses, anyway before anyone got hurt (anyway before Lawrie got hurt). Lawrie liked to feel she was being taken care of; she took it for granted that any grown-up present would naturally do this; but Miss Culver—in her mind's eye Lawrie looked askance at Miss Culver—

Patrick had turned back to Regina. At some point in the argument she had carried and was now some distance away again, the unfortunate pigeon little more than picked bones; so she should be gorged and happy; Patrick made in to her once more: advanced his fist.

There was a moment of time suspended: the falcon half-spread her wings, seemed about to fly—and then, almost as if surprised at herself, jumped to his fist, her great eyes fixed on his face. Her talons closed on bare flesh but he scarcely felt the furious grip as pain. He lifted what was left of the pigeon to keep her happy and occupied on the way home, straightened up, turned wordlessly towards the others, his eyes blazing with triumph and pleasure, and set off home.

CHAPTER THREE

A Gentleman of the Fancy

As she and Peter followed Patrick at the discreet distance indicated, Lawrie began to tell over in her head the epic to be told at school on Monday evening—an epic of near-drownings and near-shootings which it was reasonable to assume no one else in Lower IVA was likely to match. The bit about the Return of Regina (thought Lawrie kindly) should be saved for bedtime when she and Nicola were on their own; because it was really such super bad luck (for Nicola) that she, Lawrie, who was well known to think falconry a crummy bore, should have been there to see the whole thing, while Nicola, who last summer had been almost as closely identified with its mysteries as Patrick himself, should have been in London. Super utter scrudge, thought Lawrie; and, hands clasped behind her back, waltzed a few elegant gumbooted steps till Peter quelled her with eloquent eyebrows.

"Don't look now," he said next in a calm voice (Lawrie immediately did, in all directions), "but I *think* we're being followed."

"Where? What d'you mean? Who is? I can't see anyone," said Lawrie, snatched back from happy times to come into the uncertain present.

"*Don't look*, I said. What a flaming cross-eyed goon you are. If *you'd* ever tried to escape from a P.O.W. camp you'd have been recaptured before you'd even thought of going."

On the point of saying *Sorry pardon*, it occurred to Lawrie that Peter's accusation didn't make sense. She began to tell him so.

34

"That's the whole point," he told her, but she still couldn't see it. "Oh, stuff it, gel, and listen," he said impatiently. "Listen, I said. Count slowly to twenty and then be *casual* about it and take a look at the ridge."

"What am I going to see?"

"Jukie, I think."

"*I* mean what am I going to pretend I'm seeing while I'm looking for him?"

"Oh!" said Peter, surprised into respect. "Well, you could see a bird, couldn't you?"

"Another hawk," said Lawrie accurately. "I'll look and point and then you must stop and we'll both look."

"You don't have to make a three-act drama of it," he protested. "Just point at the sky and that's it."

"But if you don't look too, he won't believe I saw anything. Anyway, I'm sure it's time I'd have got to twenty if I'd been counting. Four, three, two, one, *zero*. All systems *go*. *Lift* off. Looking—*now*."

She looked. He strolled on. She exclaimed and pointed upward: he cupped his hands above his eyes and looked too: they acted argument and impatience and *come on* and walked on again. "Well?" said Peter.

"Didn't see a thing," said Lawrie.

"Oh *Lal*! If you ask me you were so busy acting seeing-a-hawk you never even looked at the ridge."

This was so nearly true that Lawrie, pink-faced, denied it loudly.

"Never mind, not to bother with it," said her brother. "Oh Lal, do pipe, as they say, *down*. I saw him for practically sure so that can count for both of us. I shouldn't have told you anyway. I might have known you'd make enough commotion to stampede every steer in Texas."

Lawrie decided not to waste time resenting this. "What are you going to do?"

"Can't do anything. Anyone can walk along the ridge. He's not particularly trying not to be seen. I just wonder why, that's all."

A Gentleman of the Fancy

So, with a strong feeling that The Thuggery, having withdrawn, defeated, should have stayed that way, did Lawrie. She tried to persuade herself Peter was mistaken: that it was an ordinary person walking there, not Jukie or a Thug at all: until a sudden frenzy of imagination suggested that the entire Thuggery were lurking there, bristling with the Ted armoury of razors, bicycle-chains and knuckle-dusters, only awaiting the signal of Miss Culver's rifle fired in the air to charge downhill and overwhelm them—

Had Nicola been there, Lawrie would have babbled this notion aloud, inviting her twin's contempt, after which she would have felt not merely braver, but safe; as she couldn't talk like that to Peter, she had either to put up with her fright or wring its neck for herself; and as they had now arrived within sprinting distance of the high wall surrounding the grounds of Patrick's home, she was able to assure herself that if The Thuggery *should* charge she could be safe behind the green door long before Peter and Patrick were finished off. . . .

Fortunately, it was all purest fancy; neither sound nor movement came from the ridge as they crossed the last of the turf. Lawrie touched the sun-blistered door in passing as if it were Home in a game of Prisoner's Base, trod the familiar cobbles of the stable yard and thought the whole Thuggery back to the far bank of the Rushton. Her hands once more clasped behind her, she pranced along the path of the hawk-house, leaving Peter to bar the door against the enemy.

Patrick and Regina had evidently gone through the high shadowy room with its rows of perches to the side-room at the far end where the hawks' furnishings were kept. (*Furnishings?* Lawrie had once asked Nicola, thinking of wardrobes, and *Hawks' tack* Nicola had translated laconically.) Lawrie followed to find him busy reclaiming his falcon: newly jessed, she stood quietly on his now gloved fist, while Patrick, his mouth shaped to an inaudible whistle, searched the drawers of a battered filing-cabinet for hood and bells. Lawrie, who had always been wary of the hawks, sidled to an inconspicuous seat on a small chest behind the door; Peter, strolling in a few minutes later, leaned his elbows on the top of the filing-cabinet and observed, in silence, the perilous happiness of his friend's face. After a while he said tentatively, "I wouldn't want to discourage you, *natch*, but you are remembering you let her go last summer because you didn't see how you'd keep her in London?"

"I am indeed, thank you *very* much for asking," said Patrick, spirits untarnished, as he laid two strips of leather on the table. "But what I've thought of *now* which I didn't *then* was that I could write to the secretary of the British Falconry Society and ask him if he knows a full-time falconer who'd keep her for me in term-time. Sense?"

"Horse-and-common," said Peter, having said his piece. After all, it was, to coin a phrase, Patrick's pigeon. He had a private internal grin over this private internal joke while Patrick said, "I've just remembered. I gave Regina's bells back to Nick because they were Jon's. Would you know where she put them?"

"In her market box," said Lawrie promptly. She meant *marquetry* but "market" had been their baby name for it and she never thought of it by any other.

Peter explained this mild dottiness to Patrick, who said, "I get you. Could you bring them over with you after breakfast, then?"

"Oh no," said Lawrie, shocked. "When it's her market box, it's *private*."

"You mean it's locked?"

"I don't expect so. Anyway, the key's in it."

Patrick saw he was up against one of those family taboos which, as an only child, struck him as both infantile and incomprehensible: he looked at Peter and Peter, who should have known better, unexpectedly sided with him. "Oh go on, Lal. Nick wouldn't mind for a thing like this."

Lawrie frowned, pondering. Then she brightened. "I could phone her at Miranda's this evening when it's cheap time and ask."

"Only I need them *now*," said Patrick. While they had been talking he had slipped on Regina's hood; Lawrie, still sure she couldn't rifle Nicola's market box, not even for Regina, thought suddenly that once a hawk was jessed and hooded it became more than just a large and savage bird: it became a—a hidden menace—

"You can't possibly ring up a strange house about a thing like that," said her brother, scandalized. "Suppose Nick was out and you had to leave a message? You'd sound quite mad."

"Well, *what* then?"

"Lift the lid and take the bells and tell Nick on Monday," said Patrick as if this were the simplest thing in the world.

"But don't you see, it's her *market* box. If it was her *shell* box even it wouldn't be so bad."

"'S all right, I'll get them," said Peter, "and she can be as livid as she likes. Anyway, I shouldn't think she'd be that dumb. So that's settled. Now can you pay attention to sir? If you've quite finished dressing Regina."

"Why? What?" said Patrick, his attention caught by an odd note in Peter's voice.

"Because something *most* peculiar. Have you got the pigeon Regina ate still?"

"That," said Patrick with a grin, "is a question with its own built-in answer."

"Funny-guts. I mean the skelington, then. Have you got it?"

"I suppose you do have to be so mysterious? O.K., here's dem dry bones. So now what?"

"So nothing," said Peter, examining the carcase. "Here's its N.P.A. leg ring. So we can identify the owner. It's an ordinary racing pigeon. Isn't it?"

"I didn't know we thought it was anything else. What would you like me to ask now?"

"If one and one makes—" And then he stopped, his eyes on Bucket who all this time had been lying comfortably spatchcocked under the table but had just come to his feet with a violent heave and was snuffing at the bottom of the door, a velvet rattle deep in his throat. "Because," said Peter, pussy-footing towards the door, "we ought to send the ring back so

that they can check which of their champs went for a burton."
He reached the door and yanked it open. "Oh do come in,
won't you?" he said, all courteous surprise. "Anything we can
do for you?"

"Ta," said Jukie.

He strolled in, thumbs hitched in pockets, and stared in-
solently about him. Lawrie, her back suddenly pressing the
wall, eyed him as if he were a lurcher of uncertain reputation
met in a lonely lane. She had never seen him close to before;
and, as the moments passed, it began to seem to her that though
his features, taken separately, weren't anything special, added
together they made the face one imagined when the grown-ups
described someone unknown as such a good-looking boy. So
it was odd that, even while she was looking at him, she found
it hard to fix his face in her mind: she almost felt she might not
recognize him next time they met unless he was wearing the
same clothes.

The silence continued. The blue-grey stare rested on Patrick
and dismissed him as a herbert, a noddy-boy; on Peter (who
still looked small for his age) and wrote him off as a short-pants
sapso; and on Lawrie as if—as if—

As if nothing. For Jukie, she wasn't there.

She should have been relieved: she found she wasn't: un-
expectedly, brow, cheeks and throat had flamed resentment.
A moment later, Jukie spoke. "I'm here for the flutter.
Give."

"The pigeon? Oh so *that's* what you've come for," said
Patrick in a highly enlightened way. "Well you *can* have it, of
course, but I'm afraid it's been picked quite clean."

"I'm not cravin' it for eats, noddy-boy. Where I come from,
the flutters is strictly for the moggies. C'm on—give."

"It's beside you," said Patrick to Peter. "Hand it to the man,
will you?"

Peter, propped against the table, picked up the carcase a
touch fastidiously between finger and thumb and tossed it
gently in the air: Jukie, who had been glancing round the room
again in a half-insolent, half-surreptitious way, was taken by

surprise. He clutched at the carcase, fumbled, dropped it. No one actually *said* butterfingers. Plainly mortified, Jukie tore the left leg from the carcase, tugged off the little metal ring and hurled the rest back. Peter ducked nonchalantly and let it lie. Jukie, still flushed, studied the ring and said, a little too loudly and immediately, "As I dreamed. It was one of our greats. The champ flutter of all time, I'm telling you." He paused; Patrick and Peter kept a noncommittal silence; so he was obliged to continue too emphatically, "See his cipher? That's Red Rocket, that was. *The* three-year-old, world-without-end. No livin' flutter could keep with him—"

"You mean," said Patrick, his voice neutral, "you know all your pigeons' numbers off by heart, just like that?"

"All the greats I do. Why the question? You wouldn't, would you, be saying the words come twisted?"

Lawrie, who had been finding his voice as hard to pin down as his looks, suddenly got it. The true north-country and the sham Yankee were easily identified: it was the third tone which had foxed her. But she had it now: it was Miss Culver's voice which came and went with the other two—

"Not twisted, natch," Peter was saying politely. "Just a touch mistaken in the agitation of the moment."

"There's no error, sapso. Red Rocket's tag I know 's if it was my own—"

A thought passed across Patrick's face, but otherwise he kept it to himself. Jukie, however, interpreted it easily enough. "They've not had me inside yet, noddy-boy. Now concentrate. 'Cause you're going to have to break it to daddy-o that when we start talking compensation he'll need to start dishing out loot like—"

"Ah *but*. Before my parent starts dishing out loot like anything at all he'll want proof the pigeon was actually yours quite apart from whether it was a champ or not."

"And whatever its name was, it wasn't Red Rocket," said Peter. "That's for sure."

"Yeh? What makes it sure, sapso?" said Jukie mechanically, still looking observantly at Patrick.

"Because that bird was a blue chequer," said Peter firmly. "So there's a mistake somewhere."

Jukie's attention came full to Peter. "What's colour on your mind for?" he said instantly. "That flutter was called for one of the sputnik whizzos. See, sapso? You won't dodge thattaway."

Peter looked at Jukie, his lips suddenly parted, but as if a suspicion had been confirmed, not as if he had anything to say. In fact, no one spoke, until Jukie, evidently thinking this as good a time as any to make his exit, flipped the pigeon's ring high in the air, caught it neatly and sauntered through the door saying, "So we'll be sending the bill for Red Rocket the champ. And tell daddy-o we'll only settle for cash in full."

"Ah *but*. It won't be you he settles with," said Patrick raising his voice slightly. "It'll be Miss Culver."

The feet stopped, then walked on. The hawk-house door banged shut and Peter looked at once into the big shadowy room; but it was so bare, there was nowhere anyone could hide and after a glance round he said, "Can one lock the doors?"

"Only from the outside. Why?"

"Because I've something serious to show you."

"*What* serious something? And anyway, why should he come back? Probably speeding home to see which pigeon it actually was and how much can he get M. Culver to claim. Go on—spill."

Peter hesitated, then decided to leave the side-room door ajar so that they could hear if anyone came in. "Well, look. You remember there were two birds Regina killed? *This* one," he indicated the carcase with his toe, "and the first one she didn't bother with?"

"I'd forgotten the first one! Poor Pa! I suppose he'll have to break the news to Maudie. What does she do? Check the lot and see who's missing?"

"I suppose. But actually, I'd be surprised if she wanted to," said Peter solemnly.

"*Would* you? Why? Anyway, we don't have this other bird. So how'd you know either way?"

"Because we have got it." He had laid his mackintosh on the table when they first came in and now his hands fumbled among the folds as his tongue fumbled among the words. "This first one—*this* one—it's this one's the one with the message."

CHAPTER FOUR

". . . Poor Airy Post"

Lawrie, incredulous but believing, said, "*What?*"

Patrick looked at him sidelong. "You don't say."

"Well, p'raps it isn't actually a message," said Peter more easily, "but it's certainly something." He had got his mackintosh open at last. The bird's body lay in a mess of blood and feathers, a capsule fastened to it by a miniature leather harness. Peter could not, Patrick saw at once, possibly have contrived this as some elaborate, idiot joke in the time and circumstances at his disposal. Lawrie, joining in now the enemy had gone, came over to look.

"Ugh, how revolting! Are you going to take that thing off and see what it is?"

"*I* think so," said Peter to Patrick.

Patrick hesitated, caught in a net of ethics; then he said, side-stepping an immediate decision, "You're *sure* this is the first pigeon she knocked down?"

"Must be. It was warm still when I picked it up. And look how its back's ripped up." (Lawrie looked away.) "*That* couldn't be anything but Regina's talons. First when I tripped over it I was going to leave it and then I saw something tied to it so I grabbed it." He scowled at Patrick, impatient of hesitation. "You know, I'm sure we should open this capsule thing. If it *is* nothing, that's fine, bung it in the post and send it back. But if it isn't, then don't we have to shove it at the police or M.I.5?"

"Well, natch. Only I don't actually see why spies should be the very first thing you think of," said Patrick mildly; and was suddenly aware of Lawrie, on the verge of eager speech, being yanked back into silence by a furiously forbidding glance from Peter. Neither spoke: Lawrie looked aside, her lips sucked in hard with the effort of holding her tongue; and Patrick, astonished, curious, but with an instinctive feeling that he'd better make as if he'd noticed nothing, went on, "I must say I can't see old Maudie Culver passing information to the enemy. She's *such* a blot-blue Tory she's practically an Empire Loyalist. And anyway, where'd she'd get any information *to* pass?"

"So what? Even if she's not in on it, The Thuggery could still let the pigeons be used to send messages."

"Well, if it has to be spies, yes I suppose they could. But why couldn't it be The Fancy sending messages, like amateur radio operators—Hams don't they call themselves?"

"Could be. Then if that's all it is there'll be no harm reading it, will there?" said Peter, his fingers itching to be busy about the harness.

"I guess not," said Patrick, common sense defeating ethics.

They had, after all, been too engrossed to hear him come back: when Jukie's voice said from the doorway "Noddy-boys, I've been doing the heavy think. Now this is a real keen notion—" they jumped as if he had thrown a thunderflash.

Lawrie backed hurriedly away, casting a regretful glance at the bird on the table: they'd never know now. And then she realized Jukie hadn't seen it yet after all because Peter was in the way. She tried to look steadily aside so that Jukie shouldn't follow her gaze and see it too, but every so often her eyes returned compulsively to the bird lying breast upward, the harness furrowing a draggled chevron of rufous feathers. An uncertainty tweaked at her mind: it wasn't a bit like—

"Lissen good," said Jukie to Patrick. "This is the sharpest. Maybe we'll not need to grab daddy-o's loot if you play it keen. Receiving me?"

"Loud and clear," said Patrick, eyebrows half-cocked.

"Keep lissening. Suppose I switch this ring to a flutter that's an also-ran, then it's the also-ran's ring I hand Maudie. 'N if I tell Maudie this was a flutter as was strickly the clipped-wing-world-without-end, due to be culled—you reading me? So Maudie's the squarest. Maudie digs the integrity racket like she's crazy for it. If Maudie's told he's a clipped-wing, Maudie won't claim."

"Go on," said Patrick, after a pause. "So then?"

"So then if Maudie don't claim, daddy-o don't pay. That adds perfect. But it still tells in the crystal that Jukie gets loot. Like you pay me."

There was a pause. Then Patrick said gently, "You know— I'm not actually scared of my pa. And anyway, my kind of pocket-money wouldn't make sense to you."

"Lissen, noddy-boy," said Jukie, evidently expecting a refusal at this stage. "You don't appreciate the favour it's doing daddy-o. It's not tens he'd be short of for Red Rocket—it's hundreds. But if Jukie gets just his rightful rake-off which he mightn't from Maudie—"

"Your brain must have worked itself loose thinking that one up," said Peter contemptuously. "How dumb d'you think we come?"

"Strickly mute," said Jukie promptly. "They come no muter, sapso."

"Then that's your bloomin' 'orrible error. You think we couldn't know less about pigeons, don't you, Razor-edge?"

"That's my gospel."

"Well, you're wrong. As f'r instance, those rings. Because *I* know they go on the squabs' legs when they're eight days old and never come off again. So you couldn't swop them over because you couldn't get them over their feet. Q.E.D."

"You instruct me, sapso," said Jukie. But though his voice was studiously satirical, his eyes were very surprised indeed.

"I'll tell you something else then. Any old birds that weren't worth keeping would have been culled last October. And you don't start culling the young birds till April. So unless Mau— Miss Culver—hasn't a clue about the whole thing, she'd smell fifty million rats. So d'you know what I think?"

"I'll make me a supposition," said Jukie coolly. "You reckon this ring tells this flutter was no champ at all. 'N so—Maudie'll

cue me no grinding of daddy-o. 'N so—no rake-off for Jukie
'n his mob. That your figure?"

"Just about," said Peter.

"My figure too, sapso. Only," said Jukie, unexpectedly
good-tempered about it, "you have to trip me by compre-
hending the flutter culture like it's ridiculous." And he gave
Peter a friendly shove in the chest.

Peter, who disliked being shoved, in a friendly way or otherwise, jerked away. The sudden movement jolted the table: and
the second pigeon, harness and all, slid with a soft heavy flump
to the floor.

Jukie looked to see what had fallen: Peter and Patrick, knowing all too well, watched Jukie. In the split second of realization,
though he remained perfectly still, his hand flat against Peter's
chest, they had the oddest impression that he shied like a
startled horse. And then his face smoothed itself clear of expression: his hand dropped: he said, his voice husky as if his
throat needed clearing, "Wha's that?"

Peter scooped the pigeon up and on to the table behind him.
Patrick said, "Just a bird. Can't be one of yours."

"How's that?" said Jukie, still husky.

Patrick said chattily, "Because it's not ringed. And I remember being told yours all were the day we came over."

Jukie, still blank-faced, tried, between a breath and a breath,
to determine the most rewarding answer. "Tha's right—'f it's
not ringed it's none of ours. Where'd you get it?"

"We found it."

"Where? When?"

"Why should you care?"

"Tha's right, why should I?" Jukie cocked his head on one
side. "Tha's a flash sort of gear on its bod. Let's have a peepful."

Plainly, he knew only too well what it was: plainly also,
this was an attempt to get bird and harness into his hands:
only, if he were to preserve the fiction that the pigeon wasn't
a Culver bird, he couldn't be too insistent. Patrick said, shrug-
ging, "It's only a bit of leather. Seems to be tangled round it.
I daresay that's what killed it."

46

"Yeh, mebbe," he said obligingly and tried again. "Better lemme make certain 'tain't ours. Best be sure."

"But it can't be," said Patrick levelly. "There's no ring on its leg."

Jukie's eyes stared boldly. "Tha's your fable. But could be you're faking, noddy-boy. Could be you add two flutters total higher than one?"

"Could be. So perhaps by now we've yanked the ring off. Then what d'you prove by looking?"

"Leastways I c'n tell Maudie I looked."

"There's that, of course. Only *suppose* we hand it over, and *suppose* you forget to give it back and *suppose* you take it home with you and your Miss Culver fancies it's one of hers—well then it could come kind of expensive for my pa, couldn't it?"

"That ud be dead crafty. Well then—you lemme look, 'n I parole to give back."

"I'm not *that* mute," said Patrick sardonically.

But Jukie stiffened: to Patrick's astonishment he looked genuinely insulted. "You weren't lissenin', noddy-boy. I said *parole*."

"We heard you," said Peter, seeing no reason why Jukie shouldn't look insulted as easily as anything else. But Patrick said curiously, "You mean you'd hand it back intact? Pigeon, harness and all?"

Jukie's eyes were suddenly steady. "My oath."

"No, not your oath. Parole."

"I've told parole."

"Only for the pigeon. I want it for the lot."

There was a brief, violent pause. And then Jukie shrugged and balanced back, flipping the ring he had taken from the first pigeon high in the air. "Why'd I parole you anyway, noddy-boy? It's nuthin to me. Tha's right what you fable—no ring, not our flutter. Even the Gestapo couldn't twist that diff'rent. An' now lissen good. You creep to the Gestapo—the police mob—'n tip them off, or that tame vulture of yours knocks down one more of Maudie's flutters—'n you know what? We'll be round one time—'n you know what? We'll dig its eyes out."

Lawrie, who had been listening with painful attention to a conversation she only half-comprehended, felt her cheeks web with sudden cold. Peter winced, narrowing his own eyes. Jukie, glancing deliberately from one to the other, smiled pleasantly. And then his eyes moved to Patrick's face and the smile became merely the planned arrangement of his features: at that moment Patrick's face could have been used as a model for a mask labelled *murder*.

The silence continued. Jukie's smile finally faded. Such expression as was left looked—regrettably perhaps—very like surprised respect.

"Now beat it," said Patrick at last.

"I'd taken off already," said Jukie defiantly, with another of those odd backward-balancing movements Peter had noticed on the Downs, as if someone—or experience—had taught him never to turn his back on the enemy.

"I'm not arguing who said what first. Just beat it," said Patrick. He set Regina down on the table, fastening her leash to the chair back. "Only this time we'll see you off."

"Who wants to stay?" said Jukie, going nonchalantly backwards through the door.

"Who wants to keep you?" said Peter.

The voices, batting the sentences to and fro like ping-pong balls, faded down the hawk-house. Bucket went with them. Lawrie remained alone, save for the motionless hooded falcon and the dead pigeon. Silence came to stay. Presently, two horrors suggested themselves: that Regina, freeing herself by some hitherto unknown means from hood and leash, would launch an attack: that Peter and Patrick would be jumped by the rest of The Thuggery, beaten up and left for dead: and then The Thuggery, razors at the ready, would come for her. . . .

"What on *earth* are you doing?" said Peter, as he and Patrick returned to find Lawrie, her eyes tight shut, her face screwed up and her fists over her ears.

". . . Poor Airy Post"

Lawrie let out a long breath of relief and opened her eyes. "You're back!"

"Of course. Where did you think we were going?"

Lawrie told what she'd thought. Peter shut resigned eyes and shook his head at her. Patrick said with a grin, "If *that's* what you thought, what's the harness doing still lying around? You could at least have sat on it."

Lawrie supposed she could. The twin terrors having proved baseless, she was now positive that if either *had* happened she would have coped with infinite courage and resource. Of *course* she would. She'd have shoved the table against the door and torn up the floorboards to make a hiding place for the harness. . . .

"Come *on*," said Peter, snapping his fingers before her eyes to catch her attention.

"Come where?" she said, startled: and then saw Patrick, Regina on his fist, going through the door, Peter and Bucket following. She scurried after them, expecting to see Patrick tying Regina to her perch; but Patrick, still carrying Regina, went straight on and through the hawk-house doors—

"Is he letting her go again, after all?" she panted as Peter bolted the doors, turned the massive key and dropped it in Patrick's jacket pocket.

"Lal, for goodness' sake! That's what we've been talking about for the last ten minutes! We're taking her up to the attics till we know what's happening. She couldn't possibly be left in the hawk-house without a twenty-four-hour guard."

"What—*our* attic? Won't Mummy—"

"Oh Lal, come to! D'you think Patrick hasn't got one?"

Abashed, Lawrie followed meekly and in silence. They skirted the stables and went through the kitchen garden to the back door. Patrick glanced over his shoulder with a look which signalled *Quiet as poss* and they trod softly in and along the passage which led past the kitchen, from which came the scents and sizzlings of breakfast cooking. *Breakfast* thought Lawrie, suddenly overwhelmingly aware that she was hollow inside—hollow and flapping. And she thought it most sensible of

Bucket to hesitate and then decide that just this moment food called louder than his worship his master, and patter apologetically through the half-open door. The rest of them trod quietly on and up the back stairs. Behind them in the kitchen a voice said, "That is the end of the weather forecast. Now before the news, here's a brief look at today's programmes. . . ." The words became steadily less distinct, but the six pips of the time signal followed them up the second flight. A whole more *hour*, thought starving Lawrie, wondering if she'd keep.

A second landing, and a third flight; a third landing and a fourth, yet narrower flight, whose bare treads sounded loudly; *surely*, thought Lawrie, a hot ache in each calf, they must be nearly there by now; and then Patrick stopped, said "Better idea" and started down again, but there was no room for him to pass and Peter had to take Lawrie by the shoulders and turn her round before she understood she must lead down: it must be morning starvation, decided Lawrie pathetically, that was making her so slow in the uptake.

She followed on along a low-ceilinged corridor with closed doors on either side. When Patrick opened one, they found themselves in a room empty of everything but motes of dust rising in the sunshine; crossing to the window, Patrick grinned over his shoulder, said "Lady and Gentleman, I will now reveal the Secret of the Moated Pile" and punched the boss in the centre of the mullion. There was a small sigh as of escaping air and a space, the height and breadth of a small man, opened beside the fireplace.

"For evermore!" said Peter, mocking his surprise and immediately examined the mechanism so far as he could and pulled the door shut with his finger-nails to admire the craftsmanship which had fitted door and panelling so precisely, shoving Lawrie and her natural curiosity ruthlessly aside as an unmechanically minded female who didn't know nuts from bolts. "But you know what, don't you?" he said suddenly.

"No. What?"

"You really are the most frightful liar. I can remember asking you at least three times when we were kids whether there were any secret passages and you always looked me straight in the eye like our Maudie and said no. Unless of course you didn't know about this then? There's always that."

"Yes, I did actually," said Patrick cheerfully. "But I was muddling then and now if you know what I mean."

"No, I don't. What do you?"

"Well, I thought—look, we must get on. Otherwise Nelly may start wondering what we're up to and if she once heard about The Thuggery she'd flap till we couldn't hear ourselves think." He punched the boss again. "You come last, Peter, and shut the door. There's no light, but we only have to keep going."

They stepped into the passage; Peter pulled the door shut; darkness, impenetrable as cloth, muffled them. Had it been an ordinary passage, Lawrie might well have besought someone to fetch a torch, squealed that spiders were dropping on her and asked Patrick several times if he was sure he knew the way out. This, however, she was able to see as proper adventure stuff, even though in the cramped sloping passage, stuffy with dust and the ages, Peter trod on her heels and sometimes she on Patrick's, while in the total darkness, even her hands groping for the walls on either side didn't save her from overbalancing every now and then. Then Patrick said, "Stop!" A door opened, narrow as the first and they stepped into a lilliputian room whose entire furnishings were a small wooden crucifix on the wall facing the door and a solid three-legged stool standing in the centre of the room. The small oriel window was screened by boughs of wistaria.

"'*Strewth*," said Peter, walking over to it and looking out. After a moment he said, "I suppose that's how it feels if you're blind. I never realized before. My goodness. It's not a bit like just shutting your eyes."

Lawrie, gazing round the tiny room, didn't answer; Patrick, eyeing his friend interestedly, waited for more. But presently Peter, who had continued to look out as if he still needed reassuring that the darkness had been temporary and external, said only, "I can see where we are now. I can see the orchard and the hawk garden. How did they hide this window before the wistaria was here?"

"It's one in a long row of windows—it hides itself if you understand me. So does that boss on the window upstairs—all the windows in those rooms look exactly alike."

"Like hiding a leaf in a forest," said Peter who had recently read the *Father Brown* stories.

"'S right," said Patrick, catching the allusion. He closed the door. Once again, no line showed on the panelling.

Lawrie said, "I suppose you don't actually have to remember where it is. You only have to remember what works it."

"'S right," said Patrick kindly, thinking (rightly) she'd meant more than she'd said. "And there are three ways out and I know them all so we shan't be lost here for ever."

Peter turned, grinning. "Yes, well, now, before we do anything else, explain those massive lies about *No* Secret of the Moated Pile. Why?"

"*That*. Well, I just told you. I got muddled. Pa showed me this room and explained it was the place where they hid the Sacrament and the priest in the penal times. Only—"

"What", said Lawrie, who thought she probably should know but knew she didn't, "*are* penal times?"

"Eh, m' dear," said her brother, "what a turble iggy female speciment 'ee do be for sure. Did 'ee niver 'ear tell 'ow our Bluff King Hal did most gloriously forbid the idolatrous sayin' o' th' Mass an' take they as disobeyed to Marble Arch for a public 'oliday of 'angin', drawin' an' quarterin' like? Splendid times those did be—"

"*Marble Arch?*" said Lawrie incredulously.

"Tyburn, then, m' dear, if so be you likes the old name better. And then 'twas Bloody Mary's reign an' she did burn us glorious Protestants as 'eretics, turn an' turn about as you might say, till Good Queen Bess sat on the throne an' put they Papists in their place, praper she did." He looked at Patrick, wondering suddenly if he'd gone too far and was relieved to see he hadn't. "That be roight, squoire, b'ain't it?"

". . . *Poor Airy Post*"

"Straight out of *Little Arthur's History of England*," said Patrick equably.

"An' a rare ol' crummy book that dü be for sure. You were saying?"

"Was I? Oh yes—somehow I got the idea the penal times were still with us and so it was still a deadly secret. So *natch* when you asked I said nay, no such thing——"

"You really thought I couldn't be trusted?" said Peter, only half-joking.

"I knew you weren't a Holy Roman. In those particular circs, from what pa said, I gathered it came to the same thing," said his friend amiably.

"And what about every Sunday when the priest came to say Mass? Didn't it seem a bit odd he just came and went?"

"No—I thought he went into hiding as soon as he'd had breakfast. Every Sunday I thought would this be the day for the brutal soldiery to burst in the front door."

"How absolutely *petrifying*," said Lawrie with a sympathetic shudder.

"I don't think I was petrified. I much more remember thinking it all madly exciting. I know I had it all worked out how very very heroic I was going to be."

"I wonder would one have been?" said Peter meditatively.

"Not this one," said Patrick quickly. "And of course, once I went to prep school, I came to. Now can we get on with this Thuggery affair?"

They agreed they better had. Peter unrolled his mackintosh and displayed the pigeon and Patrick set Regina on the stool and tied her leash to one of its legs. The rest of them sat on the floor.

"Now," said Patrick, "let's see your Top Secret message. And what d'you bet, after all this, that it says *Dear Jukie Meet Me At The Palais 7.30 Saturday Your Ever-Loving Chick Sandra*."

"Would he have a girl?" said Peter, and answered himself. "Yes, bound to have. Unless old Maudie says he's got to make do with the pigeons. She probably thinks that's what's meant by chatting up the birds."

53

He gave a hoot of laughter at such wit. Patrick said, "And what do you make do with? A half-hitch in every port?"

Peter grinned back, his fingers busy with the harness. "Practically almost. We must take our social life in hand next holidays. What do you do, young Patrick? You have more chances than the rest of us."

"How?"

"Living in London, going to day school. *Surely* you date the chicks?"

They looked at him teasingly, thinking it somehow so very unlikely, and were surprised when he flushed. But this was because he had at once thought of Ginty and it was oddly embarrassing, thinking of Ginty in the presence of her brother and sister. He said quickly, "A different chick every night of the week, actually. Haven't you got that thing off yet?"

"I have. Here." Peter showed the capsule lying on his palm. And then, as they all looked at it, he said, puzzled, "*That* doesn't look like a message-container."

It didn't. It looked much more like a shampoo sachet. Patrick picked it delicately off Peter's palm and took it over to the window. He held it against the light. He said at last, "It looks to me as if there's powder inside. Come and look."

Peter came; Lawrie stayed where she was, kneeling on the floor, her hands pressed palm to palm between her knees. Suddenly, she was wishing Patrick and Peter wouldn't bother with it. When Peter turned from the window, holding the capsule towards her, she shook her head vigorously.

"Why not?" he said. "What's the matter?"

"Nothing." Then she gave herself away. "D'you think it might blow up?"

"Prototype of the new improved mini-bomb?" said Patrick hopefully. "See the Kremlin disappear in a puff of smoke? Well, I don't know. Nothing went bang when the pigeon hit the deck. Let's have a proper look." Standing before the crucifix, he pressed its base against the panelling: a twelve-inch square opened beside it.

"I'm not a very big boy but I don't think I can get through there," said Peter plaintively.

"Oddly enough you don't have to. This is where we hid the chalice and Sacrament from Good Queen Bess. Now used by P. Merrick as a private store. Which is a bit of a come-down when you come to think of it."

"Is it all right?" asked Lawrie, half-shocked.

"Why not? It's not used for that now."

"No-o. But if it *used* to be—"

"Now you're just being superstitious," he told her kindly, groping in the recess. "Where's everything gone? There should be a volume I see before me—yes, here we are—this'll do to shake it out on—"

"If the venerable Karen", said Peter, referring to his eldest sister who was in her first year at Oxford, "could see you tearing end papers out of books, she'd—she'd—"

"Well, she needn't, because this isn't what you'd call a book. It's a journal I started like one Sam Pepys, only I got too bored with me. Only then I didn't like to throw me away. Now then."

He took a penknife from his pocket. Lawrie sucked in her lips and shut her eyes tight. Patrick held the capsule against the floor and sliced off a corner; then he held it over the sheet of paper and tapped gently. Involuntarily, Lawrie, now peeping through her lashes, shrank back. A small pile of white powder appeared. They looked at it.

"Arrh, m' dears, be so clear's mud what thaät dü be," said Peter suddenly. "They dratted pigeons, now, 'tis well known they dü stuff theirselveses wi' us poor farmerses peas. An' then, mos' like, 'tis the gales in their innards as comes to plague they. So one of they dü allus fly wi' thiccy little dose of the soda bicarb, 'case any of they dü get took bad sudden wi' the gastric—"

"Bicarbonate of soda," said Patrick, staring at Peter as if the words recalled something quite different.

"Well, if it's only bicarb it's not anything, is it?" said Lawrie, greatly relieved. "Shall you let them have it back?"

"... Poor Airy Post"

"By first pigeon post," said Peter solemnly, "natch." Lawrie looked at him doubtfully; a maggot wriggled in her thought and told her she had felt relieved too soon. "You don't think it would be just a touch queer", suggested her brother, answering her look, "to send pigeons flying around loaded with soda bicarb?"

"It mightn't be," said Lawrie, clinging to the remnants of relief. "P'raps they strap things to them for practice like—like that Russian runner who trained in football boots. P'raps it's the Culver Method—"

"Or perhaps", said Patrick firmly, "it's not bicarbonate of soda. In two of Dorothy Sayers's thrillers when packets of bicarb turn up, once it's arsenic, and once it's cocaine."

"Objection, your honour. Once when Lord Peter Wimsey *hoped* it was arsenic, it actually *was* soda bicarb—"

"And I bet a million jelly babies this is too," said Lawrie hardily. "You'll be saying it's strychnine next."

"No, I won't. Strychnine leaves a flavour as of bitter almonds on the air. Agatha Christie's libraries are thick with it."

"I bet it *is* just bicarb," repeated Lawrie desperately.

"But it *can't* be," said her brother. "Or even if it was, it would have to be a try-out for something else."

"Would it? Why would it? *Why* couldn't it just be an experiment to see how far a pigeon could fly with that much tied to him?"

"Because why not use a piece of wood? But if you're so sure," Patrick picked up paper and powder and held it towards her, "taste and see."

There was a sudden silence. Lawrie, looking from one to the other, saw that neither supposed for a moment she would risk any such thing. Pride, which rarely helped her when it was a question of courage, did quite often stiffen her in a matter of obstinacy. Deliberately, she wetted the tip of her finger with the tip of her tongue, stuck her finger-tip into the white powder, licked her finger-tip and crunched the grains——

"For goodness' sake don't *swallow* it," exclaimed her brother in alarm.

But pride had already deserted her and she was scrubbing her tongue frantically with her handkerchief. She had scrubbed it almost dry before she realized that moments had passed and she hadn't dropped dead; and just how it had tasted she was never able to say, but it certainly wasn't bicarbonate of soda. This was so self-evident that Patrick and Peter forbore to stress the fact. "So now what?" said Peter.

Patrick began to coax the grains still left on the paper back into the capsule with the point of the penknife. "Take it to the police. Now we know for sure it's something lethal."

"We really have to, do we?" said Peter, watching the point of the penknife.

"Yes, we do. Why d'you think not?"

"Oh, I don't know." Peter wriggled his shoulders. "Just all that mustn't sneak mustn't rat stuff, I suppose."

"But drug-smuggling's quite different from anything like that. It's like blackmail—much worse than most murders." He stopped his work with the penknife, his mind suddenly busier than his fingers. "Really, it is a kind of physical blackmail, isn't it? You chat people into taking the stuff, you make them so dependent on it they have the heebie jeebies if they can't get it and then you make them pay the earth to keep getting it."

"And what happens then?" asked Lawrie.

"Your brain decays, I think. Always supposing", said he, for Lawrie was looking at him in fright and horror, "that you have a brain to start with."

"Is that what's going to happen to me?"

"No, of *course* not. You didn't even swallow the stuff."

Lawrie gave a great sigh of relief. "No, I didn't, did I?"

Peter said, "I'm still not a hundred per cent keen on telling the police, but I suppose you could be right—"

"I know I am."

"All right, cocky. What do we do, then? Take it over to Colebridge? Or tell them to come and get it?"

"What for when we've our own copper just down the road? Tom Catchpole, you know. We oughtn't to by-pass him. A good juicy case like this might be a help with promotion."

"Arrh, bright 's any button be young Tom Catchpole. Allus dü look t'other way w'en my bloomin' lamp dü be troublesome." (He had recently acquired a not too reliable secondhand bicycle.) "Rackon as one good turn dü deserve another. Besides, that there young Mrs. Tom dü be a real—"

"Dishy dodo," suggested Patrick.

"Smasher. Dishy dodo dü be city talk. And anyway," said Peter, "how d'*you* come to be so with the gab? You know many Teds personally?"

"There's a coffee-bar I go into on my way home from maths coaching. It's always crammed with the kiddoes and the chicks yapping away and being with it like mad. And anyway, that's not Ted gab. Teds—the real issue—are something quite else. Even Jukie—"

"Even Jukie what?" said Peter as the pause lengthened.

"I was going to say even Jukie and his click are only semi-Teds, if that. But don't you *see*?"

"See what?"

"Jukie. We always thought they called him Jukie—short for Juke-box."

"Yes. Well?"

"Suppose it wasn't? Suppose it was Junkie?"

"Suppose it was? Junkie short for load of old rubbish. So what?"

"No, but it wouldn't be. Junkie—in their language—means drug addict."

CHAPTER FIVE

A Brush with the Enemy

<hr/>

It was almost breakfast time. Patrick opened one of the casements, moved Regina into a patch of sunshine and put the harness and capsule away in the secret cupboard. They were no longer talking much: even on the way home Peter only spoke twice: once to say "Don't tell Mum any of this", the second time to say "I'll have to give my 'tosh a scrub before anyone sees it." To both these pronouncements Lawrie agreed mutely *No she wouldn't* and *Yes he'd better*. The Thuggery was nowhere to be seen.

Doris, who now came daily from the village to help in the house, was crossing the hall as they went in. By signs and grimaces they impressed on her the need for silence concerning their muddy looks and bolted upstairs. They paused at the bathroom, rinsed the bits of them that showed, and rushed on to their bedrooms. Sitting on the dressing-table stool, Lawrie yanked off her gumboots, felt her socks, decided they'd *do*, pushed her feet into her plimsolls, and wriggled round to face the mirror and comb her hair. Her face looked back at her, clean—but *homely*, thought Lawrie dispiritedly: that was what Jukie had seen when he'd looked at her and seen nothing worth his notice.

Morosely, she made an inventory: hair—pale yellow; eyebrows—pale brown; eyelashes—long but ditto; eyes—blue; mouth—just another cakehole; chin—just a face-end; nose— Lawrie regarded her nose and her spirits rose slightly. It was, when you came to look at it, rather a super nose: not too long, not too short, perfectly straight and thin as a nose could be.

A Brush with the Enemy

Lawrie stroked it approvingly: only it did seem a pity such a jewel of a nose should have such a—a plastic setting.

She continued to study her reflection. Presently inspiration visited her: not in a blinding flash, but in a gradual illumination which sounded like common sense. She got out the three-tier theatrical make-up box she had been given the Christmas before and which was now nearly full. Peter acquired tools and wood for Christmas and birthday presents—Lawrie acquired powder and grease-paint, liners and lipsticks.

She had quite often cheered up a wet afternoon inventing a make-up for some unlikely character part—Oberon, Caliban, one of Macbeth's witches—but this was the first time she'd made-up as herself. The result ravished her: under shadowed lids, between mascaraed lashes, her eyes were suddenly vivid; the line above her upper lashes continued to the outer corners made them seem larger just as the fashion articles in the women's magazines at the hairdressers said: the pale lipstick—

Someone hit the door with the flat of their hand and marched in: Peter. "I've come for the hawk bells," he said on his way to Nicola's market box, "and if you don't want to know, just don't look—*Lumme!*"

Lawrie stiffened her shoulders defiantly. Peter, who was rarely deflected from his immediate aim, searched for and found the hawk bells. With these in his pocket, he transferred his attention to his sister's face. He stood beside the mirror and gazed at her seriously, blinking at regular intervals. This was so unlike any reaction she had expected that she took heart, saying hopefully, "*Well?*"

"What *exactly* are you supposed to be?"

"*Me.*"

"That's what I thought. Just thought I'd better make sure."

"Well? Go *on*. What does it look like?"

"Arrh me ol' darlin', 'tes wot I bin askin' meself ivver since I clapt eyes on 'ee. Do 'ee look turble now, I asks meself or do 'ee look—?"

"Do I look *what*?"

60

"Thaät's whaät I dü be askin' meself, me ol' darlin'. 'Tes the same's I dü ask meself w'en I dü see they chicks in they coffee-bars. All painted up they dü be, wi' ribbons in their 'air—praper little ol' Jezebels, like—"

"Do I look," said Lawrie desperately, suddenly lighting on the fit and proper word, "*dishy?*"

Peter's eyes widened; and then he grinned—a long, slow appreciative grin that seemed to grow for ever. "Eh, m' dear, so that's whaät 'tes all you lassies dü be arter. Droivin' us poor lads woild wi' they false eyelashes 'n that—"

"My eyelashes *aren't* false!"

"Eh m' dear, but how can us poor lads be sure? 'Tes all of a deceivin' an' a deception, like—"

Lawrie gave up. She should never have started it, not at this hour of the morning. And there was the breakfast gong, bellowing like mad in the hall. Peter, still grinning, sauntered towards the door, the tale obviously for the telling and quite useless to ask him not to. He'd only tell with even greater relish.

Lawrie scrabbled for cold cream and tissues. But newly put on make-up isn't easy to remove in a hurry and enough mascara and lipstick remained to bear out Peter's story: enough also to convince Lawrie that, however funny Peter might be, it *did* make her look dishy. Shiny round the hairline, defiant to the point of sulkiness, Lawrie stumped down to breakfast.

Breakfast, however, was eaten peaceably. No one commented on Lawrie's appearance, so either Peter hadn't told or (more likely) Mummy had said not to tease her. And since of the rest of the family only Rowan and Ann were also at home this week-end, Lawrie felt fairly safe. Rowan, who had left school the previous summer to learn how to run the farm, seldom concerned herself with Lawrie's upbringing: and Ann was too kind to tease anyone—though she was probably, thought Lawrie hopefully, being shocked rigid by her youngest sister's blue eyelids and might well start a campaign to get Lawrie back into the school Guide Company in the hope of putting a stop to such goings-on. *Ha ha*, thought Lawrie, *some hopes*, and battered down the shell of her egg.

The post came, bringing a card for their mother with the *Cutty Sark* on one side and on the other *Having fab time. Keep this for me. Love to everybody. Nicola*. Lawrie thought *Return of Regina, ha, ha* and *Little does she know, ha, ha*; her mother, apparently reminded by Nicola's card that Lawrie and Peter and Ann were having their half-term holiday too, asked, as she poured second cups of tea, "Is there anything special you three would like to do today?"

"I shall be over at Patrick's, thank you, Ma, *very* much for asking," said Peter promptly and shot Lawrie a look. "And so will Lal too, *won't you*, gel?"

"Ye-es," said Lawrie, suddenly not sure about this. "It depends. What's on at the cinemas?"

"Nothing for you," suggested Peter, jerking his eyebrows up and down. Inevitably, it was Ann who got up to find and look at yesterday's copy of the *Colebridge and District Chronicle*. There were two cinemas in Colebridge—the Regal which was small and shabby and showed the classic films of the past and the Majestic which was large and shabby and screened the current releases six months late. As Ann picked up the newspaper, Peter shot Lawrie another look, a caricature of menace and boding, and took a banana: it just wasn't on, he told himself, biting hugely, leaving Lawrie on the loose with Ma and Ann; she'd be telling them the whole thing inside five seconds—

"*The Magnificent Ambersons* at the Regal," read Ann from the Entertainments page. "And *Cobweb!* at the Majestic."

"Useless," said Lawrie, as if it were Ann's fault: for the Regal showed *The Magnificent Ambersons* so often that Lawrie had seen it twice already, and *Cobweb!* could only be science fiction. Karen and Rowan described such films as "The 20,000 Fathom Thing From Outer Space" and found them very funny. But Lawrie was scared by monster tentacles and towering shapes and wouldn't go.

"P'raps Rowan would like to go instead," suggested Peter

helpfully, glancing towards Rowan who had consumed her breakfast in a steady hungry silence and was now pushing back her chair. But Rowan said, "Not today, thank you. Today's the day I clear Poggs Acre of couch grass."

"It *is*? You don't say! Now what can you possibly mean by that I ask myself?" said Peter. But Rowan, having caught her mother's eye, got up and merely grinned briefly at him as she left the room.

"Such application as the girl has," said Peter, deciding yet another banana would do him all the good in the world. "Does she enjoy herself, does anyone think?"

"I'm *sure* she'd much rather be at school still," said Ann whose own sights were trained on the virtual certainty of a prefectship in two years' time and thought it terribly sad Rowan should have missed all that. But Mrs. Marlow, who always tried to nip gossip about absent members of the family in the bud, said quickly, harking back, "If you don't want to go to the cinema, we could still go into Colebridge and do some shopping and have tea at Romilly's. If you'd like that," she ended doubtfully, as if it now seemed a rather dull suggestion after all.

Ann, anxious no one should be hurt, said, "It's an awfully good idea, only there's this nature thing the Company's doing. My Patrol's collecting the tree specimens and I'd like to get mine today and make sure of them."

And Lawrie, who thought all feelings but her own cast-iron, said candidly, "It sounds utter scrudgey. I expect I'll—oh, *I* dunno," said Lawrie, abruptly and acutely aware of Nicola's absence. "I just needn't do anything."

"That's absurd! You surely aren't going to spend the whole week-end moping round the house just because Nicky's staying with Miranda? There's no need for anyone to go into Colebridge if they don't want to, but for goodness' sake find yourself something to do and don't go around like a wet week in a fog."

Her mother's attack was so unexpected that Lawrie's eyes filled. She spun her napkin-ring round and round her finger, muttering, "Why did you say let's go then, if you didn't want to?"

"Come and help me," suggested Ann quickly. "I could do with some."

Lawrie shook her head vehemently, silently. Peter, his chin propped on laced fingers, his eyes on Lawrie, awaited developments. His mother said, "Then go with Peter. You and Patrick won't mind, will you, Binks?"

"'S right, Ma," he said, still watching Lawrie, mildly sorry for her.

Lawrie stared tearfully at her empty eggshell and crumby plate. Her mother said, "Oh, come on, cheer up, Lal. You surely don't expect to have Nicky on a string for ever? She's entitled to her friends just as you are to yours. Don't be so selfish."

"I'm NOT selfish!" thought Lawrie passionately. "It's not FAIR! It's nothing to DO with Nick! It's I just don't want to muck about with them and their beastly pigeon!"

The obvious thing was to say so. For some mazy, half-thought reasons (that Mummy mustn't be worried; that Mummy was being a BEAST and she never even *tried* to understand how Lawrie felt) Lawrie said nothing. She lifted her head, tears standing in her eyes and glowered at Peter; and Peter grinned affably back; and there they were.

Patrick had sealed the cut corner of the capsule with a piece of sellotape and was holding it in his left hand in his jacket pocket: the pigeon and its harness were hidden in the carrier-basket of Peter's bicycle on which he was free-wheeling as slowly as possible so as not to draw ahead of the other two: Lawrie, still bruised in her feelings, was walking silently between them down the hill to the village, telling herself that in fifteen . . . twelve . . . ten minutes they would have handed the evidence to Tom Catchpole and after that it would be all over and done with. . . .

"Do you see what I see?" said Peter suddenly, standing on the pedals to see properly.

A Brush with the Enemy

"No. What?"

"Don't stop. Keep going as if it didn't matter."

"As if *what* didn't matter?"

"You'll see as we get to the village. The Thuggery have invaded."

"*Have* they," said Patrick: a statement rather than a question.

"'S right. Green Stripes and Black Check are outside The Shop and Purple Streak's at the bottom of the hill just round the corner."

"Is Jukie anywhere?"

"I don't see him. What now?"

"Well, we obviously can't go back." Patrick thought. "Have you any money on you?"

"Only jingle."

"That'll do. Then before we call on Tom Catchpole let's go to The Shop and buy stamps and peanuts—for camouflage, you know—as if it wasn't important, the seeing Tom bit——"

"Roger. And then—look here, this is rather good—when we're on the post office side buying stamps, let's ask about trains so's they think it's the Colebridge police we—"

"Do post offices know about trains?" asked Lawrie, bewildered.

"Shouldn't think so. The point is we ask so's we can talk about it loudly so's The Thuggery hears."

"And then we'll say loudly about going the long way home and that'll take us past Tom Catchpole's. And then I'll say *very* loudly that I'll just nip in and ask if my watch has turned up yet."

"What watch?"

"The watch I'm pretending I've lost so's to get us into Tom Catchpole's Without Arousing Suspicion," said Patrick patiently.

"Then hadn't you better take off that peculiar round brass object on your left wrist? Or p'raps they won't be as taken in as you think they will."

Patrick grinned, unfastened his watch and dropped it into his pocket. Then he jostled Lawrie and, surprisingly, didn't apologize. What he said next was, "Can you ride a bike, Lawrie?"

"Natch." Then, too late, she thought it might have been safer to say she couldn't.

"Then don't you think, Pete, it would be a good idea, in *case* they jump us, if Lawrie has the bike so that she can make a dash with the evidence?"

"Sounds fine on paper." Peter made a last reconnaissance from the pedals and got off. "Here you are, gel. First sign of a punch-up and you leap to the saddle like Jorrocks and me."

"*Stirrup*," said Patrick in pained parenthesis. "*Joris*."

"Where to?" asked Lawrie, disconcerted by all these mobilization plans, though relieved to be told officially she might bolt for cover.

"Use your half-loaf, gel! Tom Catchpole's if you can make it, The Shop if you can't—even the nearest hefty grown-up would *do*."

Lawrie nodded, clutching the bicycle handles and feeling more hampered by the heavy old machine than she'd expected; one of the circling pedals hit her ankle. And then they were at the corner. Music, thumping and frenzied, blared suddenly as if a band had struck up in the village street. Startled out of her skin, Lawrie ran the front wheel over her toes.

Purple Streak leaned against the hedge and seemed not to watch them pass. Ostentatiously enveloped by the thumps and stridulations of the request record being relayed by the transistor radio slung from his shoulder, he combed his hair and jived from the hips up.

"One way of sounding 'action stations' I suppose," said Patrick when they were far enough away to hear themselves think.

"Is *that* what it was? I thought he was just bored with waiting."

"Don't think so. Otherwise we'd have heard it while we were still on the hill—unless the acoustics are peculiar. Besides, look how alerted Black Check and Green Stripes are looking."

A Brush with the Enemy

"So they are. And I take it Purple Streak is now following on. Isn't that Cliff Richard and The Shadows coming up fast behind?"

"The only thing I'm sure of at this distance is that it's not Cilla Black. So now what? Do we still go to The Shop? Or full steam ahead to Tom Catchpole's?"

"Like two destroyers convoying one oil-tanker," suggested Peter. "No, I think still The Shop as if it wasn't at all urgent. And I know what—we'll leave Lawrie and the bike outside as if neither of them matter a hoot, yes?"

Patrick saw Lawrie's face and wondered if they should. But on the other hand, he thought Peter's reasoning sound and after all, she wasn't *his* sister.

Black Check and Green Stripes lounged outside The Shop and watched them come. Cliff Richard and The Shadows were succeeded by "Strawberry Fair", swung. Black Check and Green Stripes placed themselves so that, if anyone wanted to reach The Shop door, they must either walk through or round them. Peter and Patrick made blank faces and walked round as if that had always been the way they wanted to go. Patrick said over his shoulder "Wait for us, Lawrie. We shan't be a sec", whereupon Green Stripes gave an imitation of lah-di-dah and Black Check and Purple Streak became convulsed with laughter. Lawrie stood, gripping the bicycle handles, petrified. Black Check strolled into The Shop.

Even Purple Streak couldn't talk against "Strawberry Fair" swung at that volume: he turned it down but not off, so that Lawrie could hear them talking, but not what they said. Striving to act nonchalance and ease, she gazed first at a puddle near the front tyre, then at a dog snuffing by the wall, then at a line of washing swaying in the wind in the back garden of one of the cottages. But all the while their eyes looked at her, pulling at her own, till at last she had to turn her head and try to eye them with the indifference Nicola would have managed without any difficulty at all. They looked at her and talked about her, and she tried to comfort her hot misery of embarrassment by telling herself that now she had make-up on they did see *something*, not nothing, like Jukie. Then, after a while, something else happened. Green Stripes took a packet of cigarettes from his pocket, lit one, looking at her as he did so, and then flipped the carton accurately, impudently, into the carrier-basket.

Lawrie gazed at it. It lay half-hidden in a fold of the scarf which covered pigeon and harness. She would have hurled it out again, only that she was afraid—in general that they would turn ferocious if she did, selectively that they might shove it back and uncover the pigeon. A voice in her head said firmly *It's not a bit of good your crying* and she knew how true this was; but it was only by a very narrow margin that Peter and Patrick arrived before her tears, saying loudly and encouragingly, "Come on, Lal. Let's go home the other way. There's no train now till half past two, so there's no rush."

Purple Streak and Green Stripes watched them pass.

"I thought you'd never come," said Lawrie shakily. "You were *ages*."

"You're telling us," said her brother. "We thought we'd never get out. There was an absolute *mob* of old age pensioners and Ma Pedder was doing her Wilfred Pickles nut."

"And then she did hours of Ma Glum to Pa Pedder upstairs, finding out about the train. It was just completely hopeless. I say—listen. Isn't that 'Seventy-six Trombones' tailing us? Now let's do this properly. We stroll past Tom Catchpole's and then Lawrie reminds me I wanted to ask about my watch and we go back. Yes?"

They did this to perfection; so that they all—Patrick, Peter, Lawrie; Green Stripes, Black Check, Purple Streak; and Seventy-six Trombones—reached the little gate with POLICE on it simultaneously. The Thuggery pulled up, lounging but attentive. Patrick, pushing open the gate, seemed not to see them. Young Mrs. Catchpole, who had just wheeled her daughter's pram into a patch of sun and was settling her for her morning nap, looked up apprehensively.

"Good morning, Mrs. Tom," said Patrick clearly into the sudden hush—the radio was suddenly a mere whisper—"I'm sorry to bother you, but could I ask Tom if he's heard anything about my watch?"

"Tom's not here," said Mrs. Catchpole, shaking a strand of blonde hair off her forehead and looking past Patrick at The Thuggery. "But I can look and see if there's been any watches brought in if you want."

"Oh——" said Patrick blankly. "Is he—d'you know where I could find him?"

"He's over to Great Toft. Some persons lighted a fire in St. Mary's. Piled all the cassocks and hymn-books in the vestry and poured petrol over them. I wonder some people don't fear to be struck dead."

She was looking directly at The Thuggery, who looked back with all the candour in the world. "Shockin'," they said to one another and "Cor! Did you 'ear that?" and "You be an 'ones' lad 'n own up now" and one punched another playfully and they fell to scuffling.

"Only it never seems to work out like that," said Patrick regretfully. "Oh well, not to bother with it, Mrs. Tom. I'll try to see Tom on Monday morning before I go back. Goodbye."

They went on. The still scuffling Thuggery were capering all over the village street and seemed not to notice their going. But as they crossed the green beyond the cottages it became plain that someone with a long memory had requested "High Noon". The Thuggery drew level and passed them and their words had nothing to do with the song.

"Have a drag, herbert!"

"Make sure you scan the drags good before you teeter out again, herbert!"

"Belshazzar it, herbert! Be right niggled if you don't, you will!"

And then a burst of laughter and distant now, going away in front of them, the final urgent entreatings of "High Noon".

But soon the only sounds were the bird noises in the hedges and, farther off, the clankings of the steam roller on the main road. Peter, breaking off a twig of hawthorn and nibbling reflectively at the first green stipplings, said, "What *I* ask *my*self is *which* wall?"

"Do you? Why? What are we talking about?"

"Oh, Patrick! Belshazzar it, that hairy character said. Writing on the wall. What else can he have meant?"

"My word! Hats off to sir!" said Patrick, bowing profoundly. "To be absolutely and entirely frank with you, my dear Bond, I hadn't even begun to work it out yet. But *why* write on the wall? Wouldn't paper be easier?"

"Not for those hairy characters. Natural born Piltdowners those are. But not actually dangerous, would you say? They did all keep their distance."

But Patrick said dubiously, "I don't know. . . . That was a much too convenient fire over at Great Toft. It got Tom Catchpole out of the way very neatly."

"You think that was them? But it was a fairly piffling fire, wasn't it? Just hassocks and cymn-books—sorry pardon!— *cassocks* and *hymn*-books."

"But only piffling because it was found in time," argued Patrick. "Otherwise St. Mary's could easily have been burnt out—it's terribly small and ancient. Mrs. Tom obviously thought it was them."

"Yes, but that could be mad, blind prejudice, couldn't it? Because when you come to think of it, they are the Culver's mob. She wouldn't have them there at all if they were *completely* criminal."

"That all sounds terribly sensible and it really is the most complete nonsense," said Patrick, tossing a flint ahead of him. Peter flushed scarlet. Lawrie looked apprehensively from one to the other. In a silence on Peter's part offended, on Lawrie's alarmed and on Patrick's contemplative, they walked on: till at last Patrick, having worked it out and wholly unconscious of either offence or apprehension, said, "What I mean is this. One: they are criminal or they wouldn't be smuggling drugs. Two: so far as Maudie Culver goes *either* she has to be in on it with them *or* she genuinely thinks they're dead keen Edinburgh award types. I know one wouldn't think she'd be in on it, but I have read somewhere that being on the selling end is one of the easiest ways of making money, and I suppose Maudie *could* have a thing about lolly."

Peter said aloofly, "Jukie said something this morning about old Maudie Culver digging the integrity racket like she was crazy for it. So she couldn't be a smug druggler——" He checked, trying not to laugh, failed, and knew that was the end of being haughty; you couldn't keep it up once you'd laughed. "I mean *drug smuggler*," he got out at last.

"Not sure I don't prefer smug druggler actually. And talking of integrity, Jukie has something. I remembered when he said that this morning. You know Jon and I visited her ruddy pigeonry?"

"Seeing I was listening to all that argey-bargey on the downs this morning—yes, oddly enough."

"Well, it really is a terrific affair. What's called a pigeon palace. Brick lofts and white paint everywhere and troughs of running water let into the floors and everything knee-deep in sawdust. Absolutely no expense spared, every modern convenience—"

"What about the pigeons?" asked Lawrie.

"Oh, they were there too. I must say I think it's a most peculiar hobby, this fancy pigeon business. As far as I could gather, someone dreams up the most improbable bird they can think of and then perfectly sensible people spend the rest of their lives trying to breed one exactly like it, never mind whether the poor beast can actually breathe or see or not. Anyway, M. Culver has the *lot*. Pouters and Carriers and Archangels and Russian Trumpeters and Nuns and Almonds and Frill-backs and Jacobins—oh, and Tumblers. Now Tumblers are rather good. You let them fly, a whole flock of them, and they go quite high and whizz about for hours, turning somersaults and rolling like mad. Those I did like."

"And now do we get to Maudie's integrity?" said Peter as they climbed a stile to take the short cut. "Or have I missed it?"

"Wait for it. That's the background stuff. Well, so, the whole object of the exercise—of breeding these freaks—is to have an exhibition and win cups. Now every kind—so Maudie told us—has its own special 'properties' on which you win marks. Pouters have legs like baby storks and puff out their crops. Carriers have great masses of wattle above their beaks and round their eyes. Russian Trumpeters have feathered hats and bell-bottom trousers. Nuns are pied and the black and white should make a definite line where they meet. Does sir make himself clear?"

"As mud," said Peter nodding sagely.

"Glorious mud. *So*—it's all very difficult because what you're trying to get is an extreme exaggeration of a natural quality—"

"My word! Get you! Yes, all right," said Peter, "we're alongside."

"—and so *because* it's so difficult there's a sort of recognized minimum allowance of cheating. You may slightly trim the wattle with scissors to make it a better shape. You may cut out one or two feathers if they're spoiling the markings. If you breed one with rather a washy colour you can stroke the feathers with a very little oil to make the colour look deeper. You call it Improving and apparently you're allowed as much as you can get away with."

"Arrh m' dear, that dü sound fer to be a crafty ol' sport an' all."

"Well, I suppose if everyone cheats a little, no one does, if you know what I mean. *Anyway*. We were trotted around and Jon was being polite and impressed, natch, and asking how many cups and suddenly Maudie did an atomic explosion about so-called judges, y' know, who have their friends, y' know, who never go away empty-handed, y' know——"

"Now there you do surprise me," said Peter. "I'd have thought old Maudie would have been the sporting loser to the nth."

"Ah, but that wasn't her point. What gets her is that she breeds her birds as good as it's possible to breed them (*she*

72

says) *but* being such a four-square honest type, she doesn't go for Improving and she thinks they ought to mark her dickies higher than the ones which have been clipped and plucked and whatever."

"Not absolutely sure I don't agree with her."

"So might I too if it were someone else," said Patrick candidly. "Anyway—I don't know how long Jukie'd been with her by then, but he was around, rather skinny and boiler-suity, toting a broom, and Maudie kept pointing out special dickies and telling Jukie to grab them for her and explaining how the wattle properties were *so* and the markings also *so* and the colour deep and true—perfection, unsurpassable. And Jukie had the oddest sort of expression. Jon didn't notice, but I was trying to catch an occasional eye. Only Jukie wouldn't. He was looking at Maudie—not *knowing* exactly—more— quizzical perhaps. I know I thought at the time it was a very grown-up sort of look."

"Like this?" said Lawrie, interested, making an expression.

"No-o," said Patrick, regarding her. "No. It wants to be kinder than that. That's too sarcastic. I know how he looked— *indulgent*! It was a nanny face."

"Like *this*?" said Lawrie, altering her expression.

"Yes, that's it! That's it exactly! Lawrie, The Only Living Identikit!"

Lawrie thumped her chest, delighted. Peter said, "I suppose I'm being slow. *Why* was he looking like her nanny? Weren't the pigeons actually much good?"

"Oh yes, they were. That was what I wondered too, not knowing anything about them. But when I asked Jon, he said no, they were genuinely good birds so if Jukie was looking anything it was probably contempt that she wouldn't do her bit of allowable cheating and get her cup and be done with it."

"I furrows me brow," said Peter, doing so. "I should have thought that her way was what Jon would have madly approved of."

"Well, but so he did. He only thought she needn't make

such a huha. And I'll tell you something else on the same lines, only you must keep the lid on it because it was one of those tremendous local flaps that no one's supposed to know anything about only everyone does, if you know what I mean."

"Go on," said Peter, nodding, while Lawrie went through cut-throat motions of swearing secrecy.

"Well, this was to do with her racing pigeons—one of the big races—Great North Road or something. I don't know how much you know about pigeon racing—"

"Ah ken it a'," said Peter; but Patrick, supposing this to be more comedy, went on "—but pigeons don't cross finishing lines like sensible animals. They clock in at their own loft and then they find the winner by calculating which one has flown at the highest average m.p.h.——"

"Yards," murmured Peter.

"That's right, yards. And they have a most complicated way of timing it—each owner has a special clock which is officially set and sealed before the race and there's a special ring they put on the pigeon's leg and when it gets back to its loft the owner takes the ring off and jams it into the clock and that stops it at the time of arrival——"

"'S right," murmured Peter.

"—yes, well *but* these clocks are supposedly tamper-proof. Only this particular time the Culver clock had been tampered with—very skilfully done, apparently—only what the eager beaver *didn't* know was that if a bird gets home *before* a certain time it's disqualified just as much as if it arrives too late. So the judges impounded the Culver clock and took it apart and said 'Cor! See this!' and there was a terrific scandal which was supposed to be hushed up and Maudie Culver's birds didn't race for a year. The cover story was she'd had a fly-away, whatever that may be, and everyone pretended to believe it——"

"A fly-away—" began Peter.

"No, wait a sec. The point was, she wasn't barred officially from racing, because it was proved the clock had been fixed by an over-keen Thug and no one was prepared to say Maudie should be hung for that. But all *that* being settled, Maudie penalized herself. And if you want to know what Jon thought, he said there was such a thing as being more Catholic than the Pope."

"Well yes. Or else—"

"I'll tell you what it reminds *me* of," said Patrick. "Those super-pious types at Mass who cross themselves each time they genuflect and say their rosaries very very slowly with their eyes half-shut. And bet your life they've got an old age pensioner doing the garden and they're paying him a bob an hour if he's lucky."

"Actually, Maudie's rather brisk in church," said Peter, slightly missing the point. "And you could read it another way, couldn't you? I mean, that she planned for the Thug to fix the clock, so when they were rumbled she did this terrific penalty huha to show everybody what clean hands she'd got."

"But—." Patrick blinked. "Yes, I suppose it *could* be."

"I'll bet it could." They arrived at the high green door. "Now let's see what this Belshazzar wall is they're talking about."

CHAPTER SIX

Communications Cut

This riddle was solved as soon as they entered the stable yard. Old Sellars, the Merricks's groom, harassed and angry, met them with a tale of unlawful-sounding noises heard coming from the hawk-house and of how he'd arrived just too late to catch the intruder who'd escaped through the small window, smashing the glass in his hurry. "And the *mess*, Master Patrick! All your tack embrangled on the floor and the table thrown over and the lid of the chest stove in! And scribbles all over the walls—"

"Word scribbles?" said Peter triumphantly. "What do they say?"

"Some shatterpated drivel. I tried to find young Catchpole on the blower, but—"

"Great Toft," said Patrick unguardedly. "We know. A fire in the vestry."

"Eh?" said old Sellars acutely. "Were you down to the village to find young Catchpole too, then?"

"Oh, not specially," said Patrick instantly. "We saw Mrs. Tom in passing." The prevarication was instinctive: and in a moment he knew why: old Sellars was much too ancient to risk involving him in something which looked like turning rough and tough any moment now—a chivalrous conclusion which enraged the wiry hard-as-nails sixty-year-old Sellars considerably when he heard of it a week later from Patrick's father.

Old Sellars had not exaggerated. The side-room looked as if someone had not only been searching frantically but had also been told to make the confusion as vicious as possible: as for writing on the walls, HAVA DRAG was chalked repeatedly on each. This, as they did what they could to tidy up, floored them all for a time, until Peter had a sudden inspiration which he had to keep to himself because old Sellars was still there, hammering strips of wood across the window frame. In time, however, the window was adequately barred and everything else had at least been picked off the floor; as for the walls, old Sellars thought they should be left for young Catchpole to see. Patrick nodded, though he couldn't see anyone being much interested in a mild case of wall scrawl when they had something as luscious as drug-smuggling to get their teeth into. They locked the doors behind them, old Sellars went back to the stables, and the other three made for the house. Peter began to speak as soon as they were out of the stable yard, but Patrick said, "Not here. Wait till we get inside. We'll go into the library. No one'll hear us there."

So they arrived at the house in silence. Peter propped his bicycle beside the back door, bundled scarf and pigeon under his arm and followed Patrick along the flagged passages and through a green baize door, Lawrie padding anxiously behind. As they went, the cigarette carton fell from the folds of the scarf and Lawrie kicked it, let it lie and then, in the same breath, picked it up after all. They went into the brown-leather, turkey-carpet stillness of the library and, instinctively, sat down—Patrick at his father's desk, Peter and Lawrie in the enormous leather armchairs either side of the empty fire-place. Lawrie extended a languid foppish hand over the broad arm and fastidiously let fall the carton into the waste-paper basket beside her.

"HAVA DRAG", said Peter, bursting with it, "means 'smoke a cigarette' like 'hava pinta' means 'drink some milk'."

Patrick, who had been frowning absently at his hands clasped on the blotter, looked up with a sudden grin. "How terribly inventive of you." He thought about it. "Now say what it means."

"It means 'smoke a cigarette'. I just—"

"Yes, I see *that*. But what do they mean it to mean to us? F'r instance—here's pa's cigarette box. How's that going to help them, suppose we do have one?"

"Oh," said Peter, deflated, having been too pleased with his translation to wonder what it meant. But Lawrie squeaked and scrambled round in her chair to hang head downwards over the arm, more out of the chair than in. "What *are* you doing?" said her brother, thinking poorly of this display.

Lawrie, unabashed, got her finger-tips to the carton and, crimson-faced, retrieved it. "They chucked this into the carrier when I was outside The Shop," she said, falling back into the chair again. "I thought they were just being disgusting, but if HAVA DRAG means cigarettes, they'd mean this, wouldn't they?"

"Would they be tempting us with reefers?" said Peter, as he took the carton from Lawrie's outstretched hand and shook it before passing it on, automatically, to Patrick. "It sounds full of emptiness to me."

"It is too," said Patrick, pushing up the tray. And then he was still and silent. Even Lawrie, who didn't often notice that sort of thing, saw he had gone quite white. And Peter, peering round the side of his armchair, got up hurriedly, saying, "What's the matter?"

Patrick said nothing: he simply went on looking at the open cigarette carton. So Peter went round behind him. The carton was empty all right; but on the inside of the flap, someone had printed: PLAY IT SEHR CRAFTY NODDY-BOY. IF THIS MOB IS SPRUNG THE CLICK IN THE SMOKE WILL HAND DADDY-O HIS HEARSE TICKET SHARPEST.

Peter read this aloud. Lawrie said, "What's all that mean?"

In an unnaturally level voice Patrick translated. "*Take jolly good care softy. If our lot are caught the part of the gang who operate in London will murder your pa.* I wouldn't know whether *sharpest* means razors or just fast."

Lawrie's eyes and mouth grew round and alarmed. Peter said, "Is it a genuine threat, d'you think? Or are they just trying to scare us off?"

"If it was anything except drugs," said Patrick after a moment, "I'd say it was probably just a try-on. But as it is, this sort of set-up sounds so much more likely."

"Why? How?"

"Well—we've sort of been assuming, haven't we, that this is a super-teenage stunt with Jukie and his click selling dope to the types who live it for kicks and all that caper. *Except* that someone has to get hold of the stuff and bring it to this country and *that's* not so likely to be someone our age. But if Jukie and his click are just small fry who've been roped in because of the pigeons, and all they do is collect the stuff from the birds and send it on, it starts sounding a lot more likely. Don't you think?"

"So there has to be a proper gang in London, complete with razors and cosh-boys, to keep everyone in line?"

"That's what the message says—implies."

"You keep talking about pigeons," complained Lawrie, looking at the body which had fallen on the rug when Peter got up. "But it doesn't look a bit like a pigeon to me. It's got a face like Mr. Punch without any chin."

Peter straightened up and spoke with the overdone casualness of one who knows he's about to make a sensation. "It is a pigeon though. Actually, it's a Scandaroon."

The sensation came off in the most gratifying way. The other two gaped at him and said such things as "The how much? The which what? Come again?"

"A Scandaroon," repeated Peter, very pleased with himself. "It's the name of the place where they were bred, like there's a strain of racers called Antwerps. Only Scandaroons are a terribly ancient breed—the Syrian merchantmen used to have them aboard so that they could fly them ashore to let their agents at their home port know when they'd be arriving."

"You don't mind," said Patrick cautiously, "if we ask how you know what you're talking about?"

"Yes, madly, actually. You know my friend Selby at Dartmouth? Well, he has a Belgian grandfather. And the Belgians are fantastic about racing pigeons. They'd never dream of keeping them in the garden like we do—they have their lofts in the tops of their houses, which makes it all a bit whiff and buggy, Sel says, if you mind that sort of thing, which he doesn't."

"And Selby's grandfather keeps Scandaroons?"

"Oh 'strewth, no. Granpa's birds are racers—*so* first-class that the strain's called after his family, which is *the* top honour. So natch he wanted to give Sel a pair and start him off in dad's trad—only it's mum's trad, actually."

Patrick nodded. Lawrie made a long leg, put her toe under the scarf and pulled it over the pigeon: it looked too dead for her comfort.

"Well, Sel was quite pleased, natch, but he thought he'd better look into it a bit—I told him about you and the hawks for one thing. So we got hold of some books and asked around and as far as we could see Sel'd have to retire from the Service straight off and make it his life's work. Only his ma didn't want to offend granpa, so his pa's going to be responsible for having them looked after."

"And now do we get to the Scandaroons?"

"Well you wanted to know how I knew, didn't you? All the books we looked at had a chapter on The History of the Pigeon and they nearly all had a bit about Scandaroons. And one huge book had full-page illustrations. I knew sort of when I picked it up only it didn't actually click till just now. There's been so much going on."

Patrick nodded, thinking. Lawrie said, "But why didn't they use a carrier pigeon? Aren't they the kind that carry things usually?"

"If you mean ordinary racers like Red Rocket, yes. I don't know why not—yes I *do* though, it's just this minute come to me! In one of these books we read there was a whole lot about the ways pigeons were used during the war——"

"The Hitler one? But they *couldn't*. They had wireless by then," said Lawrie. Then she doubted herself. "Didn't they?"

"'S right, gel. But when it was absolutely essential to send messages without breaking wireless silence they still used pigeons. Or when they had to send back plans or films. Don't you remember that man on steam radio who went over on D-Day with four of them—Blood, Toil, Tears and Sweat? Anyway, they used enough for the Germans to have to have a special falconry unit to deal with them."

"And those were Scandaroons?" said Lawrie, trying hard.

Peter sighed. "No, gel dear, those were ordinary racing pigeons. But ordinary racers have a thing about crossing long stretches of water—if it's a lake they fly round and if they must cross the Channel they nearly all fly along the coast and use the Dover crossing. So the book said. But if the ancient Scandaroons always flew from boats, perhaps their descendants don't fuss either—*'strewth!* That must be it! The smuggling must either come from France or from a ship in the Channel! And that'd be sense because then they'd never have to risk the Customs."

"It all sounds madly logical and dove-taily," said Patrick. "Only I've just this moment thought of something too. When Jon and I were at Monks' Culvery we saw a whole lot of most peculiar-looking birds, but none of them, I'll absolutely swear, looked anything remotely like that Scandaroon."

"They must have."

"They didn't you know. None of them. Not that it makes much real difference because The Thuggery's as good as said they're mixed up in something." His eyes fell on the message on the tray of the cigarette carton. "You know, I think the thing to do now is telephone my pa and tell him what's happened and let him get the cops moving his end." He lifted the hand-piece and waited.

"Are you going to warn him about the threat?" asked Lawrie anxiously.

"Natch. That's chiefly what I'm phoning about." He jiggled the receiver rest impatiently. "And now she'll say *Ay cen't answer ef yew keep movin' the receiver ep en deown yew kneow*."

But no voice spoke annoyance in his ear. And he suddenly realized that this pause had none of the normal clicks and mad voices in it. It was just blank: empty: nothing. He handed the receiver to Peter. "Listen."

Peter listened. "I can't hear anything."

"That's what I can't hear either."

"You mean it's out of order?" said Lawrie. "What an awful bore."

Patrick and Peter looked at one another. "Or else", said Peter, "The Thuggery have cut the wires."

Patrick replaced the hand-piece. "We'll have to try the call-box in Diprose Lane."

"Why not ours? There's an extension in ma's bedroom now —no one'd be likely to hear us."

"And The Thuggery can't jump us there. I'll just sling the pige in the priest's room and say a word to Regina—"

At which point the front door bell pealed loudly and they all jumped. "We'd better answer it," said Patrick, getting up in a hurry. "You lurk behind the front door when I open it, Pete, just in case."

"Me and my little hatchet," agreed Peter, but finding no weapon more lethal than the poker. He heard Patrick shout to Nelly that it was all right, he was going, and hurried after, leaving Lawrie hesitating, tense and disorganized, on the edge of her armchair.

He took station beside the front door, poker poised, and nodded to Patrick. Patrick flung the door wide, stepping back as he did so. And then both felt uncommonly foolish, for only Rowan stood there, asking if she might use the phone.

"Do come in," said Patrick, becoming very much the son of the house while Peter stood the poker discreetly among the other fire-irons in the great fireplace. "Only sorrow to the nth, but our phone's not working either."

"Oh lord. Nor's the call-box. Apparently Westbridge is completely cut off. I must drive over, that's all."

"Drive where?" said her brother, as Lawrie emerged from the library and hovered, listening.

"To Compton Marshall to fetch Mr. Farringdon." (This was the local vet.) She added, in answer to the boys' questioning looks, "Some unspeakable lout took time off to heave broken milk-bottles into the cowpond in Old Pasture. Marigold and Fancy have cut feet and Jenny's torn her muzzle." Lawrie clutched her own nose and mouth; the others made sounds of horror and disgust: and Rowan added, "If I knew who was responsible I'd take him by the scruff of the neck and push his own face in it. Thanks anyway. If I pass a call-box that's working, I'll call the Exchange and let them know about our phones."

She ran down the steps to the jeep parked at the bottom and drove off in a flurry of gravel. Patrick closed the door and they stood looking at one another.

"It could be," agreed Patrick allusively. "As a warning to you two to stand clear."

"Then they've got another think coming. If it *was* them it's *so* disgusting we can't *be* warned off."

"Can't we really?" said Lawrie distressfully. "Why can't we? Can't we just stop and let the police find out about it? I do hate all this. It's gone all beastly suddenly."

"How," said her brother tartly, shamed by her, "are the police supposed to find out if we don't tell them?"

"They would some time, wouldn't they?"

"You mean when someone who isn't an Old Yellowstreak sticks their neck out?"

Lawrie's face quivered. She turned away saying something about Mummy being simply beastly and now him and went back into the library. Patrick, an embarrassed spectator, said quickly, "Look—I was thinking. Suppose one of us takes the evidence to the police in Colebridge, while the other one does decoy-duck stuff here?"

"You don't think we'd better stick together? One and one won't stand much chance if they get caught."

"Nor two to seven."

"I suppose not. I wish we could think up something *really* masterly—"

They gazed hopefully and attentively at one another, as if the masterly something might be conjured from some mental hinterland where it must, surely, be lurking. As they stood there, caught up in the myth that every problem has its solution, Lawrie came out of the library, buckling her mackintosh belt, acting haughty, not looking at them, going home now. They let her pass in silence, seeing no help for it if that was how she felt; and then, as she put her hand on the iron handle of the front door, Patrick remembered something. "Just a sec, Lawrie! Let me have the capsule!"

"*I've* not got it!"

"You have you know. I put it in your pocket when we were going down to the village and we decided you'd better beat it on the bike if they jumped us."

"You never said." Resentfully, she felt in both pockets. She shook her head. "You can't have."

"Of course I did. It *must* be there. Look properly."

"I *have* looked properly," declared Lawrie, coming suddenly to a high and dudgeonly boil. "*Look! That's* my hanky, *that's* my purse and that's absolutely *all*. I'm not joking."

"Oh 'strewth," said Patrick slowly, realization and dismay coming together. "Then you must have dropped it. It could be anywhere."

"I did not drop it," said Lawrie, enunciating very clearly indeed, "because I did not know I had it. Therefore I did not take any special care because I did not know I had to and it is not my fault so sker*wash*."

"No, all right, it's not," said Patrick, acknowledging the justice of this. "But that doesn't make any difference to what's happened. It's gone just the same."

"I know!" exclaimed Peter. "She must have dropped it in the library when she was dangling over the arm of the chair. Come and look."

So they went back to the library and the boys searched the chair and the carpet, the rug and the waste-paper basket, and Lawrie watched from the doorway, chewing her lips nervously. But the time came when there was nothing else to search: they came to this conclusion almost simultaneously and sat back on their heels and looked at one another.

"The only thing I can think of now is for you to pray to St. Anthony," suggested Peter half-seriously; and was considerably disconcerted when Patrick said, matter-of-factly, "I have."

"Oh. Have you. Well, that's good, because I don't see how we can possibly find it ourselves. It could be absolutely anywhere in the village—or the way we came home—"

"And if we go looking for it and The Thuggery see us and guess what it is we're looking for, they'll know they're safe."

"How? We've still got the pigeon and the harness."

"But there's nothing criminal about those. We can't prove even that they belong to The Thuggery."

"We couldn't *prove* the capsule does."

"No. But if we had that the police would be bound to investigate. I should think. They could at least go to Monks' Culvery and see if there were any more Scandaroons."

"I suppose", said Lawrie, much against her will, but unable to stop herself joining in, "the absolute evidence would be if they caught a Scandaroon flying into its dovecote at Monks' Culvery with its harness on and everything. Only before you said when you went to Monks' Culvery there weren't any."

"There weren't. . . . *Lawrie!*"

"What?" said Peter, catching the infection of excitement as Patrick scrambled to his feet, his eyes very yellow and shining under his dark brows: Lawrie came properly into the room.

"What Lawrie said," said Patrick incoherently, "the dovecote at Monks' Culvery. That's what we never looked at. That's where they must be."

"I don't get it," said Peter. "You said you saw all her lofts—"

"Yes, the ones she built herself. But not the dovecote. That was there when Monks' Culvery was a monastery. She never showed us that."

"Yes but *I*'ve seen dovecotes. The pub at Compton Marshall keeps fantails. You couldn't—"

"Yes but not that kind. The Monks' Culvery dovecote is a *building*. It's *huge*. I'll show you a drawing of it." He was already at the shelves, searching with the impatience of someone who knows exactly the book he wants if only he can put his hand on it. Peter and Lawrie waited, glancing at one another occasionally, but mostly watching Patrick. "Here it is," he exclaimed triumphantly. "Aunt Eulalia's magnum opus on the antiquities of the county: privately printed in 1834 and copies sent to every member of the family."

"You mean 1934," said Lawrie as Patrick carried the calf-bound gold-tooled folio over to the desk.

"I mean 1834. I always leave out her 'greats' because they go on too long—" ("To the nth" suggested Peter helpfully.) And Patrick grinned and went on, still talking to Lawrie, "So don't *argue*. Come and look."

He opened the book and they leaned their arms on the desk-top on either side of him and looked obediently. The illustrations, detailed and accurate as an architect's drawings, were interleaved with the text. Churches, bridges, follies, houses, flicked past under Patrick's impatient fingers. At last he said, "There! That's it."

"*Gracious!*" exclaimed Lawrie. "Good lord!" said Peter.

There were two drawings: that of the exterior showed a structure like a mammoth beehive; that of the interior disclosed row upon row of square holes, the lowest just above ground level, the topmost just below the spring of the roof: a pillar, its base on the floor, its top reaching the crossbeams which carried the roof, stood in the centre of the dovecote, supporting ladders on the three arms which sprang from either side; in addition, two circular platforms were set about the pillar, one not far from the ground, the other about half-way up.

"That's a queer-looking thing," said Lawrie. "What is it?"

"Doesn't Aunt Eulalia tell us?" said Peter, glancing from the drawing to the text. "Yes, look: *Monks' Culvery: The Great Dovecote. This Massive and Imposing Edifice* (I'll say) *stands at a distance from the House on the gentle southern slope in that part of the park known as Dovecote Pleasance, well set off by the noble trees which crown and adorn the higher ground. The building was completed by the holy Monks of the Order of St Benedict in the year of Our Lord 1303 as may be seen from the inscription above the original Doorway: ANNO MCCCIII COLUMB: AEDIF:. The Circumference of the Outer Walls of the Rotunda is a full Ninety Feet, the Walls themselves having a Thicknesse of Four Feet by which means the Temperature within is kept Constant, neither an Excessive Heat nor an Unclement Chill——"*

"You see now, don't you," said Patrick, "why Aunt Eulalia's public was just the family? *Unclement Chill*, indeed. There's nasty for you."

"Not to be so choosy," said Peter reprovingly. "I think Aunt Eulalia was proper literary. Where was I? Oh yes, *Unclement Chill. The Entire Edifice is of Stone, the Height from the Ground to the Eaves being fully twenty-eight Feet. Three great Buttresses support the Walls, in which, lest Four-Footed Thieves should seek to Invade this Fortress and carry off a Delicate Re-past——"*

"Huh?" said Lawrie.

"In case cats and rats get in and eat the pigeons," said Patrick.

"—a Device, called by Masons a String-course, has been built Three Feet from the Ground and yet another Halfway between Ground and Apex. What's a string-course exactly?"

"Like a small overhang—a narrow ledge with a scooped out underside. The rats are supposed not to be able to climb past it."

"Bet they think of something all the same. Rats are highly intelligent types they tell me. *The Entrances are Two. The Original Doorway, of stout Oak, set flush with the Wall between two Upright Stones, is approached by three stone Steps: a Third Stone forms the Lintel and bears the Inscription already quoted. Thus the Doorway assumes an Imposing Aspect; but in fact the Aperture is no more than Two Feet Two Inches Wide and Three Feet Nine Inches in Height. Thus the Enquirer might well suppose that the second Doorway, built in 1593 A.D., would have allowed more ample access to the Interior; but on the contrary, this additional Doorway is placed high in the North Wall and may be reached only by a common Ladder and once reached is no more than One Foot Eleven Inches Wide by Three Feet in Height. The Reason for this Inconvenience I could by no means discern."*

"But I discern why Maudie Culver doesn't use the Dovecote and doesn't know what's going on there—if she doesn't," exclaimed Patrick. "She's too fat! She can't get through either door! It's as simple as that!"

"Then let's hope Aunt Eulalia wasn't a buxom wench or we shan't get in either," said Peter. *"Before we leave the Exterior of this Noble Rotunda let us briefly observe the Roof. This, too, is of Stone and, so I am told by the present Owner, Mr Sacheverell Culver, once admitted Light and Air by means of a Square Aperture in the Apex. Later, in or about 1496 A.D. this Aperture was closed by a Stone Slab and a Tier of Holes resembling external Nest Holes was contrived to allow the Feathered Tribe to come and go at Will. Again, in 1749 A.D. the Roof was Crowned by a Lantern which bears a Weather Vane in the resemblance of a Pigeon. And but a few years ago, Mr Culver himself added to the Amenities of the Edifice by constructing a Trap (so-called) on which his Birds might alight on returning from a distance, when engaging in the new Sport of Pigeon Racing.*

"Passing now, albeit with some difficulty, into the Edifice, the Enquirer finds himself at the head of a Flight of six Stone Steps which end on a paved floor below the level of the ground, so that the Height Within is Greater than that Without, being a full Forty Feet from Floor to Apex. If any be so venturesome as to enter by the second Door, he—it will scarcely be she—must make his way to the pavement by means of struts driven into the Wall.

"And now we discover the Main Purpose of the Edifice—the housing of the Feathered Tribe. At frequent intervals, Apertures, one foot in Height and Width, recede into the Walls to a depth of Fifteen Inches. In all the Nestholes number Nine Hundred and Ninety-nine, being contrived in Twenty-seven Tiers with Thirty-seven Nests in each.

"But the greatest Marvel of the Edifice is surely the Potence which

rises like some strange Tree, bearing yet stranger Fruit, from Pavement to Roof."

"That's that thing," said Lawrie, unnecessarily, pointing to the drawing.

"We know," said her brother impatiently. "Now I've lost my place. Where was I? Oh yes. *This central Post is of Ash, roughly squared and girt about with two Platforms on which the Feathered Tribe may take their Ease. On either side, three Beams extend, branchlike, bearing a Ladder of thirty Rungs. The Base of this Engine rests on a Beam laid into the Floor: and the Mechanism is so delicately devised that the mere Touch of a Weak Woman's Finger is sufficient to set it in gyrational motion. By this means, two Men, one on each Ladder (or one Man alone if need be) may search the Nesting-holes and bring forth such Birds as be required, whether as now to show forth their Airy swiftnesse or to delight the table as formerly*." He stopped reading.

"Is that the lot?" asked Lawrie.

"That's it. Well, there's a bit about the lock on the door being worth a look and what a lucky Feathered Tribe to have such crafty quarters, but that's all that's really about it."

The room was suddenly silent. Peter and Lawrie straightened themselves and stood frowning at the open book, hoping they looked as if they were thinking deeply and constructively when really their thoughts were more like a log-jam. All this stuff about the dovecote—it ought to help, there was so much of it, but they couldn't see how—

"Say we do *this*," said Patrick at last, evidently having got his log-jam moving—if indeed, he had had one. "I go over to Monks' Culvery and see if I can grab one Scandaroon complete with capsule. Peter careers about the countryside being decoy-duck. Lawrie takes our Scandaroon and harness over to the Colebridge cops and tells all we know. Fool-proof, yes? Masterly, that's what."

"Except bags me take Monks' Culvery," said Peter at once. In case that sounded as if he wanted to be a hero he added quickly, "It sounds a lot safer if you ask me."

"That's why I've bagged it," said Patrick promptly. "The

89

other reason, if you'll excuse my mentioning it, is that you don't madly like climbing about high up and it sounds to me as if one was going to spend the whole afternoon up ladders."

Peter raised his brows as if he'd never heard of any such disability before and said, "Oh, I don't know." Still, it was plain he accepted the position. Lawrie, coming out of her stunned silence, said indignantly, "What d'you *mean*, me take all that stuff over to Colebridge?"

"Well, it won't exactly weigh you down, will it? One pigeon complete with harness?"

"But I've never *been* in a police station."

"Aren't you lucky? If you'd been run in drunk and disorderly as often as I have——"

"You've been run in drunk and disorderly?" exclaimed Lawrie incredulously. "*Really?*"

"Oh '*strewth*! That was a *joke*. Look, Lawrie. All you do is walk in, grab a passing cop and say you've come to report something. You can do that, *surely?*"

He was only impatient at the check to his plan, but to Lawrie he sounded contemptuous, as if she were the person he most despised in the world; and put like that, it didn't sound much. So she took her seething protests off the boil and said meekly, "O.K. After dinner do I go?"

"On the two-thirty. And mind you catch the five-twelve back. If you miss that there's nothing till the eight-five."

Lawrie nodded, knowing that. Peter said, "And what about your pa? How will you warn him now?"

"Lawrie will have the carton with her. The cops will cope," said Patrick, who'd been wondering too and was relieved to find the solution suddenly so easy.

"And how do I cover you? I suppose", Peter answered himself, "by being seen marching in the opposite direction in a most conspicuous way. So—"

"So you have to know how I'm getting there. Look—one staircase from the priest's room leads to a tunnel under the grounds which comes up in Tanners Gorse and gets me part way there before The Thuggery knows I'm out. And from

Tanners Gorse—look, it's easy!—I go by the Fosse! It's completely overgrown and it actually goes under Monks' Culvery's wall and through the park! Couldn't be simpler!"

"You can't miss," Peter assured him. "But I have to do the opposite of all that. If I'm to make them chase me—"

"Like Old Man Kangaroo," suggested Lawrie pertinently. "Very much run after by four o'clock this afternoon."

"That's me. Suppose I take my bike and go—"

"The other way."

"Yes, but *which* other way? Doing what? If I just mill round aimlessly they'll know I'm harmless and not come after me."

"Suppose—" began Patrick, but the idea got away and it hadn't been much of one anyway.

"Suppose you—" began Lawrie, not to be left out. And then she did get a notion. "You can be looking for the powder and then look as if you'd found it."

"Fab. And how do they get to know what it is I'm looking for?"

Lawrie raised her brows and sighed patiently, positive that had *she* been given the role of drawing off the hunt, she could have made it clear as crystal what she was seeming to look for. However, since the last thing she wanted was that anyone should say *All right you do it then* she didn't say so. She said instead, "If you come down to the station with me we can talk about what you're going to be looking for on the way back."

The boys worked this one out. Then Patrick said, "How d'you know they'll hear you?"

"I thought you thought they were tailing us like—like—"

"Arrh," said her brother, "lurkin' be'ind they 'edges an' up they gurt trees they do be, mos' prab'ly."

"Could be," said Patrick. "Anyway, no harm trying. And while you're about it, you might say as well what a stew I'm in after reading their cigarette carton and how I've backed out and let you down and all that caper. The less they're watching out, all the better for me."

"All right. And we'll try and make it sound as if we thought there wasn't a thing we could do unless I find the capsule and we couldn't do anything till Monday anyway. And we'll say Lawrie's going into Colebridge just to—to what?"

"To change the library books?" suggested his sister with a nervous giggle.

"Then mind you take them with you," said Patrick warningly. "It's not bad camouflage as a matter of fact, because you can put the evidence at the bottom of whatever you carry the books in and pile the books on top."

"It's Karen's music-case we use always," said Lawrie, going into unnecessary, nervous detail. "The one from when she used to learn the violin, only—"

"Yes, all right," said her brother impatiently. "No one's interested in Kay's defunct music lessons. 'Strewth, is that the time? If we don't flash home and gobble, Lawrie'll miss her train."

CHAPTER SEVEN

The Costume for the Part

The way home was mainly across open country and it wasn't till they reached the Trennels fields that they were able to walk beside hedges making loud indignant conversation about Patrick's lily liver for the benefit of any Thug who might be lurking on the other side. Even Lawrie found it harder than she'd expected to talk convincingly at an unseen, very likely non-existent audience.

Table-talk during dinner was almost entirely about the glass in the pond and the silent telephones, for though individual lines went out-of-order fairly frequently, never before had all failed together. Although she was doing her best not to look at him, there came a moment when Lawrie met Peter's meaningful lively gaze across the table. He, with considerable relish, was thinking *Sabotage!* But Lawrie was thinking *It's like a siege!* and she was frightened.

Dinner ended. Rowan returned to her tractor, Ann piled plates and table-silver on the trolley and pushed it out to the kitchen followed by Mrs. Marlow. Lawrie vanished upstairs. Seizing the opportunity, Peter ran Karen's music-case to earth on its peg on the hall-stand and retreated to the cloakroom where, behind the locked door, he shook the dead pigeon, the harness and the cigarette-carton from his mackintosh, wrapped them in the hand-towel and stowed them in the music-case. Then he strolled forth to the sitting-room, flushed the covey of library books from their book-ends and rammed as many as possible in on top of the pigeon. Then he took the stairs three at a time in search of Lawrie. If only she'd get a move on before his mother and Ann could finish the washing-up—

"Oh honestly! Not *again*!" he exclaimed, skidding to a halt at Lawrie's bedroom door.

Her hair combed back under an Alice band, Lawrie was using an eye-liner, her lipstick renewed, her lashes darker than when she came upstairs. "I shan't be a sec."

"Rot the secs! Come *now*. Mum and Ann are still hard at it. We'll only have to yell good-bye and rush."

"The library books—"

"*Here*," he said, swinging the music-case at her.

"Did you only take the ones they've finished with?"

"I took what fitted. How should I know which they've finished with and which not?"

"They put the ones they've finished with on the other side of the book about roses. Is that where you——"

"*I* wouldn't know. So what? They can get them out again."

"We can just as well take the right ones," said Lawrie, beginning to put the dressing-table elaborately, unnaturally tidy.

"For goodness' sake *come on*, gel! You'll miss the train if you muck about much longer." His eyes met hers in the mirror: he said acutely, "Or is that what you're trying to do?"

Lawrie said hurriedly, getting up, "No of *course* not," and Peter made as if he believed her. They rushed from the room and down the stairs.

But the washing-up had been left to Mrs. Herbert and Doris, and their mother and Ann were coming into the hall through the green baize door. "You sound like an elephant dance," said their mother, not particularly amused. "Where are you off to in such a rush?"

"Into Colebridge to——" It suddenly struck Peter that these words lacked tact but it was now too late to do anything about it, "—change the library books, Ma."

"You are? Lawrie, you're surely not going into Colebridge looking like that!"

"Looking like what?"

The Costume for the Part

"Like the worst kind of teenager. The house and garden is one thing, but you can't *possibly* go outside dressed like that! What *are* you thinking of?"

"But I'm ready now! I can't—"

"Now look, Lawrie. I'm not saying you and Peter can't go into Colebridge on your own. But unless you change into your coat and skirt and take that make-up off, you certainly don't go."

"But I'll miss the train if I stop to do all that!" exclaimed Lawrie, suddenly seeing this as a calamity.

"I can't help that. If you don't want to change, you must stay at home."

"Anyone would think I was going to London!" muttered Lawrie, backing up the stairs.

"In London no one would look at you twice. Colebridge is quite different. And I won't have people supposing I'd let a child of mine run around looking as you do at this moment. Now do as I say."

"Oh all *right*," grumbled Lawrie. She glowered at Peter who was standing by in a silent fume and rushed back upstairs, muttering.

Mrs. Marlow went into the sitting-room. Ann, having been visited by something which two minutes later she was calling inspiration, was already there, looking for her library book and finding it gone. There followed question and answer and an emptying of the music-case (so far as books were concerned) while Ann remarked unreproachfully at intervals, as she sorted those to go from those still being read, how lucky it was they'd discovered this easily made mistake before he and Lawrie had gone. To all this, while tacitly refusing her help in repacking, Peter replied in rigid monosyllables of extreme, barely controlled fury. He rebuckled the straps, bowed and clicked heels (which was one of his best ways of expressing exasperation) and went into the hall, shutting the door briskly behind him. The front door, unlatched, blew slowly open. He looked out and, as he had half-expected, saw Lawrie, face, hair and clothes unmodified, signalling wildly from the end of the drive. They did not waste words. They ran. Still, they could not run all the way. And when they did drop, panting, into a quick stumbling walk and Lawrie looked at her watch, they found they had more time in hand than they'd thought. "Where," said Lawrie suddenly, doubling Peter's little finger painfully, her eyes sidelong, "are you going to start looking?"

Just in time Peter got the message and didn't squeal: for all kinds of sounds belong in hedges and ditches; hedgehogs and blackbirds grubbing among dry leaves can sound uncommonly human: but nothing else sounds quite like the heavy twig-snapping of an unpractised tracker; nor, of such chirrupings as may be heard in early March coming from behind a high bank and thick thorn hedge, do any much resemble a transistor radio murmuring its desire to be Bobby's girl. "I don't know exactly. I thought I'd go back and get my bike and then I'd go over the ground we covered this morning, and then if I do find that capsule thing, I can take it straight to the police."

"That's a good idea," said Lawrie clearly. "And you could go to you-know-where and get the pigeon as well, couldn't you? That'd be absolutely conclusive evidence and Patrick needn't come into it at all if he's in such a blue funk, need he?" She paused. She said brightly, "I suppose I couldn't do anything about it while I'm in Colebridge?"

"How d'you mean?" said Peter startled. The raving clot! Surely she—

"Well—go and have a word with the police or something. But I suppose", she said regretfully, "it wouldn't be much use without that capsule thing."

No. She wasn't being a raving clot, oddly enough. She was being rather clever—over-clever so far as he was concerned. For if they now believed Patrick to be out of it and Lawrie on her way to Colebridge on some innocuous errand, the whole Thuggery would be free to concentrate on him. He didn't think he altogether went for that. Still, he could only follow her lead.

"No, there's no point your doing anything. We can't do

a thing unless I can find the capsule and Patrick said he hadn't a clue where he dropped it. It could be anywhere."

"Exactly." Lawrie looked at her watch. "I say, we'd better run again. Mummy'll be livid if I miss the train."

They had reached the long steep slope to the village. They clasped hands and ran, faster and faster, miraculously avoiding loose stones and flints rampant. They reached the village street. No member of The Thuggery, with or without transistor accompaniment, was visible or audible—

"Come to the station with me?" entreated Lawrie, eyeing the innocent scene like a scary colt.

"You should worry. *You'll* be all right," said her brother with involuntary bitterness.

"How d'you mean?" she said, half, though only half, relieved by this assurance.

"You made it crystal clear back there that I was the only one they had to bother about."

"Well, wasn't that right? I thought—"

"Yes, it was perfectly right."

"Then what did I do wrong?"

"Nothing. Nothing at all. Not a thing. *Why* are you got up like that, anyway? Ma's quite right. You do look a proper Espresso chick."

"Do I?" said Lawrie, not at all put out. "Do I truly?"

"Yes, just. Why d'you want to?"

"Not to feel so like me." Lawrie lowered her voice. "More like a James Bond kookie who does this all the time." She patted the music-case he still carried. Hastily, he handed it to her, wondering exactly which James Bond kookie she had in mind: she didn't look in the least like Pussy Galore to him. He said, "I'd have thought you'd much more have got there without being noticed if you'd just looked ordinary."

It was, of course, quite the worst thing to say. Lawrie stood still and gazed, first at him and then down at Giles's stained old mackintosh and her jeans in sudden and growing dismay. "Honestly? Would I really? Had I *better* go back and change?"

"No," he said, holding temper and impatience on a tight

rein. "You hadn't. There's exactly three minutes before the train gets in. You've just time to get your ticket and that's *all*. Not to worry. No one'll even *look* at you."

"Oh," said Lawrie, as if, perversely, she wasn't sure she liked that particular reassurance.

But already the train's whistle could be heard in the cutting. There was, as Peter had said, only just time to buy her ticket. He gave her a shove towards the station entrance and she ran for it.

CHAPTER EIGHT

Old Man Kangaroo

Peter waited until the train had chuffed into distance and silence, half-certain Lawrie would come bolting back: when she did not reappear his spirits rose wonderfully and he sauntered back to the village, whistling cheerfully to himself: so now go home, collect the bike, and ride round the countryside in search of the capsule. One never knew: one might even find it.

He walked back up the hill to Trennels, neither seeing nor hearing anything of The Thuggery. As he walked he planned that if, by luck and St. Anthony, he found the capsule, he would go straight to the police; if The Thuggery made that impossible and a post office were handy, he could send it to them by registered post; and if neither were feasible he would hide it in the nearest safe place and continue as Old Man Kangaroo. . . . At which point in his thoughts he arrived at the Trennels bicycle shed outside which he had left his bike.

It wasn't there.

Perhaps Ann, that tidy, helpful girl, had shoved it inside for him. He looked. She hadn't.

So he could now reasonably think what it had been jumping to conclusions to think before: The Thuggery had half-inched it.

So where was it now? And was it playing their game or his own to go looking for it? After all, he had to make them follow him: if he merely kept out of sight all afternoon he wasn't helping anyone.

There was a puddle near the shed. Whoever had taken his

bike had wheeled it through the water and left a brief trail pointing to the main road. At least, that's where you'd fetch up if you were a crow flying. Peter stood, considering: wondering whether he should borrow Ann's fine and magnificent velocipede. Partly saved for, partly an advance birthday present, she had had it only since the beginning of term and though it had gone through a couple of excursions with the school Guide Company, she had cleaned and oiled and polished with such devotion that it still looked like new. It seemed hardly right to treat it as he had intended treating his own; for what he had had in mind was that first, he must find The Thuggery or as much of it as had been detailed to keep its eye on him; then he must seem to find the capsule in such a place that he could leap on his bike and get away well ahead of them, leading them to the estuary, but in such a way that it looked as if he were being driven; and once there, pick up his canoe and return up river. Once in the canoe it was a piece of cake; the only thing was that sooner or later he would have to abandon the bike in some place no self-respecting owner would choose. This would scarcely have noticed with his own but Ann's was another matter.

However: in all the circumstances: dreadful necessity: the devil drives. Feeling more crafty than seemed fair, he pedalled fast along the footpath through the shrubbery-cum-coppice behind the house which ended on the bank bordering the main road. He arrived just too late to see the accident take place.

It had happened some yards to his left where the road was under repair: he cycled slowly along to look, and remained, straddling Ann's bicycle and looking down on the shouting, gesticulating group made up of Matt Carter and his steamroller, Purple Streak, Black Check and Yeller Feller, and the rest of the road-gang. It wasn't an accident in the literal sense, partly because the only casualty had been his bike, partly because what had happened had plainly been intentional. This he knew for a fact, because, as in the simpler kind of film, everyone kept telling everyone else what had happened, which was that Purple Streak, Black Check and Yeller Feller, despite repeated appeals to take themselves off, had taken turns to play Last Across with Peter's bike in front of the steamroller till at last the inevitable, the intended happened: Purple Streak had skidded, fallen and somersaulted out of the way, while the bike had been flattened into the soft tar. And now everyone was very angry indeed: Matt Carter and his road-gang genuinely so, The Thuggery setting up a clamour about This Valuable Machine and Writing to Their Solicitors.

Peter concluded he had found his allocation of Thuggery. One, probably, was watching Patrick's house; and presumably they couldn't all go off and leave Maudie's pigeons unattended. So he had three, and think himself lucky. His next move was obvious: he waited for a pause in the rumpus and then announced clearly, "As a matter of fact, that was *my* bike, that was."

There was a sudden upturn of startled faces. He stared down at them, seeing them all, but especially the three Thuggery faces, bunched together and wearing almost identical expressions of derision and defiance. In that moment he noticed Purple Streak's broken tooth, Black Check's heavy eyebrows and Yeller Feller's long pointed ears.

"*Yours?*" demanded Matt Carter angrily.

"You saying we nicked your bike?" said Black Check, deeply shocked and quite unable to believe his ears.

"'S right," said Peter.

"Man, you want to be careful," said Yeller Feller. "A bike ain't no trophy to us."

"Not," elaborated Purple Streak, "w'en it's a sad crump of broken-down tin like that old drosky there. Man, that machine was just glued together with rust. We jus' did it a kindness. We put it outa its mis'ry, man."

"It was still my bike," said Peter firmly. "*Which* you took from outside our shed."

"Man, we declare to you. We found it in a hedge."

"Only I know that you know that I know you're lying. So now what?"

"Man, you want to apologize, I tell you sincerely. Like we told you——"

"We all heard," said Matt Carter suddenly. "'N I know which tale I'd believe. But that's not my business. That there's my business." He nodded towards the soft glistening tar in which the bicycle lay embedded. "You put that there deliberate—right? Ah, quit yapping. We all saw you. So now you're going to get it out again for us, just as deliberate. And if it mucks up yer pretty clobber that's just too bad and we're all as sorry as can be. Now who'll try first?"

After five minutes of forceful unavailing protest it was Black Check who tried first. Not because Matt Carter said they had to, but because Matt Carter and his gang were nine, all larger and stronger than The Thuggery and all armed with pickaxes, spades and sledge-hammers.

Peter sat down on the bank to watch. In the ordinary way he would have taken himself off: he could feel how they felt, surrounded by that grinning circle of men's faces as they tried, clumsily and unsuccessfully, to get the bicycle clear. But unless he stayed the most likely thing they'd do once Matt Carter let them go would be to belt back to Monks' Culvery and change: which wouldn't do Patrick any good. So, to the unnoticed accompaniment of the hoof-clopping melancholy of "Marching Through Madrid", relayed by the transistor radio Purple Streak had put down on the grass verge, he watched each Thug in turn lay hold of the pickaxe one of the gangers held out and try to prise the bicycle out of the road while in the process their shoes, their drainpipes, their pullovers, their hot faces acquired large smudgings of tar: till presently Matt Carter, arms folded on the steering-wheel, gazing sardonically down on the sullen youths in the road, said, "Pitiful's what I call it. You're as much use as one old woman, the three of you. You take yourselves off now and don't you come playing your fool games on my stretch of road again. You stay over to Monks' Culvery and don't make no more trouble. Or maybe there'll be more waiting for you than you bargain for."

Yeller Feller, who was currently using the pickaxe, let it fall at his feet. Purple Streak, who was standing on the verge, said, "You don't want to talk to us like that, mugsie, not 'f you want to stay healthy. 'S a free country. We go anywhere we please."

"'Cept when I tell you hop it. An' then you hop," said Matt Carter, unruffled. Determined not to seem chivvied, The Thuggery stood on the crown of the road, glowering. Matt Carter looked at Peter and said, "What'll we do with your bike when we get it out, son? Heave it in the ditch? Won't be more 'n scrap by then, y' know. Maybe Miss Culver'll stand you a new one as it's her lads as is responsible."

"Maybe," said Peter: perversely, he was suddenly allured by the notion of cleaning and polishing and tinkering and after many days rebuilding a bicycle better than brand-new. "Anyway, leave it in the ditch for me and I'll pick it up on my way back." And then words came and he spoke them. "Actually, I'm on my way to Monks' Culvery now. Something I think Miss Culver ought to know. Something I've found."

The three Thuggery faces turned towards him, attentive as cats sighting a bird: and then he was cycling bumpily along the top of the bank and swerving crazily down beyond the road-works. If those three peasants used their combined loafs they'd remember the long curve the road made to the cross-roads: if they tottered across the fields they could get there first and head him off; and then he could turn sharp right and be chased to the sea. If they didn't use their loafs, he'd have to go through the motions of finding something wrong with Ann's bike to let them catch up with him. . . . But as the road curved he looked towards the fields and saw three purposeful figures running hard in the direction he wanted them to go.

"This", Peter admitted to himself, "is more than I bargained for."

Till then, the chase had gone as he had imagined and intended, with himself keeping just sufficiently ahead of The Thuggery to evade capture and keep their appetite whetted for the chase: and he had been congratulating himself smugly on his success when stones (he thought) began to hum past; it wasn't till the reports also registered that he realized they had a gun and were shooting at him.

The lane twisted between high thorn hedges and he went down it at top speed, forgetting they could see the glint of metal through the leafless twigs till a flint became flying splinters seconds before his front wheel passed it. Plainly, the time had come to ditch Ann's bike.

He wasn't greatly alarmed by the shooting, beyond thinking The Thuggery stark ravers to start loosing off like that. (Anyone'd think they wanted to kill him!) All the same, in the context of escape and pursuit, the high hedges and narrow lane were suddenly enclosing as a city alley. The chained gate, sun-greyed and lichen-gilt, coming into view on his right was so obvious an exit that it seemed the entrance to a trap. Then make its obviousness work: chuck Ann's bike down beside it as if you'd hopped over in a hurry and go back up the lane along the ditch on the other side—

The bicycle fell on its side, the wheels spinning: as he ran across the road he heard, coming towards him along the far side of the hedge, the jigging jangle of a steel band striking out a calypso. He was reminded, hilariously, of Captain Hook and the crocodile and, snorting with suppressed laughter, crawled over the edge of the ditch. The rank screening grass parted and he fell five unexpected feet. Fortunately, The Thuggery were deafening themselves with their own noise as they crashed through a thin piece of hedge.

Above him in the lane shoes gritted on stones. He lay momentarily half-stunned, a cold earthy smell in his nostrils and muddy wetness seeping into his clothes. A voice said, "Look's like the sapso's jinked thattaway."

"Looks like. Or would it be *only* looks like?"

"How you figure then, Kinky?"

"I figure we scared him good. So then *mebbe* the sapso jinked

as we aimed 'n now he's steering for the gravel pit *also* same's
we aimed likewise."

"But no, Kinky?"

"Just mebbe no. Mebbe he's playing creep hereabouts,
waitin' f'r *us* to steer thattaway so then he c'n take his wheel
'n drift f'r home."

Congratulations thought Peter ruefully, trying to shift his
hipbone. The calypso makers were still at it.

"So you dream we take a shufti hereabouts first?" said a
third voice. It seemed to Peter this third voice sounded a touch
uneasy. Perhaps he didn't like playing hide and seek.

"I dream, Mr. Luke. You seek that side, Siberia this, 'n I'll
seek him the back side of the hedge."

Peter eased himself over until he was lying pressed against
the road side of the ditch. It was the best he could do and
anyway it could be only a matter of minutes before he was
found. As Mr. Luke (which was he? Peter wondered) jumped
down into the ditch twenty yards away, he groped about until
he found what felt like a hefty piece of wood. He quite saw
he was going to take a painful and humiliating clobbering
not five minutes from now, but all the same he'd try to leave
his mark on at least two out of the three.

Mr. Luke shuffled nearer. For a moment, as the tension of
waiting tightened, Peter wondered whether he might not stand
a better chance if he leapt out now, taking them unawares;
and then remembered the ditch was too deep for anyone but
Garth to leap from: better to trip Mr. Luke and clobber him,
which would drop the odds to two to one: and when Siberia
or Kinky came looking for Mr. Luke do the same again—more
Captain Hook stuff: *"Fetch me out that doodle-doo—"*

With infinite precautions against noise, he began to gather
himself into a kneeling position; the natty drainpipes advanced,
the rest of the body still screened by the grass and furze growing
from both sides of the ditch: his hand gripping the wood,
he drew his knees under him—and then, before he was ready,
the drainpipes stumbled and Yeller Feller was on hands and
knees, gazing at him.

For a moment they stared at one another, petrified: then Yeller Feller grimaced violently, grotesquely, conveying as clear a warning as Peter had ever seen. He was so startled that he stayed obediently motionless while Yeller Feller straightened up and, stepping delicately past him, went on along the ditch.

His thigh, tensed in a half-kneeling position, began to ache: he pulled a cautious leg under him, overbalanced, and toppled sideways on to the piece of wood: it splintered, water-rotten, and a sliver drove into his palm.

Momentarily, it was all-important; a black inch and a half, it had driven in rather than along, and it was going to be hell to get out. And then, bent over, clutching it, he thought, "You flaming clot! What did you let Yeller Feller go for? You get away from here before he brings the others."

He began to crawl along the ditch in Yeller Feller's wake. As he did so, trying to put his wounded hand where it wouldn't hurt and rarely succeeding, he heard Siberia call, "You spy summin', Mr. Luke?"

"I spy nuttin', Siberia."

"Me too. This bog is void, man, void. How's with you, Kinky?"

Kinky's words were muffled; from what the others said, Peter gathered he was as firmly held in a blackberry tangle as any of the Sleeping Beauty's suitors. His pals, seemingly, did not go to his aid: apparently, they clambered from their respective ditches and, leaning on the gate, gave maddeningly good advice: Peter crawled on, obsessed by his efforts to avoid setting his hand down on its resident barb and wondering whether Yeller Feller's actions were matching his words: he could so easily talk nonsense over the gate and simultaneously indicate Peter's whereabouts. Still crawling, Peter heard scrambling sounds as if Kinky were getting over the gate and braced himself: any minute now—

What he heard next was a heavy clang as if Ann's bicycle had fallen over—only it was on the ground already. And almost immediately Siberia's voice was raised in protest.

"Hey, Kinky, quit crunching the chick's wheel! We c'd flog that good. Mr. Luke 'n me are skint."

A second clang followed: Kinky's voice, heavily exasperated, said, "Let me relieve my feelin's! Tell me good. How do we flog a wheel as'll be second prize when the Gestapo drag the gravel pit?"

There was a third clanging thud, followed by silence. Then Mr. Luke said loudly, "You don't mean that, Kinky? You ain't really out to crunch the sapso? Jukie never said——"

Peter stopped crawling.

"Who's Jukie now? Tell me, just. From now he's the last. From now the Boss Man's going to be lookin' for a new Number One boy 'n 'f I cull the sapso, who but me?"

"You get topped," said Siberia, with a hoarse little laugh which derived more from nerves than humour, "'n you won't be even Number Ten boy."

"Man, I can't *be* topped. Me eighteenth ain't for a year yet. I keep on 'n on *tellin'* y'. Likewise there can't be no toppin' cause there'll on'y be a nasty sad accident like the sapso rode over the edge 'n broke 'is neck 'n drownded, pore chap. Cause 'f it's not curtains for 'im after we've lofted 'im over, we'll 'old 'is 'ead down."

He means it thought Peter incredulously, his hurt hand pressing unfelt on a stone. *He really does mean it.*

"I don' wan' with it," said Mr. Luke; also meaning it. "I'm for out, Kinky."

"You mayn' wan' with it, but yore goin' a be. Or I'll spiel the Boss Man 'n you know what? The mob'll knock on yore door 'n carve you one dark night."

"Aw c'm on, Lukie," said Siberia encouragingly, as to a bather hovering on the brink from one who is finding the water pretty cold himself. "We can't be topped neither, we're just the innocent kiddos. Come for the kicks, man. You're a great w'en you've crunched one, ain't you Kinky?"

"*I'm* the great. Yore jus' the lookers-on. But I'll spiel the Boss Man you aided——"

"No," said Mr. Luke, his voice jumping. "I'm takin' off. I'm goin' for Jukie. He on'y said to keep 'im runnin'—"

There was a sound of scudding feet, a scuffle, a yelp in one voice and two squeals, followed by loud whimpering, in another: then Kinky's voice panted, "Lissen Mr. Luke. Lissen very good. Before I put the boot in. You come with us 'n help reel fancy or you'll be found in that crummy wood up there, corpsed like it must of been another sad accident w'en some herbert was shootin' them destructive rabbits. You comprehend me?"

Yeller Feller, gasping and tearful, comprehended.

"That's good. That's correct. So you hoist the wheel over the gate 'n we'll go seek the sapso up the hill."

Even when the noise made by Ann's ruined bicycle and the excitements of the steel band had faded, Peter stayed so still that a wren, alighting on a branch of furze, overlooked him. He knew the gravel pit, a gorse-patched crater with a black pool in the centre of the basin. He imagined himself dragged struggling to the edge, the awful push, and the fall which would last for ever. Since he was a small boy he had had a secret conviction that the thing you most feared was the way you were going to die. And now, perhaps, this was it.

Abruptly, the wren ceased to regard him as part of the furniture and chattered at him furiously, six inches from his face, before darting away.

"Braver than you, she is," he told himself, not liking himself particularly and ashamed of the sweat cold on his face. "Braver than me and Mr. Luke both."

He had a sudden fellow feeling for the unhappy Yeller Feller, suddenly, like himself, in the midst of an adventure which had turned into something huger and blacker than he had bargained for. He pictured the opposite slope with Yeller Feller, Black Check and Purple Streak toiling upwards, dragging Ann's bicycle and beating the gorse bushes as they passed: and all the while Yeller Feller knew—

Yes. And if Yeller Feller let slip that he knew, it wouldn't

108

take Kinky ten seconds to kick the details out of him—and then they'd come tearing back—

"Yes, well, you don't have to sit and wait for them," he told himself. "Move, matey."

He began to crawl rapidly forward, uncaring where he set his hand. The ditch became a drainpipe and dived, the far end showing as a pennyworth of light. After a moment's hesitation he crawled in. There was room, just; and if you stopped breathing it was almost possible not to know too much about whatever it was which had used the drain to die in a while back. The too-sweet stink came closer, was overwhelmingly beneath, was left behind. His teeth shut tight against his revolted stomach, he wormed his way to the drain's end which hung just above a shallow tinkling stream. He was in it on hands and knees and crawling still, till it occurred to him that he could now stand up. It felt quite remarkable to be able to do that. He paddled along ankle-deep, and his head began to clear and be able to think again.

So far as Old Man Kangaroo went, he'd done his job: The Thuggery would probably go on beating the countryside for him till dark. So now he had only to get home. Only *how*, exactly? Where was this stream taking him? At this, memory threw up a useful piece of information. *For every river* it told him *flows somewhere safe to sea*. Safe to sea. To the estuary. To the canoe. As he had intended all along. Which was very highly comical in its own particular way.

The little stream flickered on through a tunnel of alders. Peter squelched steadily on, wondering mildly what his mother was going to say about his shoes and amusing himself by imagining his ears unfolding like an African elephant's to catch the first sound of a transistor radio belting out one of the Top Ten; but there was nothing for them to hear except the wind in the tree-tops and his feet sloshing through the water.

The little stream kept the rules: it led him seaward till it became a water-splash across the lane dividing the last of the fields from the first stretches of marram-grass. The wind from the sea blew strongly, riding and driving the incoming tide as it flowed across the mudflats, already only yards from where they had beached the canoe.

He broke cover and ran out to it across the singing, streaming grasses, half-certain his appearance would be greeted by a yell and the crack of the air-gun. But not even a gull cried as he turned the canoe over and dragged it to the river's edge, suddenly remembering something which that morning he had forgotten: the Rushton was a tidal river; he would not, after all, have to battle with the stream.

He half-launched the canoe, got in and thrust the paddle into the sand to push her off. Instantly the sliver, which had merely throbbed while he was walking downstream, stabbed in his palm. "Oh lawdy," he said aloud, as the tide slid beneath the keel and brought the canoe to life, imagining the same thrust to every paddle-stroke; he made a hasty pad of his wet and filthy handkerchief and took her out on the hurrying, tugging waters: his hand still hurt, but manageably.

And the canoe was an altogether different craft from the morning's unhappy ship. Passenger-free, she rode buoyantly, obedient to his paddle. He pointed her bows upstream and let her go.

Still listening for the Top Ten, he heard nothing but the river-chuckle about his boat. He came to the place where the tree-crowned banks steepened and the river narrowed and was aware, without looking, that the wind-crippled trees gave cover to an enemy with an air-gun along the one stretch of river which was too narrow to make hugging the far bank an effective defence: the only thing to do was to drive the canoe through as fast as possible.

His arms were aching and his heart pounding before the river widened, the banks shrank to the level of the water meadows and the spaced line of pollarded willows marked the river banks. He heaved a great sigh of relief and unclamped his hand which was now hurting with a steady savage throb; to ease it, he let it trail for a moment in the quick cold water, letting the canoe go with the stream and as much steerage as he could manage one-handed.

The canoe struck, shuddered and hung still, the water piling at her stern.

Instinctively, he tried to drive her on. She went forward perhaps a foot and jammed again. He tried to backwater but the current held him fast. As from many years ago, he remembered the sapling which had nearly been the wreck of them that morning and which now, with the incoming tide, must lie just below the surface. He edged cautiously forward and groped under water, trying to find something he could break away. But the roots, slippery and resilient, could barely be grasped, much less broken: and as one more right and proper part of the disaster he saw The Thuggery tumbling over a gate and running towards him across the water meadow.

They ran silently and purposefully, Yeller Feller lagging a little, Black Check carrying the gun. Still struggling to break the roots, Peter had one of those uncanny spells of foreknowing —that the canoe was going to tilt and the water pour over the bows, that Black Check was going to fire and the bullets rip into the wood, that the canoe was going to settle, still held fast by the roots, and that he was going to go overboard and be gasping in the cold tugging hurry of the river.

The sapling's roots felt like a petrified octopus. Momentarily entangled, he could steady his feet on the trunk and keep his head behind the half-submerged canoe. But not for long: the river was achingly cold.

One way and another the sapling had been disturbed: not enough to free it, but enough to loosen some of the clottings of leaves and grass and driftwood which had silted up in the roots all winter. As each clump floated past, Black Check banged off at it—perhaps for target practice, perhaps because he thought it was Peter's head. So he was relieved to see more splashes in the river than hits in the target area.

So—how if he freed all the muck he could to distract Black Check's attention while he swam underwater to the other bank? He wasn't exactly a rave at underwater swimming, but come to that, there wasn't all that far to swim. He groped around, freeing all the clots he could. Then, while Black Check blazed away, he let himself sink and struck out for the bank.

His waterlogged clothes made the sinking part only too easy: it was swimming once sunk that was difficult. His lungs felt like paper-bags blown full to bursting-point and as an idea it had been quite the most stupid—

He had to surface. He had to surface *now*.

He tried to kick upwards and failed. He felt leaden and numb, there was an enormous pulse in his head and in a moment he would have to breathe. He would breathe water. He was going to drown. . . . His feet touched bottom.

He drifted and floundered another step and eyes, nose and mouth were above the surface. He gasped and choked, wading frantically forward, forgetting it mattered if he were seen. But he had surfaced by chance in as good a place as he could have found by intention: the undertow had carried him farther upstream than he yet realized, and behind him a willow leaned just above the surface, masking him from The Thuggery who were still watching the canoe. He stumbled against the bank, clutched at tussocks and roots and after a blind, deaf, heaving struggle got himself on to the bank.

After a while, sight, hearing and thought came back to him. He raised his head cautiously and looked about him. Along the bank the line of willows stretched as far as he could see: away from it, the water meadows lay flat and open. Trying to picture the lie of the land, he recalled that a short distance past the lock a stone wall stood above a sunken lane which led eventually to the main road. Once he hit the main road, he might even thumb a lift as far as the lane which led to Trennels—or on second thoughts, maybe not. Even the best-natured driver would draw the line at a passenger as whiff with river mud as he was.

Still lying flat, head raised, he listened. The voices and the bang-bang-bang of the air-gun still sounded from downstream. He got to his knees and peered through the willow branches. Black Check was still firing at the canoe, doubtless hoping to put a bullet in his head as he clung there too scared to move. But it had to occur to one or other of those keen yobbos some time that the sapso had vamoosed. It was time to get weaving.

For a time the willows gave excellent cover, especially while The Thuggery had it firmly fixed in their minds that their quarry still clung to the canoe. But presently the river bank began the long gradual bend which ended at the lock: on its outer curve, Peter would soon be all too visible to The Thuggery if they chanced to look upstream. For a time he did not realize this: until, peering from behind a round squat trunk to make sure they were still happily employed, he found he was gazing clear down to them with only the trunk between.

His heart gave a great thud of surprise and fright, his last reserves of courage seeming to leave him all at once like the last grains of sand running through an egg-timer. He leaned his face against the tree and surrendered to defeat, to the heavy, wet, smelly coldness of his clothes, to his throbbing hand and exhausted body. He would stay where he was and they could come and get him. . . .

But they couldn't: they were on the other side of the river; he had only to keep going away from the bank and he could still be home and dry. If he crawled away, keeping the trunk between himself and them, he might still reach the stone wall, the lane, the main road.

So he crawled, vaguely aware after a while of something different: missing: not simply the sun which had given way again to fine pelting rain: something else which—which wasn't there like a hole in a sock wasn't there. His mind continued to chafe and fret over this non-existent presence, until a chorus of triumphant yells was followed by the bang-bang-bang of the air-gun.

He knew then what had been missing. Scrambling to his feet, he saw The Thuggery still some way behind on the other bank breaking into an arm-waving run. He ran too, heading for the stone wall. But their respective banks were now in The Thuggery's favour; once they reached the main road they'd be between him and Trennels. Only they weren't making for the road. They were—where *were* they making for?

They raced along the bank, making for the lock. They took the steps three at a time and skidded to a stop on the cobbles beside the first pair of lock gates. Peter, coming to an astonished halt, saw Black Check kick off his shoes and place them neatly side by side. His pale blue socks advanced. He wasn't—he couldn't be going to try to—

He was, though. The pale blue feet were stepping on to the top of the gate itself. Poised and balanced as a cat he was preparing to cross.

Peter, who had already moved four unconscious steps forward, broke into a run. He tore across the wet grass as if he meant to do a Bannister and if the wooden tops of the gates hadn't been slippery with rain, he still wouldn't have got there in time. As it was, he hurled himself up the steps and grabbed the handle of the windlass just as Black Check reached the centre. He wrenched the handle round—and round—and the gates jerked open.

"Stuff it, yer bloody peasant!" yelled Black Check. "You wanna throw me orf?"

The question was so absurd, the answer so obvious, that Peter grinned and nodded and went on turning. The air-gun fell, throwing up a silver jet and a rush of silver bubbles. And then, with a bellow both frightened and furious, Black Check toppled into the chamber. There was an immense splash, the water swirled muddily, and then Black Check's head and shoulders reappeared, spitting and spluttering. Purple Streak and Yeller Feller squatted concernedly on the cobbles. The radio merseyed "*She loves you—yeh, yeh, yeh,—she loves you—*"

"Kinky! You all right?"

"I can't swim! You gotta ge' me out! I can't swim I tell yer!"

You don't have to, thought Peter to himself. Like you're standing, man. You only have to wade across and climb out.

Yeller Feller seemed to draw back a little. "We can't swim neither. C'm on, Kinky. 'S not far."

"I'm rooted, I tell yer! The mud's suckin' me! Do sumthin, carncher, do sumthin!"

The mud was doing no such thing as anyone could see. You pore chap, thought Peter, waiting to see what Kinky's pals would contrive. But though they muttered together while Kinky's panic grew, they seemed short on ideas; until Yeller Feller called across, "Wot you goin' a do about it, sapso? It's yore fault 'e's there!"

"Technically, yes m'lud," said Peter, having a joke all to himself. "But my counsel will be entering a plea of self-defence." He bowed deeply. "The defence rests."

"You can't leave 'im there!"

"*I* can. It's you who can't. Have you got a rope?"

"Wot ud we hava rope for?"

"Don't tempt me, matey. Well then, all I can suggest is you tie your pullovers together by the arms and give him a heave out thattaway."

"Don't you do nuthin about it, will yer?"

"No," said Peter. "You're right. I won't."

They looked at him and saw he would not. Grumbling, they peeled off their pullovers. Yeller Feller began to tie the arms of his own together and was put right by the maddening sapso across the water who told him, by way of preface, just what kind of steaming nit he was.

"Aw, shake it! Lift me out!" yelled Kinky. "It's suckin' me! I'm sinkin'!"

Shoulder-deep in water, knee-deep in mud, he doubtless felt as if he were. Peter eyed him sympathetically, remembered himself crouched in the ditch hearing Kinky's plan to drown him in the gravel pit and decided sympathy was misplaced. He said instead, "If you yell like that again, you'll do yourself a mischief."

Kinky shot him a glance of pure hatred. Yeller Feller said "Go on, Siberia, loft it" and Purple Streak dangled the pullover rope out over the water. He made some useless casting movements, looked across at Peter and said unnecessarily, "He can't reach."

"No of course he can't," said Peter, bored. "You'll have to go down those pegs, get it to him from there, and then heave. And Yeller Feller—sorry pardon, Mr. Luke—will have to hang on to you. Try working that one out for yourselves, dead crafty yobbos that you are."

He got up and went down the steps as Siberia began, cautiously, to negotiate the wooden staples. Presently, as he walked in the rain across the grass, he heard another wild yell and heavy splash. Siberia. "The pore brave lad," he said aloud, his mouth lifting a little at the corners. "Wotta shame." But now, at least, they should be within hand-clasping distance and could pull one another out.

He reached the stone wall and climbed over and down into the lane.

There was no more need for hurry. He wambled up the lane, reached the main road and walked along the grass verge in the flaring after-rain light of late afternoon, feeling spent but peaceful, while cars whizzed past in both directions. His thoughts grazed placidly on such pasture as hot baths, dry clothes and supper and wondered how Patrick and Lawrie had got on. Presently he took his wounded hand out of his pocket where he had put it for safety, looked at it, disliked what he saw and put it back again. He must make sure no one else saw it, Ann especially. If she got even half a sight of it she'd rush at him in an appallingly competent way with hot water and tweezers and agony, when all it needed was rest and quiet and a very *very* small bit of splinter removed at intervals and only then if it really felt like it. (What it got was Surgeon-Commander Leitch and his probes and lancets and considerable pother and botheration, but this unforseeable huha was still a week away.) Thinking of Ann, he remembered her unhappy bicycle, presumably past repair at the bottom of the gravel pit. Since he had "borrowed" it he supposed he was responsible, and frankly, he couldn't see how *that* was going to help Ann.

Old Man Kangaroo

Apart from those untouchables, his Savings Certificates, he was worth exactly twenty-five and tuppence. Which meant his mother would lend the ducats and he'd be in debt till A.D. 2000—unless Maudie Culver could be asked to contribute. After all it was her smashing Thuggery who'd . . . He turned automatically to take the short cut through the shrubbery-cum-coppice.

And then his feet halted uncertainly. For the first time since he had walked away from the lock, apprehension elbowed him. He tried to push himself on with the picture of The Thuggery floundering, as he had left them: but apprehension insisted that was ages ago. Then if they were out they should be on their way home to Monks' Culvery: should be. He stood gazing into the darkening, rustling coppice, remembering the threat to Yeller Feller. The gun was in the lock, but even so—

He'd go home by the lane.

He retraced his steps and went on, very tired. He tramped doggedly along the level beginning of the lane, thinking hopefully how much easier it would be when he came to the downhill part. Another five strides, man, and he'd have reached it.

A girl's voice told the world she'd blown in from the windy city. And there they were: Yeller Feller, Black Check, Purple Streak, soaked and muddy as himself, streaked and patched with tar, strung across the lane half-way down waiting for him. If he'd not funked the coppice he'd have missed them.

It was too late now. And in any case, even though it had been to keep them away from Patrick, he'd run enough. Without consciously thinking anything so explicit, it was the traditions of a service whose exemplars included the destroyer *Glow-worm*, destroying herself as she rammed the cruiser *Hipper*, and the merchant cruiser *Rawalpindi*, turning to engage the battle-cruiser *Scharnhorst* while her convoy scattered, which dictated his next actions. He stooped, picked up the two biggest flints which came to hand and went striding down the hill.

Black Check and Purple Streak were the targets—if Yeller

Feller were left on the sidelines the chances were he'd stay there. When he got closer he'd charge, hurling the flints at close range, and perhaps he'd get through. As the distance closed he saw the flick knives in their hands and thought how he would hurl the flints full in their faces—a pity he had no sand—

The ground began to shake.

At first he thought fear or excitement was making it seem to do so. And then he heard noise as well and looked over his shoulder. Matt Carter and the steamroller were on their way home.

He felt much, perhaps, as H.M.S. *Glow-worm* might have done had she seen a battlewagon storming up in support as she steamed into her last action. He saw Matt Carter lean from his seat, shouting something, and he jumped aside into the hedge, thinking that was what Matt meant. But Matt was shouting, "Come up! Jump aboard! Three to one! Three to one! We'll give the daisies three to one!"

He did not slow the steamroller, but Peter jumped, trustfully, for the step. A hand seemed to grab him in mid-air and hoist him to safety as he would have hoisted a pup. Clatter and rattle, the reek of smoke and hot oily metal, the shout of Matt's voice were all about him. "Evens now! Three to three!"

"Much better odds!" Peter shouted back.

"They an' their knives an' their three to one! Nuthin' but dirty Teds, the pack of 'em! Sarah an' you an' me'll show 'em! An' they don't jump out the way we'll flatten 'em!"

He sounded—and looked—as if he meant it. Bounced and rattled by Sarah's steadily growing pace, Peter gazed ahead to where The Thuggery stood their ground as Sarah, a baby Juggernaut, bore down on them. But even as he watched, Yeller Feller broke, flattening himself against the hedge: a moment later Siberia was backed against the hedge opposite. Only Kinky remained, half-crouched in the centre of the lane, knife in hand, daring Matt to run him down, sure the peasant hadn't enough nerve—

"Ch-ar-ar-ge!" yelled Matt, his foot down on the accelerator; and Peter yelled too, letting out the breath he'd been holding in his apprehension.

At the last possible moment Kinky sprang aside. As they rattled past in a black smother of smoke Peter, grinning like an idiot, held both hands above his head in the V-sign. Siberia gave him a loser's grin and a half flick of a salute: Kinky stared up, his pontefract-cake eyes and freckled mud-splashed face blank with defeat: down the hill, Matt slowed Sarah preparatory to turning into the Trennels drive and depositing Peter at his front door; and Yeller Feller, made bold by the passing of danger, shouted a threat of which only the word "tomorrow" was distinguishable.

But of course, once in every lifetime, tomorrow never comes.

CHAPTER NINE

Character Part

O nly meaning to be helpful, the guard had pushed Lawrie into the nearest compartment and slammed the door on her; and since she had intended to inspect all four carriages of the panting steaming local, Lawrie wasn't pleased; she liked to have active adult males as her travelling companions, not because they were more entertaining but because if there were an accident they would naturally devote themselves to seeing that Lawrie, being women and children, was rescued first. From this standpoint, her present companions, a stout, elderly woman dressed in navy, her feet bulging over her sensible shoes, and an even older man wearing a dark shabby suit, his tortoise neck rising from a collarless shirt, were a dead loss. They looked at Lawrie, looked at one another and without a word spoken united against her. The woman, surrounded by an atmosphere of mothballs and curiously strong peppermints, even contrived to suck hostilely.

Lawrie gazed resentfully out of the window: the guard's flag was still furled, he was still slamming doors: there'd have been *oodles* of time for her to look. But even as she thought this the guard's head backed past the window, his whistle shrilling, and the train gave a jolt and a heave. As it did so the compartment door was jerked open and a boy swung himself in, smoothly and competently, as if in this way he always boarded trains: Lawrie tucked her feet out of the way and looked up, ready with an admiring face if looked at. And then, with a sense of shock like a guitar-string breaking, she recognized Red Ted.

Her heart gave a grasshopper leap of panic: the music-case on her lap seemed enormous, conspicuous, transparent. Red Ted sat down opposite the elderly woman and stretched his black leather legs deliberately along the seat, not looking at anyone in particular, daring someone to tell him to take them off. Once it was established no one was going to he looked at Lawrie.

She looked quickly out of the window again. There was no corridor, so she was stuck. Her face and neck scalded, her heart hurried and her breathing choked her; and she suddenly remembered the time her mother had sent her with a message to a house where there were two bull terriers: as she had scurried up the drive, one had lumbered from the bushes to sit on the front steps and, as she backed away, she'd seen the other standing on the gravel behind her. They had neither barked, growled nor wagged their long whippy tails: they'd simply looked at her as Red Ted was doing now.

That hazard had ended with her mother's friend running out calling "They won't hurt you, Lawrie—don't cry, dear" something which, till then, her terrified eight-year-old self hadn't even known she was doing: this time, hurt or not, cry or not, there wasn't a rescuer in sight.

So, since there was no one else to fall back on, Lawrie said to herself such comfortable words as Nicola might have said if she'd been there: that the journey to Colebridge Junction took only forty minutes and some of that must have gone already; that there were two other people in the compartment, it wasn't as if she were alone. Feeling very slightly better, Lawrie fetched a deep sigh and made her breathing come right.

The train slowed into Crowlands Halt. Lawrie bated her breath, but neither the elderly woman nor the old man moved to get out. The woman still sucked and breathed peppermint and the old man sat with his eyes shut. The train, which had barely stopped, gathered speed again. Seven minutes gone, thirty-three to go. She looked fixedly out of the window, holding fast to the thought that when she reached Colebridge she'd go straight to the police station and then straight back home and there she'd stay till she and Ann went back to school——

All at once, the compartment, like Prospero's isle, was full of music—the hoof-clopping melancholy of "Marching Through Madrid". Lawrie looked round, startled into thinking Red Ted was singing to himself and adding a nice line in sound effects; this flattered him: both song and sounds came from the hand-size transistor radio he was holding to his ear.

The old man opened his eyes, blinked and sighed; the stout woman sat straighter, her habitually accusing gaze fixed on Red Ted who, without straining himself, was able not to look back. "Never mind the rest of us, will y'?" she said at last, the gaze plainly having had no effect.

"Na," agreed Red Ted laconically, his dagger-toed shoes moving gently to the beat.

"Never 'ave the manners t' ask w'ether the rest of us mind 'avin' t' lissen t' that catterwaul, will y'?"

"Wasser marrer? Doncher dig th' tunefuls?" His glance hooked Lawrie's—an in-league, rot-the-squares look. She was so relieved to find herself on his side that, almost without thinking, she gave him a similar look back, and then thought how well it went with the clothes she was wearing.

The train jolted to a stop at Upton and Great Toft. No passengers boarded or left, the usual crate of chickens was dealt with. The carriage rang with "You'll Never Walk Alone" and the stout woman said, "I've a good mind t' call the guard."

Red Ted said, "Call 'im, missus—don' make no mannerve diff ter me," and exchanged another glance with Lawrie.

The stout woman said, "Any more of your lip an' I will."

"I'm tremblin'," he said scornfully, turning up the volume, his eyes on Lawrie, who suddenly realized that all this defiance was just 'showing off' for her benefit.

Panic breathed its last: flattered and oddly excited, Lawrie gave him a quick slanting smile; and so easy was it for her to take her cue from this new climate that it seemed quite natural to say pertly to the stout woman, "Why don't you go sit some place else?"

Character Part

The train jolted and went on again. The stout woman glared at Lawrie and said, "Don't you take that tone to me, you painted little piece. Getting yourself up like that at your age. Just how old are you, I'd like to know?"

"Fifteen," said Lawrie boldly. Since no one questioned this she added, "and a half."

The stout woman snorted and looked to the old man for support; but he only watched Lawrie as if, though he didn't know what to make of her, he wasn't going to join in any argey-bargey either. The radio sang pensively "Another Spring" and the stout woman fell into an angry frustrated silence.

The train stopped at Bishops Ash and the old man got out. The next stop, six minutes away, was Colebridge Junction. The odd sense of excitement still simmering inside her, Lawrie wondered what would happen then.

The platform was on Lawrie's side of the carriage, so she was first out. She walked towards the barrier, the music-case heavy in her hand, hearing without seeming to the radio voice behind her singing "P.S. I Love You". And then she was out-side, walking across the station forecourt. As she had been nearly sure he would, Red Ted drew alongside. He said, "What's new, slicklet chicklet? Do we rove to the caff and have ourselves a ball?"

Twenty-four hours earlier, school-uniformed, on her way home for half-term, Lawrie Marlow had regarded any teds who crossed her path as a caste of Untouchables whose very shadows were to be avoided. Now, hand-in-hand with one, she was looking through the windows of a motor showroom while Red Ted indicated the various models he intended own-ing in the near future and she was nodding attentively, fasci-nated by their reflections, thinking how right she looked. When he'd asked what call she answered to, she'd told him Sophia—Sophia Lawrence—a name she had twisted from her own some months before against the day she became a professional actress. (As a matter of accuracy, Lawrie's second name was Sybil, but she resolutely refused to admit this: Lawrence S. Marlow she would say firmly when she must, thinking Sophia, and sometimes, if hard pressed, saying it.) Her family reacted to Sophia with amusement or scorn as the mood took them: Red Ted, however, was impressed. "That's class," he said appreciatively, which was, of course, what Lawrie thought too.

So for now she both watched and was Sophia Lawrence sauntering hand-in-hand with Red Ted towards the market square. It was just grotty Sophia had to lug her music-case around with her; and she naturally thought it gear when Red Ted offered to carry it for her.

The coffee-bar stood in one of the paved lanes leading from the market square. The windows were darkened by flourishing house plants and the decorations derived from film-studio African and travel-brochure Spanish. Still clasping Sophia's hand, Red Ted, calling greetings among the crowded tables, led her to the back of the T-shaped room where there was a round table meant for eight and holding twelve. This crush, it seemed, were his particular friends and Sophia found herself wedged beside him, sharing a bit of his chair and a bit of the next, a member of the circle with no difficulty at all.

They were seven teds to five chicks and the teds were the sprucer and the better-looking: the chicks, thought Sophia contemptuously, were mostly very amateur. One in particular, whose pallid hair fell limply down the back of her pale blue shift, caused Sophia pain: her too-long neck was topped by a too-pretty, small-featured face and her pale blue cuff-button eyes peeped between unclipped false eyelashes which had been stuck to lids painted black all over. She didn't look like a clown: she didn't look like someone who'd been at the blacking; she just looked like someone who couldn't read the instructions properly. (Like, thought Sophia wittily, someone who couldn't read, period.) On the other hand, the chick opposite was very professional indeed: her black hair flopped exactly on the shoulders of her black shiny jacket, her black pullover had the proper bulkiness, and her short skirt and kinky boots revealed black lace knees. She wore no make-up and her grey eyes, neither friendly nor hostile, watched Sophia: Sophia, unobtrusively copying the way she held her cup in both hands, the handle pointing to the centre of the table, also copied her look; and after a while the chick smiled faintly and gazed into her cup.

But this was by the way: what was important was that Sophia was beginning to understand the language and had become part of the noisy to-and-fro free-for-all table-talk. Eight transistor radios stood one on top of the other in the middle of the table and when the jigging jangle of a steel band struck out a calypso the teds and the chicks practised hand-jiving: an arm (not Red Ted's) circled Sophia's waist and a hand drummed out the rhythm on her ribs: the fair chick kept leaning across to give the owner of the arm and hand a slap and a cry of "Creep, I'm *watchin'* " and each time the arm merely hugged her closer.

She was quite blissfully, shiveringly happy and so far as she knew the ball never came to an end: it just happened that Red Ted decided he and she should leave.

Afterwards Lawrie had a distinct memory of the black-haired chick watching her leave as if (so Lawrie interpreted the look then) she hoped Lawrie knew what she was doing. But at the time it was just a look and then she and Red Ted were crossing the market square, leaning against one another, arms round waists, with the street lamps coming on and the Beatles merseying from Red Ted's pocket "*She loves you—yeh, yeh, yeh,—she loves you—*"

They slowed under a lighted portico; Red Ted said "Like we take a shufti at the big dark?" and walked her up some steps. He slapped down a pound note for two four-and-sixes and Sophia, blinking around her, saw photographs on the walls: Jack Lemmon and Shirley Maclaine. Before she had

quite taken this in they had gone through door and velvet
curtains to darkness ending in a lighted screen filled by a
monstrous spider, all eight legs on the move forward.

The golden lacquer of pleasure which had gilded the afternoon cracked open. Eyes averted, she went where Red Ted
led her to seats beside the wall, thwarting the usherette who
had wanted to seat them in the centre block. The music-case
bumped against her knee as she sat down. Like the jolting
remembrance on waking of preparation not yet done, she
thought *I've still got that to do*. The crack in the lacquer widened.

Red Ted slid down in his seat, his feet on the back of the
empty one in front. Sophia-Lawrie followed suit, discovering
that from this angle one need hardly see the screen if one didn't
want to. This suited them both since it was soon plain that
Red Ted had not come primarily to see the film. His arm
went round Sophia, hugging her as close to him as the seats
allowed. On the screen dreadful things were happening to a
character who had blundered into a monstrous spider-web and
Sophia-Lawrie's immediate reaction was to grip Red Ted's
free hand tightly. This suited Red Ted very well. His head
against hers, he was muttering such phrases as, "Yore my slick
chick, yeh? Yore the Firebird, you know that? S'pose we was
to take orf for the Smoke 'n leave the mob guessin'?" Presently
he said, "You chuffed I made Jukie make you my watch this
noon 'n night?"

Sophia (she still had a few moments of life left) nodded
and said, "Chuffed, highly chuffed." It was true she was hating
the film, but she was also profoundly interested to find herself
sitting in the back row of a cinema behaving in a way no
Marlow would dream of doing—

—And then her thoughts caught on a mental trip-wire and
went sprawling: he'd said *You chuffed I made Jukie make you
my watch this noon and night?*

Sophia, that glam, with-it chick, blew out. There was only
Lawrie now, the arm of the seat hard against her side, her
cheek hot and sticky against Red Ted's jacket. A cold choking
panic began in her stomach and spread. Then—he hadn't taken

her on because she was dishy: their meeting in the train hadn't been an accident: it had all happened simply because he was the Thug who'd been told to keep an eye on her.

Part of her had never felt so flattened; so sker*washed*. The rest of her, tense with fright, only wanted to know how on earth she was going to get away. As so often happened with Lawrie, someone else settled this for her: the usherette tapped them on the shoulders whispering, "You two quit the heavy snogging if you want to stay. The manager's on his way down an' he don't dig your sort."

Loud enough to provoke hushing noises, Red Ted gave his considered opinion of the manager. All the same, he released Lawrie, took his feet off the seat in front, sat up and seemed to watch the screen. Lawrie did the same. People were coming into their gardens to find cobweb, stout as ships' cables, slung from chimney-pot to chimney-pot: the Spider brooded monstrously above; he had them in his larder to devour at his leisure. Tinily, in her ear, someone told her, words and music, that she'd blown in from the windy city—

"Turn that thing off or get out!" said a peremptory voice above her head.

Red Ted turned it off: under the manager's eye he put it away in his pocket. Only when the manager was out of earshot did he mutter his opinion of him.

Lawrie watched the manager stroll on down the aisle, every moment making it that much more too late to ask him to get her away from Red Ted to the police station. Especially she had to get away from Red Ted and she couldn't think how. If she walked out, he'd walk with her. And suppose he meant it about taking her to London? For he could, easily. The express trains to London stopped at Colebridge Junction. If he chose his moment, he could pull her aboard——

The Spider's legs reached down through the web, selecting its morsel; an ash-blonde nitwit, who had dashed out of her house to rescue her laundry, was running screaming. . . . Lawrie watched unmoved. What was happening to her was worse than any old spider-legs. And anyway, all was now ending happily: the armed forces of the United States were coming by land, sea and air to drive the Spider away and drop atom bombs on it—

"You nourish the flavour 'v the month?" said Red Ted as the Spider exploded and the ice-cream girl passed with her tray. Lawrie nodded and said, "Deliver, kiddo." Even though she had dwindled back into herself she had to go on being Sophia to him.

It was a good flavour; it was just a pity she couldn't enjoy it any better than if it had been frogs' eggs tapioca. A Tom-and-Jerry cartoon was succeeded by a thriller introduced by Edgar Lustgarten. Usually she liked those; now she looked and listened and neither saw nor heard.

The manager had left the auditorium. Red Ted was sinking down and putting his feet up. She could *try* just walking out— tell him to get knotted, she was bored rigid—but if Jukie had made her his watch—

On either side of the auditorium EXIT signs shone tantaliz-ingly. Red Ted put his arm round her saying "Closer, Fire-chick" and as he did so she read the other sign. The one place he couldn't follow her. LADIES.

She sank down, obeying the voice inside which said *Don't rush it now* rather than Red Ted, and put her head against his coat where she could watch the clock to the left of the screen. Ten past five (oh gosh! no more trains till eight-five now)— wait till twenty-past—

"Le' me up."

"Whyfor?"

"For I have to."

He said "Uh-huh. Hurry back, Firechick" and drew his legs on to his seat to let her pass. Picking up the music-case, she edged past him. He grabbed at it, saying "Leave me the souvenir, Firechick" and she tweaked it away, whispering urgently, "*No*—I have to have it." Whereat he looked mildly surprised, but let go.

She walked down the long lane of tired carpet, past the

intent scattered faces gazing at the screen and pushed open the door under the lighted sign. There was a short passage, steps and a green door. Lawrie went in. The small lobby, the two cubicles, were empty. Her knees both stiff and shaking, she bolted herself into the nearest cubicle: and suddenly her head swam. It seemed to spin, faster and faster, the floor tilted horribly and a far-off bit of her mind said *If you're going to faint you ought to put your head between your knees.*

A long time later, still feeling uncommonly odd, she found herself at a basin trying, by using her hands as a cup and her handkerchief as a sponge, to do for herself as other people usually did for her when she felt mouldy. She wasn't too successful; as she dried her face on her sleeves, she felt tearfully sorry for Lawrie, so alone and so ill. The only consolation was her mirrored face which, under the blurred remains of make-up, was white as the tiles with splendid dark smudges under the eyes.

Only what now?

If she waited till the programme ended and tried to slip out with the rest of the audience, Red Ted might spot her walking out on him and turn violent like teds did if crossed. An inveterate reader of newspapers laid over washed floors, Lawrie knew all about people who'd been kicked to death only because the teds hadn't liked the way they'd looked at them; so what would happen to a walker-outer—Lawrie shut her eyes and told herself desperately that if it came to the *absolute* worst she could stay where she was till the Mrs. Mops came next morning: even Red Ted would have given up by then. This seemed the perfect solution till she imagined the huge emptiness of the closed cinema: then it wasn't. Her eyes were brimming, this time with tears of pure fright, when she saw the window.

It was a small deep window, high in the wall of the cubicle. If you stood on the lavatory seat, perhaps you could heave yourself (and your music-case) on to the sill.

The shiny green walls were covered with the usual scribbles telling who loved who. Lawrie wondered who cared anyway.

She hefted the music-case on to the sill and clutched, sprang and scrabbled. It was a desperate business and in any but a desperate moment she couldn't have done it. But at last she was crouching on the sill; it only remained to get through the window.

Metal framed, the window swung on a horizontal bar so that when it was open the square space was sliced into oblongs too narrow for anyone but a monkey to squeeze through. But where the bar went into the wall it was rust-eaten and the plaster itself cracked and crumbling. In desperation, Lawrie shoved: one end snapped: the window swayed outwards: its weight pulled the other end of the bar out of the wall.

Too preoccupied to be wholly aware how much noise the crash had made, Lawrie stuck her head out and saw an alley cluttered with battered dustbins. She dropped the music-case out and a cat which had been crouched in alarm since the window fell fled with a spit and a screech, knocking over three milk bottles. It was quite a drop from the window, but that she didn't mind. She wriggled round, eased her legs out, hung by her hands and let go. It was purest luck that though she landed among the broken glass she wasn't even scratched.

She pulled the music-case over beside her and sat where she was, dusting dirt and rust from her hands. Presently, she looked up and saw, with surprise, that a knot of people had gathered at the entrance to the alley, with alarm, that a very tall young man in white crash helmet, black jacket and leggings was walking a motor-cycle towards her. She looked for a place to run and there was nowhere. The alley was a cul-de-sac.

The young man stood over her, tall as a tower. "*Well*," he said. "What's all this for?"

Lawrie gazed dumbly up.

"Hurt yourself, have you?"

She shook her head.

"Better get up then, hadn't you?"

She did so.

He took out a notebook. "Now then. Let's start with your name, shall we?"

Lawrie found her tongue. "You're the police!"

"That's right. What's your name, miss?"

"Sophia Lawrence," said Lawrie instantly, though afterwards she could never think why. "Oh please *could* you tell me where the police station is? There's something terribly important I'm supposed to have told them."

He looked at her non-committally. "Is there? Well then, I daresay it'd save time, wouldn't it, if I were to take you straight there now?"

CHAPTER TEN

Telling the Tale

S oon after her arrival, a policewoman brought Lawrie a
cup of tea and a bun; she drank the one and ate the other,
but she couldn't stop shivering—not so much from cold
or fright (though she felt both in a routine sort of way) as
because her body *would* do it; and though that was as im-
pressive in its way as the black smudges under her eyes, she
wished it would stop: it was uncomfortable.

What she couldn't understand was why everyone was so
unfriendly. All her life, till the tall young constable had walked
her into the police station, she had accepted the hypothesis
that the police were her friends: in time of need they told
you the time, lent you money, found you if you were lost,
and generally saw to it that no harm came to you. Now she
kept telling her story over and over to different policemen
and not one of them looked at her as if they believed her
or were going to be the slightest help.

What she didn't realize was that while she knew she was
Lawrence S. Marlow, youngest daughter of Captain and Mrs.
Marlow of Trennels, with a perfectly true, though admittedly
highly coloured, story to tell, what the police saw was a
scruffily dressed girl who had been apprehended leaving the
Majestic cinema in a highly irregular manner, causing damage
to commercial property; who now claimed to have given a
false name on being apprehended; and who had, in addition,
a quite incredible story to tell which no one, so far, had been
able to make head or tail of.

She had just finished telling it to the Inspector on duty and he was the unfriendliest of the lot. It was true he had features specially designed (Lawrie thought) to look as cross as possible, but he didn't have to look at her like that. He exchanged an all-too-readable glance with the pin-neat poker-faced police-woman who had taken charge of her when she arrived, and then they both looked at her in a silence whose hostility was underlined by the ordinary friendly noises of doors closing and people walking and talking in the passage outside and the sound of music from the Radio and Television shop across the street. The contents of the music-case had been neatly laid out on the Inspector's desk and he now looked from them to Lawrie: his eldest girl would be twelve tomorrow and Lawrie, at that moment, looked like the kind of teenager he hoped Angela would never become. He said severely, "I'm going to take you through your story again. First—you told the constable your name was Sophia Lawrence. But now you say it's Lawrence Sophia Marlow. Well?"

"I——" Colour rushed into Lawrie's white face. They waited. "It's Lawrence Sybil *really*, only I—"

"Lawrence *Sybil*? Not Sophia?"

Lawrie nodded, blushing deeper still.

"Can you prove that? Have you by any chance a letter on you addressed to you?"

Lawrie shook her head, her eyes round, surprised, alarmed.

The Inspector picked up one of the books. "Suppose I contact the public library. In whose name shall I be told this book has been issued? Yours?"

"No—I don't know—I expect it's Mummy's—"

"But the surname will be Marlow?"

Lawrie nodded hard with relief. Of course it would be!

"Very well." He said into the telephone "Get me the public library" and while he waited, watched Lawrie. He so obviously thought her a liar, she felt like one: her eyes glanced furtively, her face and neck were burning, she was trembling violently. "Is that the Library? This is Inspector Allwood speaking. I have a book here, number 4956, due for return on the fourth of this month. Would you kindly tell me to whom it's been issued?"

Lawrie held her hands together. In a moment the librarian would tell him Someone Marlow, Trennels Old Farm, and he'd have to start believing her—

"Yes. . . . What? . . . Will you repeat that?" He wrote on the pad in front of him, said "Thank you" and put the receiver down. He looked at Lawrie steadily and then read aloud what he'd written on the pad. "Miss D. Gates, 4 Waterside Row, Brook Lane, Westbridge."

Lawrie gasped. Her wits deserted her. "But it can't be because it *isn't*! There *isn't* a D. Gates. They—they—"

"Yes?"

"They must have muddled the tickets—they're always doing it—that thin girl who—she's—"

"Now don't let's have any more nonsense. What does D stand for? Doreen, Doris, Dorothy—"

"Oh!" exclaimed Lawrie. "*Doris!*"

"Doris Gates. Very well. Will your parents be in by this time? Are you on the telephone?"

"Yes, only the telephone's cut off. I *told* you. Peter and Patrick think The Thuggery did it—"

"Now just listen to me," said the Inspector, leaning forward on his desk. "First of all, *no* one cut off the telephones. That was due to a fault at the exchange. And secondly, as I've already told you, we know all about these boys you call The Thuggery. We've been in touch with Miss Culver all along and she gives them a perfectly satisfactory report. But what are we to make of *you*? You're apprehended for hooliganism, you give us two false names, you tell us a wild story about pigeons and drug smuggling and *furthermore* you tell us that Mr. Merrick's son has spent the afternoon trying to steal a valuable bird from Miss Culver's lofts. And all you can offer by way of proof is a dead bird you say you picked up on the downs. Now *I* think this is all a pack of lies. But if you still insist it's the truth—why didn't you come straight here the moment you got to Colebridge?"

"Because I was with Red Ted. I—"

"Yes, you were with this boy. So then you quarrelled, I take it—"

"No honestly. It was just suppose he made me go to the Smoke and the gang crunched me sharpest—"

"Doris," said the policewoman. "Is your gang trying to make things hot for Red Ted's mob? Who helped you concoct this story?"

"No one. I'm not in a mob. *Honestly*. And I'm not *Doris*. She helps our Mrs. Bertie. That must be how that was her ticket—I expect we change her books—"

Their exasperated, wholly unbelieving faces defeated her. Tears burst out of her in a way which would have reflected no credit on the proper pride of a three-year-old. They told her to stop that noise, to pull herself together, to get a hold of herself. Presently their pardonable testiness changed to a certain concern. A glass of water was brought, the policewoman patted her shoulder, a large necessary handkerchief was put into her hands. Still she wept. The Inspector's voice said, "But we must make certain the girl *is* Doris Gates. Find out if anyone in Waterside Row is on the telephone and if so—"

The telephone on the desk buzzed urgently.

The Inspector picked up the receiver, saying testily, "Allwood here. . . . *Who?* . . . Yes, certainly put her through. . . . Good evening, Mrs. Marlow, what can I——? She was supposed to call here earlier this afternoon? Can you give me a description? . . . Yes . . . yes . . . yes—tell me, Mrs. Marlow, do you know a Doris Gates? You do? Ah, yes, I see. Well, now, Mrs. Marlow, we have a girl here of approximately your daughter's age and appearance who claims to be either Lawrence Sophia or Lawrence Sybil Marlow, but she's certainly not wearing a grey tweed coat and skirt. . . . Yes, I'll hold on."

There was a pause. Lawrie sobbed still: but now because her mother was at the other end of the telephone and all would now come right.

"Your son says she was wearing—Yes . . . yes . . . yes, Mrs. Marlow, that description tallies with the girl we have here. No, she's quite safe. It's only that we've been having some difficulty establishing her identity. Tell me, Mrs. Marlow, can your son throw any light on this remarkable story your daughter has been trying to tell us about the boys over at Monks' Culvery? . . . Yes, I'll hold on."

This pause lasted longer. Then the small clicking voice in the receiver began again, talking fast and urgently. The Inspector broke in, "Look, Mrs. Marlow. I think it would be best if you could come here and bring your son and then we can get the whole affair sorted out. Have you a car or shall we—yes, very well, Mrs. Marlow, we'll expect you in about half an hour. Thank you." He put down the receiver and looked at Lawrie: Lawrie, blowing her nose, looked at him over the handkerchief, her eyes smarting and swollen. "*Well*," he said; and paused. "Before your mother arrives, I think Policewoman Sutton had better take you to the cloakroom and let you have a wash and brush up. Your mother won't want to see you looking like that." He looked at Policewoman Sutton. "Better bring her back here when she's washed her face, and get her something to eat. Time's getting on."

As she followed Policewoman Sutton from the room, Lawrie squinted blearily at the wall clock in the outer office. The hands stood at a quarter to eight. *Golly!* No *wonder* Mummy had phoned.

Policewoman Sutton took her to the canteen and Lawrie chose a cup of cocoa and a wedge of pork pie. She forgot to provide herself with eating irons and Inspector Allwood lent her his pocket-knife. She felt sleepy and headachey and not specially hungry, but eating was something to do while Inspector Allwood read to himself from the files on his desk and they waited for Mrs. Marlow and Peter and she wondered whether Red Ted was still waiting for *her*. . . .

In the event, Mrs. Marlow and Peter arrived almost before Lawrie expected them. Her mother said "So *this* is where you've been, darling" but her voice and expression didn't match the words. And Peter, following her in, made two grimaces in Lawrie's direction: one said Ma was *livid*; the other said Lawrie was a parboiled steaming nit to have made a bish like this.

Lawrie shrugged. She went on eating small squares of pie and listening, through a growing blur of headache and sleepiness, to Peter telling Inspector Allwood everything *she'd* told him already. The only difference was, he obviously believed Peter. Across the street a girl's voice wailed "But what if Johnnie says no?" and Lawrie found she had finished all the pie. She wiped the blade surreptitiously on her jeans, closed it, and sat turning the knife over and over, first one end tapping the desk, then the other, while she listened vaguely to what they were saying and fought the drowsiness which kept shutting her eyes for her. She came finally awake to hear the Inspector saying, ". . . the loss of the container. If we'd had that we could certainly have taken a look at Miss Culver's lofts. But as it is, all we have is this bird and no means of identifying the owner."

"That's what we thought," said Peter, his voice anxious. "*That's* why Patrick went over."

"And as I've already explained, whatever his motive, he's acting quite illegally. If only you'd brought the bird and the capsule to us straight away, we might have had the whole thing cleared up by now. This could be a most serious business —if, that's to say, you're right in thinking the bird was carrying drugs of some kind."

Peter decided it was no use saying *That's what we thought* all over again.

"And in any case, why have we heard nothing from young Merrick? We've established he's not at his home, nor yours, and he's had more than enough time to reach Monks' Culvery and take a bird—if in fact any carrying contraband *are* housed there——"

Peter had a sudden thought. "Could he have bagged a Scandaroon and gone on to London?"

"Why on earth should he go to London?"

"To warn his father. Or perhaps he suddenly thought Scotland Yard—"

"I hope he's done no such thing," said Inspector Allwood sharply. "There's no reason at all why this shouldn't be dealt with at local level—at least to begin with."

Feet in it, Peter thought and shut up. The Inspector pinched his lower lip between thumb and forefinger. Then he got up and they all got up too. "I think as things stand all I can do at the moment is contact Sergeant Jackson at Culverstone and find out if anything unusual has been happening at Monks' Culvery. In the meantime, Mrs. Marlow, I don't think I need keep you or the children any longer. You'll be returning to Trennels? Then if you do hear anything from young Merrick, please telephone me immediately."

"Of course. If only they'd had the sense to tell me, I could have driven them over directly after breakfast. I can't imagine why they should have behaved so idiotically. I do hope it won't ruin all chance of catching these people."

"I hope not too, indeed. What really worries me is that if these boys are part of some dope ring they'll have had ample time to warn the men involved. However," the Inspector smiled angrily, "we must just do the best we can."

Peter and Lawrie murmured apologetically and moved towards the door, shepherded by their mother. The desk telephone buzzed again and Inspector Allwood, who had been moving to open the door, stopped to pick up the receiver. He said "Allwood here" and he and Mrs. Marlow nodded and gestured *so sorry I can't see you out—not at all, doesn't matter in the least* and then the three of them were crossing the outer office. Policewoman Sutton came hurrying after them. She touched Lawrie's arm, saying, "Just a moment, please—"

"Sutton!" The Inspector's voice, harsh, loud and urgent, sounded from the inner office. "Is Mrs. Marlow there? Ask her to come back at once, please!"

They looked at one another and went back. The Inspector was still talking on the telephone and they couldn't make out what had happened except that something was plainly very wrong. He said at last "I'll come straight over", put down the receiver and spoke directly to Mrs. Marlow.

"That was Sergeant Jackson from Culverstone. He's had a call from Miss Culver's housekeeper, Mrs. Moxon. Miss Culver herself is in London attending a meeting of one of the pigeon fanciers' societies. What has happened is this: it seems none of the boys came across to the kitchen for their supper at the usual time and when Mrs. Moxon sent her daughter to fetch them, Olwen found their quarters deserted—except, that is, for a body lying on the storeroom floor." His listeners came, almost visibly, to mental attention; they stood silent and still and the room seemed suddenly cold. The Inspector continued, "A rug had been thrown over it and she was unfortunately too frightened to lift it and look at the face, but the right hand, which held a rosary, was showing and this—the rosary— she brought back to the house with her. Since then she's become hysterical and Mrs. Moxon won't leave her till we get there. So for the moment we can't be sure whether the boy is dead or merely injured, nor of his identity—all we know is that the rosary is ebony and that engraved on a medal attached to it are the initials P.M.A.M. and a date."

Peter's lips moved in his white face. After a pause he managed to say, "Patrick Michael Anthony Mary. He showed me once. I always remembered because of the Mary."

"Thank you. Then, Mrs. Marlow, I have to ask whether you will be good enough to come with me and see if you can identify this boy—if, that's to say, he should turn out to be Patrick Merrick."

Their mother nodded, her face very white.

"Mrs. Moxon, of course, can tell us if it's one of the other boys. Then we'd better—"

"We can come too, can't we?" said Peter, his face stiff. He looked from the Inspector to his mother to Lawrie who looked stupid with shock. "We won't come in if you don't want us to—but if it's—" He found he couldn't say Patrick's name and stopped.

"Yes—if your mother has no objection." The Inspector searched his desk-top. "My pocket-knife—what did I—? Oh, never mind—"

"That was just what I was going to ask you." Policewoman Sutton touched Lawrie's arm. "I think—when you got up to go—didn't you slip it, by mistake, into your pocket?"

Lawrie looked at her blankly. She put her hands into her pockets and felt. She shook her head. "I'm sure I saw——" said Policewoman Sutton, friendly but firm.

"Never mind it now," said the Inspector brusquely. "It'll turn up. I daresay I put it in a drawer——"

"I assure you sir, I saw what happened. I intended asking her for it before she left the station. I'm not suggesting, *of course*, there was any overt intention—"

"Lawrie, empty your pockets," said her mother sharply.

Lawrie did so. She dredged up her purse and two handkerchiefs, one her own, one borrowed. The Inspector, her mother, Peter, moved impatiently, wanting to get away to Monks' Culvery, yet held by Policewoman Sutton's insistence and the small aggravating oddity of the knife's disappearance. "Where's my return ticket?" said Lawrie fumbling. "That's gone too."

In the exasperated pause, a voice made itself heard: across the road Harry Belafonte, to the applause of a studio audience, sang of his bucket: ". . . *dear Dinah, There's a hole in my bucket, dear Dinah, a hole*. . . ."

Peter made a sound between a gasp and a cry. Suddenly he was standing in front of Lawrie, his hands digging far down into the depths of her mackintosh pockets. And then he was undoing the front buttons so savagely that the bewildered Lawrie was almost jerked off her feet while he cried, "You—you *peasant* you! You prehistoric *aborigine*! There's a hole in your pocket—"

He wrenched the mackintosh from her shoulders and arms and flung it down, lining upwards, on the Inspector's desk. He gave a great tug and the ancient lining surrendered, ripping from the hem as Peter jerked and shook it, so that the collection of years cascaded on to the desk-top.

A silver threepenny bit. Two London bus tickets. A tiny key. The return half of a railway ticket. The Inspector's pocket-knife. A Christmas cracker ring. A long-withered conker. Sea-shells. A stub of pencil—

—and a polythene capsule filled with white powder which might have been bicarbonate of soda, but wasn't.

CHAPTER ELEVEN

The Dovecote at Monks' Culvery

By the time the stable clock chimed half past two, Patrick was already making his way along the earth-smelling tunnel which, now the Merricks no longer kept it in repair for priests or smugglers, was slowly disintegrating as the tree-roots forced the stonework. He groped his way to the far end and emerged to see Green Stripes, field glasses trained on the house, squatting at the edge of Tanners Gorse. Fortunately, the tunnel's exit lay well behind Green Stripes's vantage point, and Patrick went on, unchallenged, to half-run, half-slither, down the long slope into what was said to be a Roman fosse, and follow the grassy bottom to the grid below the wall which fenced the northern, wooded end of the Monks' Culvery grounds. He squeezed past the grid, the Fosse went on, and he scrambled out to crawl along the tunnels the rabbits and foxes had made in the belt of furze; he felt bold and gay and the consciousness of being a pace or two the shady side of the law was exhilarating rather than (as no doubt it should have been) unnerving. Trespasser and potential poacher he might be, but the cause was irreproachable. After all, who was it had said only the other day that it was every citizen's duty to assist the police? The Home Secretary himself, with both sides waving order papers and saying Hear Hear. *So*.

So it was curious that the words which now came marching with steady feet down the paths of his mind should bear so little relation to his mood. They said:

> *I saw a man this morning*
> *Who did not wish to die:*

The Dovecote at Monks' Culvery

I ask, and cannot answer,
If otherwise wish I.

Tenacious as a snatch of tune, they repeated themselves endlessly. Once he had had the whole poem by heart, but for the moment only this verse came to mind. It accompanied him to the edge of the wood where he crouched in the long grass and brittle fronds of last year's bracken to take his bearings.

The sky was clouding again and the park with its artfully clumped trees looked bleak and windswept. In the distance he could see the house, the angle unfamiliar, since what he was looking at was one side and part of the back. The more familiar front faced south-west: so the back must face north-east . . . mustn't it? And according to Aunt Eulalia, the Dovecote was on a *south*-facing slope some way from the house. All this compass-boxing threw him into a fine mental confusion: he looked haphazardly towards the higher ground to his right and among the tree-tops saw what he instinctively took to be the weather-vane of a church till Aunt Eulalia's description nudged him: *crowned by a lantern which bears a weather-vane in the likeness of a pigeon*. That was it. There it was.

He withdrew into the trees and began to make his way round. His feet crunched acorns and beechmast and somewhere a woodpecker hammered busily; a squirrel watched him, head downwards on the bole of an oak; the rain came again, driving through the trees and hissing in the long grass. *I saw a man this morning Who did not wish to die: I ask, and cannot answer—*

The weather-vane disappeared behind an elm: the sun came again in shafts between the clouds and the vane swung, flashing golden as, abruptly, the trees ended; they stood back, as they had stood for centuries, about the wide wheel of turf of which the Dovecote was the hub. Patrick checked: Aunt Eulalia's drawing had not prepared him for its massive solidity, its height, its breadth, its sheer thickness. Or its chill. Peter, thought his friend, would have seen it as Childe Roland's Dark

Tower. And he shivered suddenly, a goose walking over his grave: *I ask, and cannot answer, If otherwise wish I.*

Then he saw the pigeon. It was strutting about the lantern and it was too far off to be certain whether it was wearing harness or not. But as he watched, it clapped its wings, took a wheeling flight, returned to the lantern and stood, waggling its wingtips into place.

"So let's say that proves pigeons are living there," thought Patrick. "Let's say I *think* it's a Scandaroon. Now if I were Jukie, I'd have someone watching here, in case I broke in. So do I make like an Apache and see if I can find him or do I walk into the open, bold as brass, and save myself the trouble?"

I saw a man this morning Who did not wish to die: said his mind behind his thoughts. It seemed as good a time as any to have to hand the incomparable throwing knife (no one, thought Patrick, feeling the haft settle in his palm, could expect him to walk into The Thuggery's stronghold unarmed) with which an eighteenth-century cousin, who had contrived to live like a gentleman by constant attendance at the gaming-tables, had silenced those who thought his luck might possibly be traced to collusion between himself and the proprietor of the gaming-house: which it could, and, in the end, was.

He walked boldly into the open and nothing stirred but branches sighing in the wind and clouds coming and coming above the trees and sunlight vanishing from the grass. He walked once slowly around the Dovecote and all was silent. So presumably no one watched among the trees. The thing now was to get inside.

There were, on the face of it, three possible ways in: by either door or the lantern. He thought it unlikely that the lower door would have been left conveniently unlocked, but he went up the three steps, their centres scooped by the feet of centuries and turned the heavy handle. The age-darkened wood stayed shut against him.

He jumped down on to the grass and walked round to the north side. There was the door Aunt Eulalia had described, but there was no sign of a ladder. He stood back, frowning. There had to be a way in. Impossible to go back and say *Sorry pardon, couldn't make it.*

He looked up the weathered stones with their golden splotches of lichen: to his left a buttress thrust against the wall. It *should* be possible; there were toe and finger holds and the wall's slope was with him. The upper string-course circled the wall just below the second door so he would have a bit extra to stand on; and if that door was locked too he'd just have to go on up to the lantern and get through that way.

The clouds passed above the vane and the long climbing curve of the building. He took off his shoes and socks, stuffed the socks in his pockets, knotted the laces and hung them round his neck. He moved over to the buttress and stood on the lower string-course: his fingers reached up and clung to the ridges and indentations years and weather had made. Helped by the inward slant of the buttress, his mind bounded by the nutshell of each next positioning of hand and foot, he inched his way upward.

Time went by uncounted: his tensed muscles began to ache and tremble: the holds were too tenuous to permit stopping to rest, and going on at least meant getting that much nearer to the string-course. At first he had kept looking up to see how much higher he was and each time it seemed as far away as ever. Now he refused to let himself look. He kept his eyes to the wall and fingered and toed his way up.

He reached the top of the buttress. The wall's inward slant was less. He moved now by half-inches, resolutely not thinking how if he slipped he would go sliding and scraping straight to the bottom and would surely break a leg. Both legs. He tried to think of some other thing and his mind, suddenly recalling the last verse of the poem, said *Stand in the trench, Achilles, Flame capp'd and shout for me.*

His fingers, sliding up the wall, grasped a ridge wider than any they had felt before. He let himself look up. He was clutching the string-course.

His other hand reached it. His feet found toe holds and his

hands went on and up. He got one knee on the string-course, reached on and up, got from knee to foot, and, braced flat against the wall, got his other foot beside it. After that, it was comparatively easy to sidle crabwise along the string-course till he reached the door.

The handle was very small. He put his hand to it and then checked, looking up at what lay ahead of him if this door were locked too. Above the vane the clouds came and came from the south-west till the Dovecote seemed to sail towards the sea. The last ten feet of wall went up shaped like a bow in rest. He knew that even if it were necessary he could not climb it. He knew that if it were necessary he must. He turned the knob and shoved.

There was only the slightest movement, but it was enough to assure him the door was jammed only because it had warped in the frame. Clasping both sides of the frame in case the door gave unexpectedly, Patrick thumped his body hard and steadily against the little door.

The top yielded first: then the base grated back and stood on air. He eased himself down till he sat with his legs dangling inside the Dovecote. In the light from the open door he could see the great potence with its two ladders and alighting platforms and behind them the curving wall with its tiers of nesting holes. One dangling foot found a support: he looked down and saw it was resting on one of the struts Aunt Eulalia had described. Laboriously, a very old man, he stood on the strut, turned himself round, pushed the door shut and shakily, exhaustedly, descended. His foot found a broad surface: it took him some seconds to realize he was standing on the floor. Then, almost without intending to, he found he had sat down, his back against the wall, his legs straight out in front of him. For the moment he couldn't do another thing.

Now the door was closed, light entered only through the louvres in the lantern. From the walls came a feathered stirring and soft disturbed throaty noises. He looked at his watch and saw it was just three o'clock. He thought he might take a five-bar rest.

The Dovecote at Monks' Culvery

He was looking at his leg: it lay on a surface made of beaten earth and uneven paving stones: beyond his foot a piece of timber stood upright like the base of a mast. He moved his leg and remembered where he was.

His mouth felt furry with daytime sleep. He looked at his watch and saw it was just three o'clock. He looked at it again, held it to his ear and said inwardly *Damn!* The thing had gone and stopped again: as it invariably did when he forgot to wind it. Now he couldn't even be sure it had been three o'clock when he looked at it the first time and he'd no sort of idea how long he'd been in that foul-tasting sleep. Certainly the Dovecote seemed to have less light in it, but that could come as easily from rain clouds as from dusk.

He got up, stretching to take the stiffness out of himself and thought how quiet the pigeons were now and how stationary the air. But once he was on the ladder, slipping his hand into the nesting holes, working methodically over one patch of wall before pulling himself on to the next, the pigeons began to stir again, uneasy and disturbed. Heads began to appear even on the walls he had not yet touched, and the stagnant air was quickening with skimming wings, crossing and recrossing. He could only continue to put his hand gently into the nesting holes, feel the inhabitant, if any, and pull himself on, the potence turning easily as a skewer in lard. Soon, perhaps, the birds would grow used to him and calm down or he would be lucky and come on a harnessed pigeon. . . . But time passed and the air below the roof was still alive with wings and he had found nothing. He could only say with certainty that the Dovecote at Monks' Culvery housed a considerable number of Scandaroons.

The square brick storeroom at the far end of the line of palatial pigeon lofts was equally splendid in its own way. Along the back wall, bunches of herbs hung above zinc-lined food-bins labelled PEAS, RAPE, HEMP, GROATS, LINSEED, RICE, CANARY, GRIT; cupboards, a sink and a cooking-stove were also provided together with the piece of equipment The Thuggery regarded as essential—the light panel which, connected to the landing-boards of the racing-pigeon loft, signalled each homed pigeon on race days. There was also a wooden table in the middle of the room with, at the moment, four occupants: Jukie, half-sitting on it; a transistor radio which sang to itself of one who'd blown in from the windy city: the boy the Westbridge children called Blue Bobble-cap; and the abandoned survivor of the first pair of offspring produced by the mating of a well-marked Yellow Agate hen and a Yellow Wholefeather cock.

It squatted limply in a nest improvised from a scarf. The scarf belonged to Blue Bobble-cap who had just taken a half-cooked egg from a pan of hot water and broken it into a saucer; this he tilted, one finger delicately on the yolk, letting the unset white run into his mouth; he held it there, his cheeks puffing out a little, warming his hands round the pan. Then he took the squeaker in both hands, holding it to his face so that the beak slipped in sideways between his lips and, with the tip of his tongue, began to push the egg-white between the open mandibles. He did it quickly, expertly and with affection. In a few moments the squeaker, "filled up", was laid back on the scarf; but it now had an evident interest in continuing to live. Blue Bobble-cap swallowed the remains of the egg-white, wiped his mouth with the back of his hand, and grinned at Jukie. He had very white teeth, very brown eyes and skin the colour of milky coffee. His mother came from Ireland and his father from the Persian Gulf: his gang name was Espresso.

"It comes to me, man," said Jukie who had been watching with an unconsciously puckered face, "that you are the premier flutter propagator. That I could not do."

"You never done that, man? Nuthin to it." Espresso, who had had a hungry upbringing, eyed the egg-yolk. "How'd you manage, then, when you had a squeaker whose mam flighted off and wouldn't nurse?"

"Mashed up milk and biscuit and shoved it down with a squirt, the way Maudie cued me. Lucky she never give me the *do that*, cause I'd a for sure thrown up. No option."

The Dovecote at Monks' Culvery

Espresso overcame whatever shyness had been holding him back; he lifted the saucer to his mouth and the yolk went down whole. He gave Jukie a half-defiant glance as he set the saucer down but Jukie was eyeing the squeaker. He said, "Why so much try to decorpse this one flutterlet?"

"Could be he'll live to be a Yellow Mottle," said Espresso fondly. "Me Da says that's a rare sort nowadays."

"Your Da still care for that?" asked Jukie sceptically.

Espresso shrugged, his face blank and beautiful. "Sometimes, maybe."

"It come to me, man, we owe your Da a heap lot," said Jukie, suddenly moved by a passing but genuine gratitude. "If it weren't for his say we'd all of us still be telling *Ta much* to Maudie time she tosses a nicker come Doomsday. Was your Da put us in the big loot, lettin' us in with the Boss Man."

"You don't owe me Da nuthin. You an' this place was the way himself—eased in with the Boss Man. An' the big loot likewise."

"Like——? Now that I did not figure." For an unguarded moment Jukie looked genuinely disconcerted, but he recovered almost immediately. "I mus' be slippin'. How come I missed the link? Why should your Da dole mints to us without he slicks it double for himself?"

Espresso shrugged, not looking at him. He took up the squeaker and went out to the end loft which housed the Almond Tumblers. Having returned the infant to its reluctant parents, he spent longer than he need have done among the crooing, strutting birds, planning that if by tomorrow the squeaker's parents still refused to do their duty by it he'd find a nurse from among either the Turbits or the Baldheads. For a brief spell he was just one of the Fancy who might have a Yellow Mottle to cock about when the first moult was over: besides which, the Yellow Wholefeather itself was a pretty sleek flutter, though the colour still wasn't as deep as it should be; he would cross it with a Red. . . .

He had hoped Jukie might be gone from the storeroom before he got back, but he was still there, flipping a coin and listening to Skidskid telling why he'd come back sooner than ordered. "Trees is weirdies," he was saying earnestly. "Onestercreep, Jukie, they was crowding behind me back 'n movin' down on me. I never saw 'em shift, mind, but each time I looked they was closer—*solid*. So I come back, not wishin' to be trampled. Anyways, the herbert wasn't movin'. Like the jill 'n the sapso told, he's scared rotten."

"I know how they told. That don't make it for sure. I gave you the nod—watch his manor till dark."

"But nuthin *to* watch. Ceptin' these woody weirdies 'n they don't shift while you're watchin'."

"I've a word for you, Skidskid. You take 'n lay off the spice. We take it in, we send it on, 'n f'r that we get loot *but*—we don't get to crave it. We leave that to the lollipops as think they're livin' for kicks. Ask any 'v the mob—they'll cue you once you start you can't win."

"I'm different, man. I'm the new issue."

"You're *no* diff'rent, man. You're the twitch as sees trees walkin'. You play it crafty so's you take loot off the Boss Man, not so's you toss it back."

"He don' take much."

"He don't now. Wait a time till you get the ravin' cravin'. Then he'll strip you. 'N then mebbe he'll rub you 'n why? Cause you might sing. You never heard tell how harmless kiddos doin' nuthin but walk home quiet 'n respectable get set on by wicked Teds 'n crunched for no reason? So mebbe mos' times there's no reason but it happened to Dipso 'n it happened to Napoli, 'n why?"

"Dunno. Never knew neither've them kiddos."

"Nor never will. 'N why? Cause they're in the boneyard. 'N why? Cause they might 'v chatted too loud one time the spice cravin' come on them. Not *did*. *Might*."

Skidskid's eyes slid from Jukie's face to Espresso's. Espresso nodded sombrely in corroboration. "You mean—*you* rubbed them, Jukie?"

"Na, not us. Though Kinky mebbe would 'v volunteered. Na—the Boss Man tipped the Diker mob."

"The *Diker* mob? But spice ain't their lay."

"Which is how the Boss Man figured. It was a real carve up, Kinky said."

"How'd he know?"

"Cause the Boss Man sent him to watch, private eye, case the Diker mob made a deal with Dipso 'n Nap. You gotta cogitate these things once you're Top Operator. But Kinky said there weren't no error. They tripped 'em 'n carved 'em 'n left 'em. So you deny yourself, Skidskid, unless you dream a long life is dregsville."

Skidskid shrugged and took a jiving stroll about the room as if trying to make the bravado of his body compensate for the panic in his eyes. "I *like* it, I *like* it," clamoured the radio in a shrieking undertone, helping him. He stamped and spun, recovering his nerve. Presently he felt sufficiently himself again to say, "What's with the Dovecote light, Jukie? Why's it on the blink so?"

Jukie, who had been checking the food-bins, looked round. Espresso was watching it too. The Dovecote light, the last of the row, was disconnected only when Miss Culver came into the storeroom. Dipso, an all-time wiz who had lightning eating out of his hand, had fixed it so that when the light stayed white they knew nothing was happening: when it turned red they knew a loaded Scandaroon had alighted on the landing-board: when it turned green and went out they knew the flutter was safe inside and someone went down to the Dovecote immediately to take its load. But now the light was flipping from white to red to white again. Time after time it happened, the apparent reason clear enough: the flutter was flying on to the landing-board, hesitating, and then flying off again. There were three possible explanations: one, that the signal system had gone wrong: two, that the presumed bird wasn't a Scandaroon at all, but a rook or a gull, say, who had no intention of going inside; and three, that the light was right, and the bird a Scandaroon, but that something or someone was frightening it off.

"You better both come with me," said Jukie after a moment

as the light turned white again. "Could be just a moggie on the prowl. Or could be one of the noddy-boys loafin' by. If it's yours, Skidskid, you'll be in dead trouble, I promise you."

Skidskid said noisily, "Onestercreep I *swear* Jukie there weren't no one movin'. I wouldn't a come away 'f I hadn't bin sure. Onester*creep*."

"Yeh, man. On'y could be you were sure *an*' wrong. Say the Gestapo come callin' tomorrer, that's harmless, cause first light the flutters'll be waftin' back to the steamboat. But suppose they take a shufti *this* day we'll be netted certain."

"*Yeh*, Jukie. But onestercreep—"

"Aw, stuff it. C'm on."

The light was still flickering white, red and white again as they left the storeroom. Had they delayed a few moments longer they would have seen it, at long last, turn green and go out; but by that time they were running across the park in the dusk and the thin rain blowing in on the wind. As they ran, Jukie a little ahead, the two behind him conversing by means of shrugs and grimaces, three figures emerged from the trees on the far side of the park, saw them, veered, and ran towards them, Kinky's tale and Jukie's urgency colliding in a welter of words and phrases: for some moments everyone spoke his own piece without hearing what anyone else was saying. Then Jukie prevailed. The other voices died away. He told them what they were to do and they all ran on together.

CHAPTER TWELVE

"Who did not Wish to Die"

The Scandaroon which, sensing the disturbance inside the Dovecote, had been flying uneasily to and from the landing-board, at last felt the call of home too strong, folded its wings and strutted inside. Patrick saw it enter, harness and capsule entire. Perched on the top rungs of the ladder he froze, watching to see where it would go.

It flew down to the lower platform and began to feed from a half-full grain hopper. Patrick stayed motionless; less from consideration for the tired pigeon than because he thought a sated bird more likely to come quietly. So he watched it gobble its fill and then dunk its beak in the water-pot: as it did so, a grating noise cut through the crooings and flutterings of the pigeons. He stayed still, knowing what it must be even before the pale band of light widened across the earth and flagstones and touched the far wall. *I saw a man this morning.*

His deliberate exploration of the nesting holes had brought him directly above the door and he could only watch the unbroken oblong of light. Then the sunset flared, the oblong brightened momentarily and an elongated human shadow moved into position dead centre. *Who did not wish to die.*

The pigeon preened itself. The shadow paused on the threshold, descended, stood still, looked swiftly round and then once more, slowly, to make sure it had missed nothing. *I ask and cannot answer.*

There was nothing to be done and Patrick stayed where he was, doing just that. Almost before he could wonder if

the shadow might go away now, it had lifted its feet and its
head was running up the wall as it walked forwards into Patrick's field of vision, becoming solid Jukie, intent on the
pigeon. Patrick tried to turn his thought and hood his eyes
so that neither sent out their eerie silent summons, compelling
Jukie to glance upwards. *If otherwise wish I. I saw a man this
morning Who did not wish to die: I ask, and cannot answer—*

Jukie took up the pigeon easily and skilfully, pocketed harness and capsule, and set the bird back on the platform: Patrick
measured the distance between himself, the ground, Jukie: the
pigeon, no longer interested in grain or water, shook its
feathers and took off for its nesting hole: half-turned to go,
Jukie watched its flight. So he saw Patrick.

They eyed one another in a silence which began to seem
unbreakable. But at last Jukie said, "You'd best come down
from the high place, noddy-boy. You're in dead trouble, you
know that?"

"Someone's in dead trouble," said Patrick beginning a slow
descent, "but I wouldn't know it was me."

"Then you know it now cause I've cued you. Hurry on
down, noddy-boy. We ain't got all that time."

"I've got time," stated Patrick. "Don't let me keep you
if you're really in a rush. I can find my own way out—"

"You ain't goin' no place," said Jukie automatically. But
Patrick said it with him and Jukie looked not only disconcerted
but hurt.

"I go to the flicks too," said Patrick conversationally, and,
stopping momentarily, turned sideways on to Jukie while he
talked to him so that he could ease Cousin Ambrose's dagger
from his pocket into his hand. "I even watch the antiquities
on TV. And that line is one they've been using since *Scarface*.
You dig Paul Muni?"

"Just descend, noddy-boy. There's not time for a slice of
tongue pie. Anyway, I don't dig the flicks none."

"Really not? Don't you take your chick ever?"

"Na. And why? Cause I don't have a bird."

"Don't you really? Isn't that most irregular? I thought all

Teds dated Chicks—sorry pardon—Birds. I thought it was a rule."

"Strictly for mugs," said Jukie contemptuously. "Birds drain the loot like you'd think they pulled the plug out. And it's my choose my loot stays mine. You comprehend me?"

"Yes indeed," said Patrick, coming down a little faster. "I think you're very sensible." He was level with the lower platform. "Besides—"

He swung from the ladder to the platform, giving the ladder a violent thrust as he did so: the potence spun in massive obedience and the ladder opposite caught Jukie on the side of his head. He staggered sideways and Patrick, taking two strides across the platform, hurled himself against him. They fell heavily, Jukie underneath, the zip-closed pocket holding harness and capsule under Patrick's knee. He wrenched at the zip, clumsy with haste, and it jammed. He tried to prise it open with the knife, but the blade slipped, ripping the material, and he saw leather and slashed down through the rest of the pocket. Next moment, harness and capsule were in his hand. And then he was on his feet, through the doorway, down the steps and running. But as he ran, he saw from the corners of his eyes the dark figures start from the wall on either side of the doorway and his advantage was cut to the few yards of surprise. He bolted for the encircling trees, but the twilight, levelling the bumps and hollows of the turf, disguised a shallow dip as flat ground; he stumbled headlong and The Thuggery threw themselves on him from behind.

In the first moments of the scrimmage, while he was flat under the heap of bodies with the breath knocked out of him, it seemed, from the grunts and yelped protests, that they bashed one another by mistake as often as they bashed him on purpose. Then a voice shrilled repeatedly "Put the boot in! Put the boot in!" and one and another rolled aside, the weight on his back lessened, and he could heave and struggle against the wet crushing body, reeking of river mud, which was holding him down. He lashed out with his legs and someone yelped

and people came back and sat on them. The voice shrilled
again, "Put the boot in, I tell y'! Put the boot in!" Someone
else growled "Put it in y'self, Lukie!" and there was a pause
and then, it seemed, the boot miskicked for the weight on
his back jerked sideways, shouting "Y' great yobbo! Look
what y'r at!" and for an instant he was rolling clear and
scrambling to his feet. But with confused cries, the bodies flung
themselves on him again, kicking his feet from under him,
and there was grass in his mouth and heavy breathing above
him and his arms were being dragged behind his back and
bent painfully upwards. Someone shrieked "A blade! The herbert's carrying a blade!" and something so paralysingly hurtful
happened to his wrist that his fingers jerked open without
argument. A new voice shrilled "Lemme put the boot in!
Gimme room to put the boot in!", another voice yelled
"G'wan then! Wat yer waitin' for?" and two purposeful kicks
hurt his side while he struggled vainly, unable to twist away
because of the wrench on his arms. Then the Thug who knelt
on his back and held his arms panted "Put it in proper, you
peasant! Give it 'im in 'is top!" and there was a sudden silence
and two dagger-toed boots appeared on the grass in front of
him. One swung back.

A voice shouted. The foot stopped, its startled owner wob-
bling momentarily out of Patrick's field of vision. The grasp
on his arms slackened. The immediate pain which had deafened
him a little grew suddenly less and he heard Jukie's voice,
the words jerking as he pelted up to the group, "Stuff it!
Stuff it, you kinky mobster! We need him conscious!"

"No one don't take them words to me, Jukie boy. This
kind ain't conscious even w'en they're walkin', see—"

"Like which words? Like he wasn't conscious when he
stepped past you without you noticin'? How about that,
Skidskiddo?"

There was a silence. Then the dagger-toes kicked spitefully,
but to miss, and vanished. One of the other voices, mild,
placatory, said, "Why you want him conscious, Jukie? We
thought you'd need him clunked."

"We need him conscious cause we need to quiz him. Does that add?"

"It's your say, Jukie. Quiz for why?"

"Give me patience. To learn how much they know, how much they've told 'n who to. That figure to you?"

The questioner made a snubbed assenting noise. Someone else said, "What met your top, Jukie? It grows a melon."

"The ladder met me," said Jukie shortly. "Let the herbert up, Kinky."

A knee ground viciously in Patrick's back and the weight lifted. His arms flopped on the grass. After a moment he rolled over and sat up, picking grass out of his mouth and looking at the six figures which stood about him, tall because they were looking down, shadowy in the dusk. The trees stood behind them, taller and more shadowy still. "Time to ramble," said Jukie. "On your feet, noddy-boy."

"When I'm good and ready," said Patrick; his limbs trembled as they had done after the climb up the Dovecote wall and since he was not at all intimidated by his antagonists, he found his body's treachery the more exasperating.

"Like man, you find yourself good and ready now," suggested Jukie; and then he said suddenly, holding out his hand, "You whipped sumthin off of me. Toss it back 'n stay healthy, yeh?"

Patrick looked blank. "I whipped—? Gracious! So I did!"

"Yeh, so you did. Don't stall me. *Give.*"

Patrick slapped his pocket and then gazed blankly round him. "I must have dropped it when they tripped me. I can't see it anywhere. Can you?"

The dusk and the long, trampled, leaf-scattered grass made searching an almost hopeless task. Nevertheless, The Thuggery went to work, casting methodically over the ground across which Patrick had run and on which he had lain. He sat and watched them, capsule and harness still safely though ticklishly stowed between vest and trouser-band where he had thrust them when he grabbed them. He thought it might be over-doing it to offer to help look, so he stayed where he was till,

defeated by the growing dark, The Thuggery gave up. A
breeze shifted the weather-vane. Patrick gave his mouth a final
wipe with the back of his hand and got unhurriedly to his
feet. They closed about him.

It was dark among the trees, but The Thuggery pressed
so closely that escape was impossible; in the blowy greyness
of the park, they drew away a little. Motionless clouds blotched
a quince-coloured sky and across the park the mass of the house
stood solid against the west, the windows lightless. As Patrick
looked about him, half-knowing escape was impossible, half-
despising himself for not trying anyway, Kinky trod on his
heels, jostling him, whether accidentally or on purpose he
couldn't tell. He chose to think it intentional. He shoved him
off, saying, "Stand clear, d'you mind? I take my air fresh."

Kinky aimed a running kick at him, Patrick dodged, Kinky,
unbalanced, stumbled clownishly and nearly fell. The others
laughed, not kindly. They said, "He's right, Kinky. Man,
you're real high. Man, they should of put you in the deep
freeze while it was time. Like man, you stench of the ever-
open grave."

Kinky slouched and muttered, hunching his shoulders.
Yeller Feller, evidently a natural kicker of those safely down,
began gleefully to relate the tale of the sapso and the lock
gates. "Man, was Kinky tearful-fearful. They must 'v heard
him singin' in the Smoke——"

I saw a man this morning Who did not wish to die said the
words in Patrick's mind as he glanced at Kinky who was walking crabwise alongside the group, bellowing his denials of any
such behaviour, at the same time calling loudly on someone
called Siberia to bear him out. But Siberia's corroboration,
when it came, was of the perfunctory sort, not meant to be
believed. The derisive comments of the others continued like
darts thrown in competition. And at last Kinky fell silent and
walked along kicking at nothing, looking aside.

They reached the storeroom. Blue Bobble-cap opened the
door and switched on the green-shaded light which hung
above the table; the rest shouldered Patrick inside. As Jukie

sat himself on the table and the rest stood around, awaiting what came next, Jukie caught sight of the knife in Skidskid's hand. "What's that you're heftin'?"

"I took it off the herbert," said Skidskid proudly.

"That so?" said Jukie with a glance at Patrick. "Give."

For an instant Skidskid hesitated. Then he tossed it, at Jukie, at the table. It righted itself in mid-air like a cat and stuck point downwards in the wood, quivering. "Some!" said Jukie admiringly, jerking it out.

They played with it enthusiastically, tossing it in turn and watching it fall unerringly on its point: Patrick thought it had probably not found itself in such congenial company since Cousin Ambrose was turned off at Tyburn. He glanced towards the door and began, hopefully, to edge round behind the group as if trying to see better over their shoulders. He had almost reached the spot where it needed only a step back to be through the door and away when Jukie looked up sharply saying, "Where's the herbert? Oh, that's where you've lost yourself to, is it? Espresso, why don't you lock 'n bolt? The guest's staying."

Patrick looked behind him as if in surprise, shrugged slightly and strolled to the chair below the light panel. This he straddled, giving Jukie an innocent, blinking look, half-smothering a yawn. The Thuggery looked at him and he looked back at them: Jukie was Jukie: Purple Streak was Siberia: Black Check was Kinky: Green Stripes was Skidskid: Blue Bobble-cap was Espresso—and he wondered suddenly what their real names were: Tom, Dick and Harry; Clarence, Percy, Algernon: Aloysius, Sebastian—

Siberia said abruptly, "What now, Jukie? What we do now?"

"First thing you 'n Kinky 'n Mr. Luke better do is get off those whiffy duds. 'N then, when you come back, we'll quiz noddy-boy. There's no rafty old rush."

"You sure that ain't playin' it too frigid, Jukie?"

"Yeh man. Sure I'm sure. Lissen Siberia. There's guessin' 'n knowin'. 'N even w'en it's knowin', herberts 've gotta enlist

the Gestapo. 'N even w'en they've got the Gestapo real keen,
the Gestapo say 'Proof, mugsie?'. 'N 'f you don't have proof,
the Gestapo don't move. Right?"

"Mebbe."

"Not mebbe, *is*. So they know a little 'n they guess a heap
'n mebbe the guess ain't way off. But all they got's a corpsed
flutter 'n a bit of leather, so they got nuthin. 'N first light
tomorrer the steamboat'll come 'n we loose the flutters 'n that's
the finish. They'll not use this place no more, that's for solid.
We'll be movin' on, soon's the Boss Man whistles. But till
then, we're here. Get me?"

"Yeh," said Siberia, nodding like a mandarin. "Yeh, Jukie,
I get you. So I go get me into dry duds. You comin', Kinky?"

"Yeh, I'm comin'. You comin', Lukie?"

Mr. Luke said "Yeh, I'm comin', Kinky" and went out with
them, smiling about him. Patrick, who had been watching
them both, thought Mr. Luke must be a bit of a goon. Anyone
looking at Kinky's face as he followed Mr. Luke through the
door could tell that quite soon now Mr. Luke was going to
be made sorry he'd spoken. He wondered if that made him
sorry for Mr. Luke; and decided it didn't, very.

No one spoke for quite a while after they'd gone: the only
sound was the radio, vocalizing. Jukie sat thinking, repeatedly
tossing the knife to fall on its point while Skidskid, making
blinkers of his hands, peered through the black shine of the
window pane, and Espresso moved restlessly about the room,
opening food-bins and running grain through his fingers, opening cupboards and examining their contents. Presently Jukie
took a cigarette-case from his pocket, helped himself and
tossed it to his friends in turn. He caught it the second time,
made as if to toss it to Patrick and then checked, saying, "You
wouldn't, do you, noddy-boy?"

"No," agreed Patrick. In fact, he did, occasionally, depend-
ing on whom he was with. But this time he wasn't sure he
might not be being offered reefers.

"Thought not," said Jukie. He pocketed the case, saying,
"What you peerin' at, Skidso?"

"A great big black of nuthin. I was wonderin' w'en Rigid'd be back, that's all."

"Late," said Jukie laconically. He added, "I think mebbe he'll give the chicklet a real live whirl. If she's willin' of course. 'N then again mebbe even if she's not. Does she live it, your chicklet?"

After a moment Patrick realized the question was addressed to him. He said, "Come again?"

"Your chicklet. Does she live? Is she a whirlybird?"

Since whirlybird in Patrick's tongue meant helicopter his bewilderment persisted. "I don't have a chicklet. Nor a whirlybird. I still don't get you."

"Don't josh me. She was runnin' with you this mornin'. The jill in the sordid mac."

"You mean—'Strewth! You mean *Lawrie*!"

"He finally latched on! Yeh, if her label's Lorry, that's who I mean. So does she live it? Is she with it?"

"If you mean what I think you mean," said Patrick cautiously, "no, I shouldn't think so for a moment. Why?"

Skidskid looked over his shoulder and said, "Then mebbe today's the day she'll learn. The birds get the notion real speedy from Rigid. Don't they, Jukie?"

The dialogue made no sense to Patrick. Lawrie was in Colebridge: she had gone to the police: and after, if she felt like it, to the public library: so he said, "Sorry pardon, but I still don't get it. So far's I know, Lawrie went into Colebridge this afternoon to change some books—"

"Yeh," said Skidskid, watching him. "That's sumthin like you said this mornin', you'n the sapso. The two-thirty-two to Colebridge. But things bein' dicey we didden like to let none of you out on your tod. So Rigid took the chicklet, cause Rigid goes for birds 'n birds go for Rigid 'n mebbe before they come home, they'll 've had theirselves a true ball. Latch on?"

Patrick thought he did. For five long seconds he was appalled by the joint insanity of forgetfulness which had landed Lawrie in the muck. Then it occurred to him that even Lawrie would hardly be fool enough to let herself be picked up by a Thug; and even if she hadn't sense enough she'd still be too scared. He sighed with relief, the radio sang "You'll Never Walk Alone" and Jukie said irritably over his shoulder, "For mercy's sake, Espresso, quit the prowl 'n park yourself. You're treadin' on me nerves."

Espresso closed a cupboard and stood hesitating. His dark eyes slipped from Skidskid to Jukie as he sucked his lips in. He said, "Jukie—"

"Yeh, I'm here. You can see me." Espresso was silent. "Well—*say*. What's bleedin' you?"

"Your say jus' now about movin' on. You mean that?"

"I mean it good. This place corpsed this morning."

Espresso looked away from Jukie, his thumb knuckles rubbing together. "There's the other flutters still."

"Yeh, that's right, there is. They all got two wings 'n a beak. So?"

"You know what *so*," muttered Espresso sullenly. He sucked his lips in again and then forced out of himself, "So I'm stayin'. When you quit I'm stayin'."

Skidskid gave a short laugh and assumed what was plainly intended as a sardonic, a knowing look. Jukie tossed the knife high in the air and watched it fall and stick quivering in the wood. He said, "You think your Da'll like that?"

"His like or not like is nuthin—"

"I don't think it's nuthin. Cause why? Cause the Boss Man won't like. So you lose the notion. There'll be other flutters—there gotta be."

"Not like these there won't."

Jukie looked at him. So did Skidskid. So did Patrick. In their different ways they were all reminded of a small kid about to be clouted by the grown-ups any minute now, bawling for something he wouldn't get. And at last Jukie said, "It's not me you have to convince, kiddo. It's the Boss Man. You try 'f you want. 'N supposin' you want a one-way hearse ticket, you try real hard."

Espresso turned his back and stuck his head in a cupboard

as if he looked for something. Jukie and Skidskid exchanged shrugs. They almost exchanged shrugs with Patrick too before they remembered he wasn't one of them. In some embarrassment Skidskid turned back to the window. He looked casually through the black shine and then made blinkers of his hands again. He said, "Here's Rigid now!"

"Rigid! You sure?"

"Yeh, yeh, yeh! Sure I'm sure. He's with us now."

A face appeared at the window, grimaced, vanished. Patrick ticked off the last name: Red Ted equalled Rigid. The handle rattled violently as Skidskid unlocked the door and Rigid was in, trampling Skidskid in his hurry: the normal charges and counter-charges of clumsiness were exchanged: till Rigid caught sight of Patrick and exclaimed, "The noddy! How'd he come?"

"He lurked down, private eye, to the flutter fort. Where's the chicklet that you're back at good boys' bedtime?"

"Man, she flipped me," said Rigid dramatically.

So she *had* been picked up: she'd also, seemingly, got away with it; disconcerted, and uncertain now whether relief or consternation was called for, Patrick heard Skidskid say, "Man, you're losin' touch. How'd she flip you where?"

"Yeh, where?" asked Jukie, a small, upright crease above the bridge of his nose.

"Man, where you couldn't have followed neither. To the Dames."

"Birds is always flippin' to the Dames. But they come back to you. They gotta."

"Not this chick. And mind, she was a real warm hold. I was cuein' me what a pleasure it was goin' to be for the both of us when I got her settled to the snogging session——"

"Only she flipped first," said Jukie sardonically. "She's shacked up in the Dames sooner than. When you suppose yourself she's comin' out?"

"Jukie, this isn't witty. But you gotta learn it. She's out. There I sat me, waitin' 'n waitin', 'n already she was out."

"Man, you gone for blind?"

"No, man. It goes she busted the Dames window 'n flipped through. 'N Jukie, you are now going to be very highly niggled. The Gestapo swooped her 'n rushed her to the Copshop. It's the entirely true. Spin cued me."

"*Brother!*" thought Patrick. "What for a grotty bish-up!"

"Spin?" said Skidskid in a half-murmured aside.

"The slick chick in the black altogether. She's the slickest with the mostest but she don't give nuthin—"

"Stuff it!" said Jukie in a sudden burst of anger.

"Jukie, man, I *regret*—"

"You let her flip you to the Copshop and you *regret!*" said Jukie with unexpected and withering violence. As Rigid's face went blank with surprise, Jukie said to Patrick, "What would she cue the Gestapo? Hurry! Give!"

But before Patrick could answer the changing party returned: first Kinky, wearing the creamy look of slaked vengeance; next Siberia, glancing back in malicious sympathy; and Mr. Luke who was now very very sorry indeed: no marks showed, but his lashes were pointed with tears and his walk was stiff and careful. He watched where Kinky went and placed himself as far away as possible.

"Hi Rigid!" said Siberia. "What gives?"

Rigid told him: but he kept glancing uneasily at Jukie who sat stabbing reflectively at the table-top and the narrative lacked sparkle. Jukie let him finish and then said again to Patrick, the violence and anger still rasping in his voice, "So what can she acquaint the Gestapo? Cue me!"

If Kinky and the others had not come back when they had, Patrick would have answered instinctively *Nothing*. But now he had had time to weigh the alternatives: *Nothing* would be what they expected and hoped and they had a plan for that: if, on the other hand, he said *The lot* it might, to coin a phrase, set the cat among the pigeons. He said it.

"It's on'y tellin'," said Siberia after a moment. "All you got's a corpsed flutter."

"'N that she wasn't totin'," said Rigid triumphantly.

"She was, you know."

164

"Where then? 'S fact she didn't have nuthin with her," exclaimed Rigid, appealing to Jukie.

"She did, you know," said Patrick. "In the music-case."

"As I spied. Was nuthin but a load of books."

"Only not quite," said Patrick politely, insufferably. "The pigeon was underneath."

Rigid sucked in a breath. They were all silent, looking at Patrick, waiting for him to go on, till Jukie said, "That all?"

"Not quite," said Patrick. *I saw a man this morning Who did not wish to die: I ask, and cannot answer——.* "There was that message on the cigarette carton and the harness." Into the silence he added, more truly than he supposed, "And the capsule with the spice in it, of course. Most important."

"You didn't have that!" said Jukie, pouncing. "Siberia heard the jill 'n the sapso tellin' each other——"

"As we planned you'd hear."

There was a long silence while The Thuggery looked at one another and no one came up with an answer. The words in Patrick's head said *Stand in the trench Achilles, Flame-capp'd and shout for me*, returned on themselves and said *If otherwise wish I*. And then, at last, Kinky said, his voice loud, "Jukie man, you're in real live trouble."

"All of us," said Jukie hardily.

"All of us some, mebbe, but you the most. Cause for why? Cause you're Top Boy. So the chop'll get you first."

The faces looking at Jukie showed a sudden collective relief. They seemed to edge away, drawing closer to Kinky. "Like man, this is dicey," said Skidskid after a moment. "Who thinks good we loose the flutters now 'n be on our way?"

"Like man, you're displayin' your know-nuthin," said Jukie contemptuously. "Right now the flutters'll be roostin'. They won't budge till it's light."

"We could drive 'em out," said Skidskid obstinately. "Or we could leave the doors open 'n let 'em start 'emselves."

"Drive 'em out 'n they'll roost in the trees. 'N suppose then they stay put? Lissen Skidskid. Lissen very good. This say ain't mine. It's the Boss Man's, for if ever there was real trouble.

The top thing is get the flutters away. So too bad, we can't flip till the steamboat comes 'n that won't be till morning. It's when we done that we c'n breeze ourselves. Get it?"

No one got it as well as all that. "'N suppose", said Siberia, momentarily spokesman, "the Gestapo take a shufti tonight before the flutters is flown? What then?"

"Then we try it as we're jus' the innocent kiddos who toil for Maudie. What goes in the Dovecote is sumthin we never knew."

"'N w'en he starts to sing?" Siberia indicated Patrick.

"He'll be stowed '*n* muted till the Gestapo flip."

"'N after?"

"*After* we'll be gone. Then he'll be the Boss Man's target."

"So'll you," said Kinky.

There was another glance-catching silence. Then Kinky said persuasively, "Lissen Jukie. You're for bad trouble. You know it. We know it. Say we play it this way. You stay 'n let the flutters loose while we breeze to the Smoke. 'F the Gestapo come lookin' 'n you're nailed, leastways, where you'll go, the Boss Man don't reach. 'N whichever goes, we'll talk honey for you to the Boss Man—tell him it weren't your fault the steamboat loosed the flutters in fog so they come driftin' in all week every which way."

"As he knows," snapped Jukie. "Now lissen, Kinky——"

But the relieved clamour which had broken out stopped him. Patrick heard Espresso say, "I'll stay, Jukie, like I said. You breeze with them." But Jukie didn't hear. He was watching the others, his hands clapped to his ears and saying "Stuff it, stuff it" till there was silence again. Then he said, "'F you breeze now, like Kinky's saying, you ain't goin' against me. You're goin' against the Boss Man. 'F you think that figures, breeze."

They looked at Kinky expectantly. When he said nothing they looked at one another uncertainly. Jukie relaxed a little. Then Kinky, leaning his hands on the table, said, "Lissen, Jukie. I don't reckon the Boss Man planned for us to stay to be nailed. He planned so's we'd get away easy. I say this

166

is the time to breeze. 'F you stay to let the flutters fly, then I ain't sayin' you're wrong cause you're Top Boy 'n it ain't for me to say. But I say we have the share-out now 'n those who vote to breeze, breeze, 'n those who vote to stay, stay."

They were convinced: less, Patrick thought, watching the ebb and flow of decision, by the arguments for or against staying than by the spell-binding words "share-out". When Jukie did not move but continued to look at Kinky, his hand clenched on the knife-hilt, Siberia nodded to Kinky, walked over to the food-bins and opened the one labelled GRIT. He reached down and something scraped, metal on metal. He straightened up and came back carrying a deed-box which he set in front of Jukie. Jukie looked up and round at each face in turn. What he saw evidently convinced him: he shrugged, felt in an inside pocket and brought out a crowded key-ring. He unlocked the lid and threw it back.

It was all very orderly. There was a cash-book, with a page for each name and the amounts earned clearly set down: and there was money—a very considerable amount of money—in notes and silver. Jukie reckoned totals, handed the book to the recipient to check, and counted out the cash. When it was handed over, the recipient signed his name across the total. There were no arguments and, apparently, no disappointments; Skidskid, indeed, seemed pleasantly surprised his hand-out came to so much.

"Who grafts that loot?" he asked, indicating the similar packet of notes remaining when each had received his share.

"Maudie. She dreams it's profit we make selling spare flutters," said Jukie sardonically. "Like it's the Boss Man's method of binding her, case she ever tumbled us 'n he had need to put the squeeze on."

"She don't need it this time though," said Kinky thriftily. "Not w'en there's seven pore kiddos whose pockets is goin' to get lighter 'n lighter the next few weeks."

"That's out," said Jukie, suddenly stubborn, pocketing his own share and throwing the notebook back into the box.

"On'y cause you say so?"

"Yeh, man. That's right. Cause I say so. Now breeze, Kinky, 'f it's breezing you're after."

"Now lissen, Jukie. Play it very slow. Yore in dead trouble, right? You want I speak honey for you to the Boss Man, right? Then you gotta make it sweet for me, the trouble I'm takin' for you, right?"

"Tell on," said Jukie.

The rest stood watching, silent; Patrick, only half-knowing he did so, got up from his chair.

"So I'll take Maudie's loot. 'N half yours would be sweet like treacle, Jukie. Right?"

"Wrong," said Jukie, standing up.

"That's sour, man. That's dead rotten. Yore 'gainst the wall, Jukie. You need friends. But friends gotta be treated generous."

There was a pause. Jukie seemed to be considering Kinky's face feature by feature. Then, with a sudden little shrug, he laid his hand on the lid. And shrill as a slate pencil Mr. Luke burst out, "Don't lush him, Jukie! He aims we'll topple you with the Boss Man 'f you lushed him a million. He wants Top Boy, Jukie! 'S afternoon he cued us—"

No one was trying to stop Kinky reaching Mr. Luke. It was just there were too many people standing around in too small a space to make movement easy; to step aside seemed the one way to step into Kinky's path. And now, as he spoke, Mr. Luke was shoving frantically to get away. As Kinky fought towards him he screamed childishly, rushed to the door, unlocked it and bolted through. Kinky knocked Rigid staggering and charged after him. Jukie, his arm flinging forward, yelled, "Come back, you kinky mobster!"

A sound came out of the dark, part grunt, part gasp, part surprise: and after, the soft thud of a fall.

They stood where they were, gazing at the open door, waiting for Kinky and Mr. Luke to come back while the radio wailed softly "What If Johnnie Says No". Patrick hardly knew he had moved until he found himself walking across the room, his shoes sounding over-loud on the bare boards. No one tried to stop him. He walked outside and saw a boy lying in the shaft of light. Kinky gazed up at him, trying to raise himself.

He had seen that look of bewilderment once before, at a point-to-point: in the eyes of a mare with a broken back who couldn't understand why her legs no longer obeyed her. "Wha' happened?" muttered Kinky. "Wha's got me?"

Patrick, crouched beside him, said automatically "Don't try to move. You'll be all right in a minute" and knew as he spoke that these were stupid words to say. At the same time his hand found an inexplicable thing to do. It went into his pocket and found his rosary where it lived in its case along with his penknife, a tangle of string, a stub of pencil and similar objects. He put the rosary into Kinky's hand and Kinky grasped it and his hand together.

"Wha's got me?" muttered Kinky again and lay gazing up at Patrick. Patrick swallowed, crossed himself and stayed beside him, crouching.

Mr. Luke came sidling back out of the darkness: there were muted movements and voices from behind Patrick as The Thuggery began to emerge from the storeroom and stand around, looking down with concerned faces. They said *Wha's happened to him* and *Why don't he get up then?* and *Oughten we get him inside or sum'in'?*

Patrick freed his hand and stood up and out of the way. The Thuggery, trying hard to be careful, but not very skilful about it, got Kinky off the ground and into the storeroom, speaking reassuring phrases as they did so. They laid him on the floor and the light, swinging in the draught from the open door, sent the shadows running to and fro. They stood round him, puzzled by his unwinking stare.

"You feel reel bad, Kinky?" said Siberia anxiously.

Rigid produced a rug from the cupboard. "Put this over him, we should," he said. "Didden we oughta call the pill-lusher?"

"Na, leave it," said Mr. Luke uneasily. "Why for?"

"Why for? Cause he's crook 'n needs curin', that's why for," said Rigid indignantly.

"But he's dead," said Patrick.

They turned on him faces of genuine indignation. They told him not to say them words: them words weren't lucky: them words was judas: they demanded he should unsay them. When he looked silently past them with a face as white as Kinky's they became impatiently anxious to prove him wrong. Rigid produced a mirror from his breast pocket.

"Now look—see?" he said. "Watch how me gran proved our Rita was still with us after she was in a comma from feedin' herself too many pills cause her rave took up with another doll. See? You hold it here, in front of his sniffer, 'n his puff makes it fog—"

Rigid's voice halted. He knelt in silence, his lips parting, the hand which held the mirror beginning to waver. He said at last, "Here—it's not workin'. There's sum'in' wrong with it—help me sit 'im up."

He got his arm under Kinky's shoulder, looking round for assistance, but no one moved. And then his face stiffened. He felt and looked and took his hand away, red wetness smeared across his palm. He said, the words coming in jerks and rushes, "It's the blade in 'im. It's stuck so deep there's on'y the handle to feel. You done 'im Jukie! W'en you threw the blade you done 'im!"

The pause, like that between lightning and thunderclap, was broken only by the scramble of Rigid's feet as he got himself away from the body and back to the group. And then Siberia put words to the mounting panic, "That's it! That's it then! It's breeze 'n sharpest! This isn't none of ours!"

His words touched off a stampede. He, Skidskid and Rigid jammed in the doorway, Espresso and Mr. Luke shoved frantically: then they were through and gone. The radio made itself heard once more and Patrick, finding himself beside it, suddenly switched it off. There was a moment of utter, velvet silence and then Jukie sighed and stirred, moving from behind the table as if he were leaving a barricade. His face wore an expression absorbed and almost marvelling. He stood at Kinky's feet and said at last, "It's the real strangest, isn't it?

You're here 'n then—click!" he snapped his fingers in illustration, "you ain't nowhere. How's it happen?"

Patrick was silent. The anaesthetic of shock was lifting. He began to know he had seen murder done. *Murder*.

"Kinky thought it was the strangest too," said Jukie conversationally. "He always was sayin' he aimed to see it happen. On'y he never did 'ceptin' Dipso 'n Nap 'n he was too far off when they got theirs. He was always fablin' he'd crunch Mr. Luke before he got so old they'd top him—but now you need to do it for twice, I told him, before they'll top you, so to take his time. On'y now time's gone bad on him. It's the true strangest."

Patrick heard himself say, "Yes." One should pray for the dead: but his mind refused to play that particular record, continuing instead to insist *I ask, and cannot answer, If otherwise wish I*. Then Jukie knelt beside Kinky and he was so taken aback he could only stare till he realized Jukie was slipping his hand in and out of Kinky's pockets; as he watched, Jukie drew out a wallet and the bundle of notes he had handed Kinky at the share-out. He looked in the wallet, found more notes and added them to the bundle. He put the wallet back in Kinky's pocket and looked up at Patrick, making a little joke. He said, "He c'n keep the change." And then, thinking Patrick hadn't latched on, he explained, twitching the rug over Kinky's face "I'd be a gowk to leave the loot with him. He can't never use it" and stood up, stuffing Kinky's money into the inside pocket with his own and the key-ring. As he did so, motorcycle engines started up in the distance. In the night quiet the sound was miniature and precise. Jukie raised his head, counting, as they roared tinily, one after the other, away and along the road into silence. "How four?" he said tensely. "Espresso ain't got one—I ain't there—Kinky ain't there—Rigid's is scrap since last month—should be three—no—hold it—Rigid'd take Kinky's." He relaxed a little. "Come on then. We gotta breeze too."

From habit, he pushed the deed-box deep into the bin labelled GRIT, switched off the light, opened the door, motioned

Patrick through and shut it behind them. Patrick thought *So what do I do now?* but it was like thumping on a closed door and there weren't any answers. It seemed easiest to walk with Jukie to the one-time stable yard, now converted to garages and cycle-sheds.

The cycle-shed stood open. One motor-cycle still stood in its place. Jukie walked towards it, saying over his shoulder "You can ride right behind me, noddy-boy" and even as he said it, he put his hand on the machine and it fell to pieces.

It had been most delicately balanced, most exquisitely taken apart. Jukie stood staring down at the mound of metal, his face stupid with shock, and it was Patrick who picked up the biroed note. It read: THE NUTS IS IN THE HEEP JUKIE. YOU ONNLY GOT TO LOOK.

"The mobsters," said Jukie, catching his breath. "The kinky, sordid mobsters."

"What do they mean by the heap?" asked Patrick after a moment.

"'S a rafty great mountain in the cabbage plantation," said Jukie, his voice trembling. "The gard'ner 'n us piles it with garden muck 'n the swep'-up pigeon-droppin's. No one'd find anythin' in it, never." His voice shook in a most juvenile way as he stared at the metal at his feet. "She was the real top. I on'y had her the month. The others hadn't nuthin like her. I did a ton jus' ridin' her from the mart. She was the true speedy—"

There were standing tears in his eyes. Patrick, for whom machines had no personality, looked aside, half-embarrassed, half-contemptuous; till Jukie burst out suddenly, "'N how'm goin' to breeze now? Like creepersjeez I have to blow the fastest! Say 'f the Gestapo wheels in 'n finds Kinky corpsed 'n me still daisyin' around? They'd swoop me for sure!"

"Won't they swoop you for sure anyway?" said Patrick flatly.

"Not 'f I blow speedy. I c'n go to ground where the Gestapo'll never know. I got friends—!" His voice checked as the remains of the motor-cycle caught his eye, then went on defiantly, "Not those yobbos—friends as is for real."

"I'd be surprised if any of your friends were that real," said Patrick spontaneously and as instantly wished he hadn't. He was suddenly most oddly sorry for Jukie.

His words, however, acted as a stiffener. Jukie snapped back, "Then surprise yourself, noddy-boy. I been too useful to too many. There's a heap beans I could spill." He slapped his thigh suddenly and spun round. "Onestercreep, I mus' be losin' my mind! We c'n breeze in the hearse! She don't like drivin' in the Smoke."

Brother! thought Patrick as Jukie dragged open the garage doors, disclosing Miss Culver's Mark X Seraph in all its power and glory; he watched Jukie settle himself in the driving-seat and back the great car into the yard. "C'm on," said Jukie urgently, leaning over to open the off-side door. "Hurry yourself. We got no time for dally."

Patrick got in. As he slammed the door on himself, he saw Jukie look at him in barely concealed surprise and gave him a funny little smile which acknowledged Jukie might well be surprised; come to that, he was surprised himself: he had learned enough about Jukie in the last hour or so to think a number of highly predictable things about him; but as well, there was this maverick sense of sympathy; that was the separate, decisive thing.

Jukie switched on the headlamps and infant searchlights lit the way ahead as they rolled out of the yard. Half-way along the back drive a figure leapt into the light and stood waving both arms. "That's Espresso," exclaimed Jukie, slamming on the brakes as the boy came racing up the shaft of light towards them. "Didn't those aboriginals lift him then?"

He leaned back to open the door behind him, but Espresso ran to Patrick's side of the car, mouthing urgently. As Patrick searched frantically for a handle to wind down the window, Espresso's voice sounded behind the glass. "Tell Jukie I'm staying to let the flutters go. *Tell him I'm staying.*"

"*Here!*" said Jukie impatiently, leaning across Patrick to

press a button. The air rushed in and Espresso's voice with it. "Jukie, did you hear? I'll keep me in the flutter fort and let them loose tomorrow dawn."

"Sick the flutters! We *all* gotta blow the speediest! Get *in*, Espresso!"

"I'm not blowing, Jukie. It's like I told you, I'm shackin' here for keeps. 'F the Gestapo come I'll act know-nuthin— Kinky 'n all."

"You think you will, but they'll squeeze you dry. You'll be broadcastin' before you know. Come on in, Espresso, before I knock you."

Espresso hesitated; then he smiled brilliantly, said "It's your say, Jukie" and ran round the front of the car, crossing the band of light from dark to dark. They waited. He did not come.

"Creepersjeez," said Jukie suddenly. "I mus' be simple!" He sprang out and stood staring about him in the dark. Patrick, gazing into the night on his own side, thought he could just see a figure running fast across the park in the direction of the woods and provisionally, so to speak, wished it luck.

"I mus' be *simple*," repeated Jukie, returning. He sat with his arms circling the steering-wheel, muttering "creepersjeez" to himself for some moments, then shrugged and restarted the car. The infant searchlights flowed along the shrubs bordering the drive, lit the gateposts and swung a brilliant arc along the hedge opposite as they turned into the road. The speedometer needle moved from twenty to fifty, stayed there while the car ate the stony lane, took the smoother surface of the main road beneath the wheels and moved to eighty. The road climbed constantly, the countryside fell away on either side, the fields were darker than the sky. Far away on the horizon Rum Beacon stood against the stars, impassable, for all their speed, as the hub of a giant wheel whose rim was their road.

CHAPTER THIRTEEN

The Flyaway

<hr />

"Were you expectin' I should drop you off home?" said Jukie into a silence broken only by the pft . . . pft . . . pft of approaching and passing cars.

"Not really," agreed Patrick. He felt a mounting exhilaration (*Stand in the trench, Achilles, Flame-capp'd, and shout for me*) at the sheer speed of their going, an exhilaration known before only in the midst of a headlong gallop across country with a big fence coming up fast.

"That's sharp, that's keen, cause I got things to say. You've bingoed yourself a snowball of peril, noddy-boy. You know that?"

"Yes indeed," said Patrick, with a sudden secret smile.

"That's right 'n it ain't so very highly witty. Why the dial-splitting?"

"A thought I had. Nothing massive," said Patrick, deciding not to ask if it wasn't terribly wearing, having to remember to talk in that madly special way. He glanced out of his window and saw that Rum Beacon had been left behind at last. "You were saying?"

Jukie cornered fast, the great car steady on the road. Something bi-coloured, missed by inches, swerved violently and a head came out of a window to shout after them, but they were long since past and gone. Jukie said, the speedometer needle flickering on ninety, "Like man, I conjecture you cue yourself I'm goin' t' have t' carry the full can. But the way I tell it you can cue yourself again 'n quit the smirks. It's this way: you can drag me out of the bog or I can jerk you in. You read me?"

"Neither loud *nor* clear. No."

Jukie switched on the car radio, the bruise on his forehead showing rounded and dark in the dashboard light: a female voice came suddenly, swinging "Loch Lomond". "Like man, it's this way. 'F the Gestapo net me for corpsing Kinky, my fable will be we had a stramash, 'n he had the knife 'n I tried to· grab it 'n how it got stuck in him I jus' do not know. You read me?"

"By a bright, bright light."

"But all fables need witnesses. That's Gestapo law. 'N 'f I call Siberia 'n them other aboriginals mebbe they'll prop me but more likely mebbe they'll sing. Mebbe Mr. Luke'll tell for me cause Kinky scared him rotten, so *mebbe* when he's stopped runnin' he'll be grateful." The car gulped a rise and swept down the other side.

Patrick said, "You do know we're not on the London road?"

"Yeh. I know it good."

"Oh. I thought the Smoke meant London?"

"It does. But we ain't pointin' thattaway."

"Where then? Or are we just driving?"

"Nope. We're headed Shamrock Islewise."

"*Ireland?* Whatever—?"

"Stuff it, herbert, 'n lissen. Lissen good. Whichever way they sing, the Gestapo'll misbelieve them. Siberia 'n Skidskid rate the Borstal tag 'n the others all 'cept Espresso got Approved School rating. But you're diff'rent. You're a herbert. You're Simon Pure. You swear my fable's solid 'n the cuffs'll be off like lightnin'." Patrick said nothing. Captive in the dashboard, a comedian began his patter. "Well—*sing*," said Jukie edgily.

"I'm waiting for the bit about you jerking me into the bog."

"Yeh? Well then, see, what I have in mind is if you were up beside me for runnin' drugs 'n aidin' with a corpsin'—cause it's your blade stickin' in him, you'll remember—daddy-o wouldn't be very highly chuffed, would he?" Jukie's voice became viciously toffee-nosed. "Y' see, doncher know, he' got his position to think of."

Patrick shot him a look of appreciative amusement. Then he saw Jukie was quite serious. "Good lord!" he said, contemplating him. "You really mean that!"

"Yeh," said Jukie, nettled and savage. "I do with very great sincerity mean that. So quit the smirks, herbert, 'n think on."

Patrick was silent, though his mouth twitched each time he thought Jukie's words. The car rounded an uphill bend and the band of cats'-eyes glowed in the headlights. To the applause of the studio audience, Harry Belafonte began to sing of his useless bucket. "Like man?" said Jukie furiously, breaking in.

"Like—well, like this. My pa doesn't have the kind of position that has to be kept up. He's not—" Patrick sought the just and proper word.

"What's daddy-o not?" said the edgy voice beside him.

"Sorry—can't think through the song." Patrick brushed a lock of hair from his forehead. "I know—*competing*!"

Jukie gave him a look both baffled and sceptical. "Like crazy he's not competing! Like he wouldn't be a real keen Top Citizen? Nor he wouldn't be one highly respected Talk-Shop zombie? So, 'f you don't see to play it my way, like for sure we'll fix it, me 'n the Boss Man, so's you're up beside me on such a weirdie of a charge that the news-sheets'll throw dirt till you're buried—you '*n* daddy-o." He shot Patrick a furious glance. "'N don't think that wouldn't happen cause it could—*smooth*."

A jovial orchestra played out the variety show and the virginals played in the night's play. Impatiently, Jukie spun the dial across Europe until, in Brussels, it fadged with music he found tolerable. The road levelled. He looked at Patrick's profile. "You comprehend my drift?"

"Loud and clear," said Patrick absently.

"That makes you a real keen herbert. Moreover," he said reasonably, "you'll only need cue the Gestapo my say *if* they net me——"

"I said I saw what you were getting at. I didn't say I'd do it."

"Now *lissen* noddy-boy—"

"No *you* lissen. How *could* you and your Boss Man do such a fool-proof frame-up on me that we couldn't prove it was a phoney if we had to?"

"Don't deceive yourself, noddy-boy. I've seen the Boss Man go to work—"

"And even supposing you could: my pa still wouldn't care to have me commit perjury."

"Like man, he wouldn't mind you being put inside a spell? 'N how if it finishes him for ever being Top Talk-Shop zombie?"

"You mean Prime Minister?" Patrick grinned suddenly. "Honestly, there's not the slightest chance. He's strictly amateur, you know—he only stood for the seat at all because the party was having a bad time and the local chaps thought he'd poll higher than someone from outside. And now he's there he works rather hard. But he'd stand down any time they wanted someone else in."

"Yeh man, I get you," said Jukie after a pause. "You mean he doesn't need it. He's got it all already."

It was Patrick's turn to pause and consider. Then he said justly, "I expect there is quite a lot in that. But as a matter of fact even if he were running for P.M. he'd still feel the same about me committing perjury."

"You mean", said Jukie helpfully, "he's the complete square?"

"So square he's a cube," said Patrick promptly.

Jukie laughed. "Man, that's real. 'So square he's a cube.' Man, I shall repeat that offen." They topped another rise and saw the underbellies of the clouds on the horizon pale with pinchbeck light. "What in pete's that? A fire?"

"You're welcome. . . . No, moonrise."

"Is that the truth? I never recollect seein' that before. . . . Noddy-boy, you're settin' me a problem."

"I am?"

"Yeh, you am. I thought I had you buttoned. . . . Kinky would of twisted your arm off, in a manner of speakin', but me, I see it wouldn't conclude nuthin. Ultimately."

"Why not?" said Patrick, interested.

"Say I twist your arm. So it's Hey Jukie, quit the agony, I'll sing your say. Well, but then I gotta let you go. I can't keep hold like if you was Mr. Luke 'n remind you twice a day you'll be carved 'f you sing outa tune."

"You don't think it'd be any use telling me The Thuggery would never rest till they'd avenged you?"

"What Thuggery?"

"Our name for your gang."

"Uh-*huh*. . . . Zero. 'N I'll tell you why. Cause you saw my machine fall apart. You know I'm on my tod."

"Actually, I hadn't thought of that. Why remind me?"

"I ain't. I'm more thinkin' aloud. Cause mebbe that way one of us'll inspiration somethin'. 'Cept don' tell me hold out me mitts for the cuffs. That's out from creation up."

"I don't think I would either," said Patrick, giving the matter his consideration.

"Na? I thought that was how all the good noddy-boys did when they'd done wrong? What would you do then, *pal*?"

"I don't honestly know. . . . Won't your Boss Man help?"

"Ay don' 'onessly know," said Jukie, mimicking, but nearly friendly. "Like this—he told me if ever there was bad trouble, there was this cottage in the Shamrock Isle I could shack in till he could see me right."

"Well then?"

"Well then, but does it add? Or is this cottage a real lonely lay-by where he could corpse me easy? Not himself, that's for sure, cause it wouldn't do to soil his hands seein' who he is, but one of his Big Fists could oblige."

"Who he is? How d'you mean? Who is he?"

"Now that's uncommon tackless of you, noddy-boy. You expectin' I should spill?"

"Sorry. I wasn't thinking."

Jukie shot him a quick suspicious look. Then he said in a

surprised voice, "You really mean that, don't you, noddy-boy? Y' know—you remind me of me grands, you 'n daddy-o." Patrick wondered whether he should take this as complimentary: Jukie went on, "Man, did they dig the integrity rave like it hurt us all. Though mind you, I'd not of cared to be raised in an orphans' palace. Those are very wholesome places. 'N I guess to raise me themselves was goin' against their grain, seein' I was me mam's trouble." His eyes slid sideways to see how Patrick took this: Patrick waited, attentive and interested: Jukie said irritably, "What I'm cuein' you is, me mam 'n me parent was never wed."

"That's what I thought you meant."

Since the noddy-boy was genuinely unshocked and un-embarrassed, Jukie was obliged to enlarge to show he felt the same. "Well me parent had sense. He went away so fast 'n stayed so quiet they was never able to fix him. Me mam wanted to scarper south 'n have her trouble private but me grands said no, her home was her home, 'n 'f they could hold their heads high wi' the neighbours, so could she. So I guess cause she was on'y a jill 'n kinda soft 'n scared rotten, she stayed."

"How old was she?"

"Dunno exackly. She was long way their youngest. Fifteen—sixteen mebbe. The grands never told me nuthin, d'you see, nor none of the fam'ly. They gave it me as me parent 'n me mam was killed the same time 'n it was justa coin*ci*dence as all our surnames was Clark. But neighbours can't never let well alone, can they?"

"Why, what happened?"

Jukie answered the question he hadn't asked. "Me mam had me in the push 'n a lorry came on the pavement 'n crunched her against the wall."

"How very beastly!" said Patrick, flinching.

"That's right. Not that I precisely remember, cause I were one month 'n three days at the time."

"Oh—yes, I see." Patrick let a small pause tick by. "Then how did you—d'you mean the neighbours told——"

"Yeh. Old biddy Gutch spilled it." They were cruising now at a mere seventy. "See—this happened. Me 'n my click, we useter go down to the goods yard now 'n then 'n wedge the points, like for kicks. On'y course, bein' sapsos, we did it once too offen, 'n there was me marched home by the Gestapo. So me granma cried—bein' a real easy crier, mind, any time— on'y this time old biddy Gutch was there too, 'n I'd brought shame on the fam'ly likewise—so she hit the screamin' ravers. 'N old biddy Gutch thought it time I knew what I owed so out she spoke like she had a duty, 'n there it was, the whole story, up on the wall at last. I dunno's I felt any diff'rent, not to begin with. But mebbe me grand welted me fiercer that time—he'd bin a railwayman hisself so I c'n see his angle —or mebbe I was jus' feelin' sensitive, but it came to me to wonder whether he'da given it me as fierce if me parent 'd been regular."

"Probably," said Patrick quickly, in case Jukie still needed the reassurance.

"Yeh, well, mebbe. But I still think mebbe he was weltin' me parent outa me—he hoped." Jukie shrugged and fell silent.

"So what happened then?" asked Patrick tentatively as the silence lengthened. Jukie put aside whatever thoughts he was thinking.

"Dunno as anythin' happened then. I didden seem to have much to say for meself for quite a while as I remember. There we all was, everythin' the same—'ceptin' old biddy Gutch didden get any more Welcome on the mat. The nex' real trouble was me grands wantin' me to get higher educated 'n me wantin' to opt for out."

"And who won?"

"Well—I see now I shoulda scarpered then, but I somehow didden seem to have the energy. Trouble was, me click was all workin' 'n weekends they was flashin' loot like you'd think they robbed the bank. It fair griped me."

"I know that one," agreed Patrick.

"*You?*"

"Yes," said Patrick surprised. "Why not me?"

"*How?*"

"Because there are plenty of people at school with a sight more pocket money than my pa would dream of handing me. It can be very crushing, sometimes."

"Pocket money!" said Jukie violently. "Lissen, noddy-boy. There was me on a tanner a week 'n me mates was pulling down five nicker, minimum."

"Yes, well, with me the gap's more like five bob to a pound, but——"

"There ain't a but. You got it cause daddy-o's rollin'. You got cars 'n hosses 'n butlers 'n a rafty great house 'n loot stacked in the vaults. I'm not sayin' 's I want butlers 'n that, but there's plenty other things to want for me 'n I'm startin' fr'm scratch. 'N me click was startin' in spendin' twenny nicker on a suit 'n me in me jeans still 'n the grands lookin' like I was a nutcase any time I tried to cue 'em the day 'n age."

The goad of Jukie's remembered grievances had raised the speedometer needle to ninety again. Patrick was silent, convinced he really did know how it could be, keeping company with people who had more spending money than you had, but seeing also that he would be closer to what Jukie meant if he could say that in place of his father's sober rooted income he coveted the spoils of the millionaires. Only he didn't: to sweat to buy twenty cars seemed to him wasted effort: the Merricks' middle-aged Rolls did everything needful in the way of getting them from here to there——

"Like man, they never stopped bein' savin'," exploded Jukie suddenly. "Ev'ry Sat'dy night me granma'd put the loot-box on the table 'n me grand'd lush in a bit for the rent 'n a bit for the gas 'n a bit for this 'n a bit for that, 'n the caddy with Windsor Castle'd get the holiday bit—ev'ry mortal week, till it'd bring on the screamin' ravers. So one time it got me right flamin'. There was the month's loot for the takin' 'n I whipped the lot."

"'Strewth! What happened?"

"Man, I flushed the lot. With the holiday bit there was

nearly thirty nicker. I jus' bought 'n bought. It was plushy. Then Sat'dy come again 'n that was it."

"You mean that was when they found you'd—it was gone?"

" 'You stole it' you was goin' to say, noddy-boy. That's what they called it too. Me, I never seen it like that. I reckoned they owed me a lavish, one way 'n another. Man, I explained. Onestercreep, I thought I could make 'em *see* that 'f they'd not made me get higher educated I c'd of spent me own. But it weren't no use. Man, did the old man welt me that one time. 'N what with the old lady bawlin' downstairs— man, it was a real noisy night. What the neighbours musta thought I really do not know." Jukie laughed, a not parti- cularly amused noise; and after a moment went on, " 'N it weren't as 'f it left 'em short. They drew on their savin's for the rent 'n that. It's what I always said—they'd got plenty by 'f on'y they'd a used it. But this is what curdled me. Mine that me grand couldn't load back on the shops, that he burned. Stacked it in the yard 'n poured petrol over it. Tha's what made me bitter." He looked at Patrick sideways. "You read me?"

"I can see how one would feel about that," said Patrick slowly, after a pause.

"That's real nice. It shows you got a real sympathetic imagination." Jukie gave him a quick savage glance. "But for the most of it, it's me grands you warm to." Patrick said nothing. "*Ain't* it?"

Deeply embarrassed, Patrick shoved his fingers through his hair: *No* was a lie; *Yes* pharisaical. Fortunately, before Jukie could insist on an answer, the lights of an all-night garage blazed ahead of them. "Best brim her with juice while we got the chance," said Jukie more calmly. "It's a long way to Ticklemary."

They drew in beside the pumps. The attendant, a tall pale- faced man, whose forehead reached the top of his head, came out to them. Jukie gave his order and Patrick made as if to get out. "You're not goin' no place," said Jukie, grabbing him.

"That's where you're so very, very wrong," said Patrick, indicating the board with TOILETS above an arrow.

"Yeh. Well jus' remember you ain't the jill 'n I ain't Rigid. You parole me you'll be back?"

"I parole you," said Patrick impatiently, twitching his arm free.

He walked .through the office to the Jeyes-smelling shed at the back, a trifle surprised Jukie hadn't insisted on coming too, since it would be easy enough to do a Lawrie, wait till Jukie drove off and then come back to the garage and telephone the police. So he wondered why, having thankfully removed harness and capsule from their precarious hiding-place against his middle and stowed them deep in his left-hand trouser pocket, he was walking meekly back the way he had come, through the office. Just because he had promised? Not that he didn't think promise-keeping important, but in the circumstances—yes, indeed *I saw a man this morning Who did not wish to die*—it did seem faintly fatuous. Dial 999? He stopped, hesitating, by the old-fashioned wall telephone.

Through the grime-fogged window above a desk which, besides the usual office clutter, held a pocket chess set, laid out and in play, he could see Jukie and the garage attendant talking amicably. Suppose he dialled 999—which anyway he couldn't because this was neither London nor a dialling system so he'd have to wait for the operator—and how long would they keep him explaining? *I ask, and cannot answer, If otherwise——*

Behind him, a radio relayed the B.B.C. Light Programme, music, music, music till midnight. No—not quite midnight. At 11.55 p.m. they broadcast the final news bulletin. . . . His thoughts said loudly: *Here is a police message. The police wish to interview the driver of a white saloon, number whatever, in connection with the murder of Kinky Black Check. Please get in touch with the Chief Constable telephone number whatever whatever——*

Patrick peered through the window. Then, with his fingertip he wrote on the dusty window pane PBM 533 MURDER TO IRELAND and went on out to the car.

The Flyaway

Jukie said amiably, in a very high-class voice indeed, "I was just coming to look for you, old man. Feeling better now, old chap?" And, as Patrick's eyebrows moved in surprise, said to the garage attendant, "I guess you're right. We'll take her straight back. Thanks for being so jolly decent."

He beamed wholesomely, the garage attendant nodded benevolently, and Jukie backed, turned and drove south at a gentle fifty, smiling to himself. Patrick blatantly refused to ask *What's happening now?* So Jukie told him.

"The zombie got the idea, from where I cannot just exactly cogitate, that us 'n the dray didden belong. So I explained it to him."

"Explained?"

"Yeh, explained. I fabled him good. I voiced him best Culver. Nuthin elaborate. Like we'd borrowed uncle's car 'n gone for a spin, like all high-spirited lads will do 'f you give 'em the oppo. So then he talked me back, reel nice, jus' like a father, 'n said he did oughta cue the Gestapo but on condition we spun right home, man, he wouldn't say nuthin." They came to a cross-roads and Jukie swung north. "So now I supposition as he's feelin' reel warm inside 'n goin' to tell his mates as them tearaways is reel good lads at heart 'f on'y you talk them cosy."

"'M," said Patrick non-committally, picturing the writing on the window pane and wondering whether it would be seen. It might have been better to do something more like Father Brown throwing soup plates at the wall to make sure the garage attendant remembered them. But it was three miles too late now.

They came to a market town. The traffic lights changed beside almost empty crossings and the roadway was shining black, rippled with reflected lights. Rain spotted the windscreen and the wipers, harnessed metronomes, swept their semi-circles. The Brussels broadcast became a voice speaking and Jukie moved the dial to Vienna.

"You wanta hear the resta the Jukie Clark story?" he said, out of the silence in which they had driven since the cross-roads.

Patrick roused himself. "Yes—sure—go ahead."

"We gotta talk some or I shall kip at the wheel. Or c'n you drive this dray?"

"Sorry. I can't drive anything."

"That's what I supposed, you very useless herbert. So where'd I got to?"

"There'd been blood for breakfast because you'd spent the family budget."

"That's right 'n you thought me grands were the original pies in the sky." They crossed a bridge, the water a black shine behind the ironwork. "*So*—there was this bonfire, like I said. 'N after the bonfire it seems like I got the message. From then on I was on me own. I got me a mob together 'n man, we really did rip up the town."

"Go on."

"I don' need no encouragin'. Man, am I tonguecrazy tonight! Generally, Herbert, I'm what you'd call a very reserved kinda kiddo. . . . So, like I say, we took the town apart. 'N we was too keen for the Gestapo. Wherever they was lookin' for us, we was somewhere else. Till one night me grand was homing 'n spotted us tearin' the school up. The windows we'd put paid to 'n it was just a case of gettin' to work with the choppers inside. Here, reach in me pocket 'n light up for me."

Patrick felt in Jukie's pocket for his cigarette-case, lit one and stuck it between Jukie's lips. Jukie drew deeply and the speedometer needle dropped back to seventy. "So me grand nipped round the corner 'n dialled the Gestapo. Man, were they chuffed. They came in squads fr'm all over. Was a great party, on'y me grand was niggled when they pushed me out at the copshop cause he'd thought I was at the flicks." He breathed out a long sigh of smoke. "So the nex' thing, we was all lined up in court (the juvenile issue) 'n one got this 'n one got that 'n they was goin' to put me on probation cause though I was the leader they'd not seen me dial round

there before 'n I came fr'm a good home. 'N then me grand
spoke his piece." Jukie drew on his cigarette, sighed smoke
and drew again. "Like man, I should certainly ha' known sumthin was comin' cause this was the one only time he'd not
welted me any. So what he was sayin' was he'd done his best,
but I was too much for him 'n me granma was ailin' cause
of the worry I caused. So he reckoned they was both too
old 'n he'd take it a favour 'f the Gestapo'd lift me off their
backs. So I got me Approved School."

They were passing a village hall strung with fairy lights
for a dance. There was a moment of colour and people and
gaiety and then they were past and into the darkness again.

"Not that it wasn't a highly civilized cage. There's hulks
where you stand in line 'n move at the double, but our Top
Brass didden use that jazz. He jus' cruised it real matey 'n
we got on with it nice 'n easy. Man did I make the big error
with him."

"How?"

"Cause the first week I settled he was the original marsh-
mallow 'n it was for me to play it cool. There's some goes
in kickin' 'n some as strolls it. 'N how I saw it, 'f you stay
kickin' you're liable to get broke, 'f you keep strollin' you
can stay yourself. So I co-operated. I was model. I was the
mos' reformed Yessir Nosir you ever saw. 'N in jus' one month
he had me there in his study 'n *man* did he peel the rind off.
There wasn't nuthin I could say he couldn't twist round the
way it really was. Man, he had me weepin' like it was real
tears. So I flipped. That very night I flipped. He was the mos'
dangerous citizen I ever encountered."

"What did they do when they caught you?"

"Man, don't give me shudders. On'y they never did cause
I got me head down so speedy. See, I hopped a lorry that
night 'n it took me clear through to Maudie's, 'n jus' as I
was takin' a shufti through the gate she stomped up behind.
N how it was—like it was luck I latched on so quick—she
took me for some sapso who'd come answerin' her advert
for flutter-boy in the local news-shout. 'N what was for luck

also, when she asked me where I was from, I gave her some name I'd seen as we was comin' through way out. So then it went how she told me I musta been at Ley-on-Rushton Secondary 'n that bein' so she wouldn't want references cause the headmaster was a real square 'n havin' been under him was a reference in itself. So I was in. Most especial I was in when she latched on I wasn't particular what she paid 'n I was truly anxious to live in 'n be on call mornin', noon 'n night."

"She was asking for it," said Patrick derisively. "Besides—I know Ley-on-Rushton's a good way from Culverstone but keeping that up must have been a touch tricky, wasn't it?"

"Man, it was all of it tricky. To tell for real, I thought it was clothes 'n me fam'ly in Ley-on-whatsit as would trip me, but it went the one helped the other. Like I say, she wasn't never lavish with the lushin' out, it was take the half-crown Fridays 'n fable thanks. But she did hold I oughta get to see me ever-lovin' near ones once a month 'n for that she lushed me the fare. So just in time I'd enough for new duds. Not that Maudie'd ever noticed I hadn't no luggage but the serfs was startin' to question. Was lucky what we wore in the cage wasn't painted with the broad arrow. Course, 'f I'd been situated diff'rent I'da breezed the first week, but bein' how it was I hadn't no option."

"So how did the smuggling racket start?"

"See, how it gave was this. I was slavin' unnatural cause keepin' me head down was the needful. So I'd work all hours 'n gobble the gristle the madam cook dished out 'n not make meself conspicuous payday. So Maudie reckoned she'd hooked a good thing. She notioned there was other kiddos itchin' for slavery. So how she worked it, she nattered to the padre 'n he worked it with some Youth Grouper in the Smoke to send down good keen lads who'd mebbe gone a little wrong but on'y needed a spell in the outback to help them adjust 'n turn their leaves. 'N that, d'you see, was top-class social do-good 'n likewise practically free labour for Maudie. Maudie's not slow. Light me one, Herbert."

Patrick did so. Jukie took a long drag and said, "Well, they wasn't much. Twisters as want to straighten is dregsville. 'N then Espresso came. 'N Espresso does really dig the flutters 'n he told his Da, who is—was—a king flutter operator. 'N his Da told the Boss Man who was jus' then open to bein' told a new way of importin' spice, havin' jus' suffered what you might call a crippling loss. So the Boss Man came down for a shufti—at night, seein' it wouldn't have done for Maudie to take a shufti at him. So while Maudie had her feet up with a good book I showed him what he'd come to see. Which was the flutter fort. You reading me, Herbert?"

"Loud and clear."

"So he said it was keen 'n he'd graft it so the Youth Carve-up always sent the right kiddos—innocent o' course, not realizin' the strings was jerkin'. 'N when the Gestapo locals got round to askin' Maudie, very polite, what we was all in aid of, I was kinda mixed in with the rest 'n they never looked me over special." Jukie laughed.

A woman's voice welled from the radio: honey-sweet and husky, resonant as a viola, quite unmistakable: the one and only Marlene Dietrich singing in her native German "Where Have All The Flowers Gone?". As he listened, Patrick thought a sketchy English version at the beginning of each verse: *Where have the flowers gone? The young girls have picked them all: To give to the young men: Who have gone to be soldiers: And lie in graveyards, every one: Where now the flowers grow. . . . Where have the flowers gone? The young girls have picked them all. . . . Why will they never learn . . .* the voice sighed a last note; faded. . . .

He realized suddenly that the speedometer needle was dropping back and back: that the car was slowing, had stopped and that the radio was silent, the headlamps out. In the silence, the night wind badgered the windows. And there was another sound: which he did not at once identify as Jukie's breathing.

Moonlight and tree shadows alternated along the road; moonlight reflected into the car from the bonnet, showing Jukie's face as ivory, his eyes, mouth and nostrils pebble-black.

No louder than the shuddering rasp of his breathing he was saying, "It's jus' got me—it's jus' got me——"

"*What's* got you? Jukie, what's the matter?"

"He's dead. Kinky's *dead*."

But of course Kinky was dead. That was why they were here, on this nameless road, with all the clocks in England ticking on to midnight. Patrick stared at Jukie who was rubbing his hand across and across his face in a fumbling sick fashion. And then, while he was still wordless, Jukie said rapidly "I gotta breathe. There's no air. I gotta breathe", got the door open and half-fell into the road. He stumbled to a milestone on the verge and sat slumped, his head in his hands.

Patrick got out too, wondering what came next. The night wind, damply fresh, blew between them. Presently, Jukie took his head out of his hands and stared at and past Patrick, shivering. He said, his voice unsteady, "See 'f Maudie's reviver's in the pocket. I can't seem to stop meself."

Patrick groped inside the pocket on the open door and found a bottle whose label read *Sal Volatile*. "This?"

"Tha's it. She won't carry spirits, drivin'. On'y it needs water." Jukie put his head back in his hands.

Yes, and if it needs water it needs a cup, thought Patrick, exasperated. But it struck him that Maudie Culver must know that too and, searching the pocket again, he found a collapsible picnic-cup. So now all it needed was water.

He looked crossly about him and saw that a nearish clump of trees half-hid a solitary cottage. "Look," he said, "I'm going to try there. With any luck there'll be an outside tap. I won't be long."

He waited a moment, but either Jukie hadn't heard or he couldn't answer; so he ran along the particoloured road to the low, white-painted fence and gate and lifted the latch. The cottage slept, curtains drawn.

There was no outside tap, only a cinder path which crunched. Prowling round, he came to an uncurtained kitchen window, the sink, like all sinks, just behind the pane. He gave the window a little upward push and it moved. He eased it gently up and turned the tap to the merest trickle. He held the cup beneath it and the pipe began to creak and groan and thump. In the still night the noise was enormous.

He stood petrified. Then he turned the tap to a rush, turned it off and pulled the window down. Carrying the full cup he could not run. *Stand in the trench, Achilles—*

As he edged past the back door a flutter of paper caught his eye. Held by a drawing-pin and blotted with rain the half-sheet read: *Baker, milkman. Don't leave none till Friday and oblige Mrs. Denny.* Patrick said "'Strewth!", blew the hair from his forehead and walked sedately back to the car.

Seemingly, Jukie hadn't moved. Patrick poured sal volatile into the cup and held it out, saying, "Here you are." Jukie took his head out of his hands. He gazed at Patrick and at the cup held out to him. "Your sal volatile," said Patrick patiently.

Jukie made a sound of recognition. He took the cup in shaking hands, gulped, shuddered and gulped again. Patrick waited. Jukie shut his eyes and sat head drooping, cup dangling. Presently, still looking down, he sighed and said shamefacedly, "Tha's better. Dunno what it was got me, but onestercreep it shook me rigid." He looked up and said, "You don't read me, do you? Can't say I read myself all that good. You think I'm a nut-case?"

"Of course not. But you knew that you'd—that he was dead. You knew before we came away."

"*Corpsed* I knew. *Corpsed* is what we fable each other for threats. But dead—" He stopped, reminding Patrick suddenly of a sweating, ears-back, eye-rolling horse shying from something his rider couldn't see.

"Dead is *what*?" said Patrick firmly.

Jukie's glance went away from him and down the road. Almost inaudibly he said, "The flip-top box 'n the earth piled back 'n your number's zero." Still staring away he said, "How did you know Kinky was? D'you have a secret waggle like the Masons?"

The Flyaway

"How did I know Kinky *was*? Was what? Dead?"

"A Holy Roman," said Jukie surprised. "What else?" His eyes searched Patrick's face. "Then how come you hand him the beads, Herbert? I fabled me you somehow knew."

Patrick found he had sat down in the car doorway. He knew his face had gone white because he'd felt the blood leave it, something he'd never felt before. He heard himself say, "No. No idea."

"But you handed him the beads," insisted Jukie.

"I know. I still don't know why." In his turn Patrick looked away along the road. "I wish I'd known at the time."

"Why do you scare?" said Jukie after a moment, watching him. Then, as Patrick did not answer, he said, smiling carefully, "Kinky useta scare too, whiles. Mos' times he knew it was cobweb but times it seemed like it was still under his skin. 'N then he'd say the way he was actin', he'd get Purgatory for nearly ever, even if he spilled the entire death-bed confess. 'N 'f he didn't, then he'd fry for sure. It really did hand him the shakes when he had the mood on him."

Patrick was silent, his thoughts pinned to that moment on the path outside the storeroom and Jukie watched him, his hands slack between his knees. He said, holding the smile, "Once he had me promise I'd see a priest got to him before he snuffed. 'N I gotta see he grabbed his beads 'n kissed the crucifix, I didden exactly comprehend for why—something indulgent is how it stays with me. But even supposin' I'd remembered, which I didn't, there wasn't time for a priest, was there?"

"No."

"'N you handing him your beads would be the samewise?"

"Not for a plenary indulgence. Only for an affirmation of faith."

"Is that as good?"

"I've no idea."

"You *mus'* know. Your mob all spell the book of rules."

"It's all very well to talk about rules but even the Pope couldn't tell you how God finally reckons it. Besides——"

"Besides what?"

"I don't think Kinky had any idea he was dying. I'm sure he didn't know it was a rosary I'd given him. So he couldn't—wouldn't have——"

"Put himself right?" said Jukie helpfully. "Uh-huh. Well then, there's another thing he made me promise. He said suppose it happened too quick for a priest or the beads—like it did—a priest could come and sprinkle him on condition. You know *that* one?"

"Conditional absolution. But I *think* it's only valid if it's administered up to an hour after death."

"Like man, it's too late?" Bravado clashed with uneasiness. "You *sure*?"

"Not absolutely. You'd have to ask a priest. And anyway, I don't suppose they give conditional absolution just like that. I mean—you don't just anoint someone with holy oil and say the right prayers and that's it, you're in. They'd be almost sure to want some evidence that at the moment of death he wanted to *be* in."

"Like man, you were there. You can fable."

"What on earth good would that be?"

There was a pause for mutual, exasperated incomprehension.

"You know something, Herbert?" said Jukie, his voice loud and sudden. "I need nourishment. 'S why the morbids are givin' me a whirl. Reach into Maudie's larder 'n hand the eats."

Patrick realized he was hungry too. He got up, opened the glove locker as Jukie told him and found two one-pound slabs of plain and nut-milk chocolate, a packet of Bath Olivers and a vacuum flask filled with cold black coffee.

"Maudie anticipates a tyre might blow in the wilderness 'n her miss one entire meal," said Jukie sardonically as Patrick slid from the driving-seat, clutching these things. "Dish me half of each. Man, are the pangs chewing me."

They ate and drank, not talking, but exchanging friendly glances from time to time. They could easily, thought Patrick, wondering a little, have been friends in the midst of some cheerful, idiot escapade: except that the wind-strummed telephone lines above their head must have carried their description hours ago; and by now too, the Boss Man could have sent out his orders. "If it were me I'd be scared white," thought Patrick, swallowing the last of the chocolate and a last gulp of coffee to kill the sweetness; and he glanced across, wondering what it felt like to be Jukie at this moment.

He met Jukie's gaze full. He had evidently been staring at Patrick for some moments for as their eyes met Jukie's shifted instinctively. In an almost expressionless voice he said. "How long d'you reckon we got?"

Back in the garage the radio said politely, "That is the end of the late news summary, but before we close down here is a police message. The police wish to interview the driver of a white saloon car, a Seraph Mark X, registration number PBM 533, in connection with the death of a youth earlier this evening. The police have issued the following description: fair hair, blue eyes, fresh complexion, aged between sixteen and seventeen, height about five feet seven inches. When last seen he was wearing a black pullover and cavalry twill trousers. He may be accompanied by a younger boy, between fifteen and sixteen. This boy has dark hair, hazel eyes. . . ."

The garage attendant, intent on chess, the words a half-heard accompaniment of accustomed sound, suddenly caught their meaning. A white saloon—a Seraph—two boys——

"I'll just repeat the details. A white Seraph Mark X, registration number PBM 533——"

The garage attendant raised his head, the better to listen: and on the window pane the writing showed clear and black as the moon rose above the elms and shone full on the glass.

"To get to Ireland?" said Patrick. "No idea. I suppose it depends how soon—"

"Na, not that." Jukie's glance flicked Patrick and went away again. "I mean before they drop it."

The Flyaway

"Drop what?"

"The H, Herbert, the H. Don't they speak of it where you hive? I thought mebbe they'd cue daddy-o the date."

Patrick looked at him warily, but Jukie's face was cold and blank; so he said lightly, "Well if they have he hasn't told me."

"I mean it serious," said Jukie in his edgy voice.

"But you can't honestly think the Prime Minister keeps a Super Top Secret file labelled 'Date of the Drop' for handing round among his friends?"

Jukie shifted uneasily on his milestone. "I'm not talking random. Somebody somewhere's gotta know the date. Tha's on'y sense. Lissen—when I was in Approved School there was a very famous Methuselah zombie on the talk box telling how it was a strictly dicey time 'n mos' likely it'd drop next week, but he was wrong, it didn't, so we all breathed."

"One more old man who has abolished God and is now afraid to die," said Patrick, trying out a sentence which had been in his head for some time.

"Tha's right, the same oldie as utters there ain't nuthin after, not like you 'n Kinky fable. 'N it come to me 'f we was due for cremation that fast 'n nuthin comin', it on'y made sense 'f you grabbed the loot the fastest, never mind how. 'N flushed it the fastest, natch. Cause there's no more time for me grands' loot-boxes 'n all that savin' jazz." He put his head in his hands and said, "I'm talkin' on again. It's that song always gets me. The kiddos under the grass 'n the birds handin' blooms to the nex' lot of sapsos." His voice wavered as if it were going out of control, but he went on, "'N now I've handed Kinky his 'n he's havin' nuthin for ever."

His head was still in his hands and Patrick was almost sure he was weeping. Various comments presented themselves but in the end he chose to say, "I brought the knife, so I'm in on it too." Since Jukie didn't answer, he persevered, "If I hadn't brought it, you wouldn't have had it handy to throw just at that particular moment."

Jukie moved his fingers slightly as if he were wiping tears.

He said in a thickened voice, "You don't have to worry, Herbert. The Gestapo'll never swoop you for that."

"I wasn't actually thinking of it from the Gestapo angle."

Jukie made an odd little noise, something like a laugh. He said, "You gotta conscience, Herbert. I said you 'n me grands was very closely resembled." His face came up, half-smiling and smudged with the tears he was now openly wiping away with the back of his hand. He stood up and said, "We gotta blow, Herbert. Thing is, which way to go?"

CHAPTER FOURTEEN

The Homing Instinct

Patrick got up too, not sorry this conversation seemed to be over. "You mean we're lost? I did wonder were we on the right road—"

"Which we are. Like I'm homing. I jus' query—"

"Query what?"

"Suppose I make the Emerald Isle? Suppose I make the Boss Man's cottage? How crafty would I be playing it?"

"But you said—"

"'N so did he. On'y he wasn't thinkin' murder—", Jukie checked almost imperceptibly, "—when he cued me that. Jus' the Gestapo stumblin' the flutter-'n-spice import 'n me lyin' the lowest till the Gestapo got lost."

"Oh," said Patrick slowly. "Yes."

"See, Herbert, he's a dicey kinda citizen. I never been certain he mightn't beckon me over 'n lose me in a bog. But I'da chanced it in other certain circumstances. On'y this—" He checked: and seemed to pick up the thread a sentence or so further on. "This lottery he needn't even bog me. He c'n just have a word drifted to the Gestapo's lugholes 'n I'm safe to do my twelve or whatever longest pleasures our Top Chick."

Detained at Her Majesty's pleasure translated Patrick's built-in interpreter. And then Jukie was staring at him with a blind wild look and saying, "*Twelve years!* Twelve everlastin' years! That's buryin' alive! Man, I'd be twenny-*eight* before I'm loosed!—"

Patrick, equally appalled, found nothing to say. Jukie said

in a stifled voice "Go on, get in, Herbert" and following, slid in to the driving-seat. He slammed the door and, shivering, lit a cigarette. He had smoked that and half another before he spoke again. "So where to?"

"Could—would your grandparents—"

"Me grands 'd say I'd come to me bad end 'n do a public service turnin' me in. Think on, Herbert. Me think-box is fused."

Patrick bit the ball of his thumb: the right lawful deed would be to hand Jukie over to the police: the right romantic one, to help him escape: if he had had no notion how this could be done, a prudent neutrality might have been possible, but he knew very well what he himself would have tried. Shutting his eyes, he tried to order his thoughts: *con*: Jukie had murdered Kinky and smuggled drugs; *pro*? There was no pro. Except that he himself had put the knife into Jukie's hand. He opened his eyes and said, "If it were me, I'd try the ship."

"On'y there'll be eyes on the ports 'n a passport I do not have."

He hadn't latched on. So there was no need——

"The ship you say is coming for the flutters."

Jukie struck the steering-wheel so hard that his hand slipped and the klaxon blared. "Herbert, you are a razor-edge! What hour is it? Ten past one? They'll be nosin' in sixish—"

"Where?"

"The estuary, where else? 'N 'f I give the signal they'll send a skiff. Herbert, it is the perfect! On'y—I gotta get there before the flutters."

"Well, we've time enough for that. More probably."

"How?"

Patrick glanced at him. Carefully unemphatic he said, "Because the police are bound to have been to Monks' Culvery. And they'll know about the Dovecote because Lawrie will have told them. So Espresso may never have a chance to get the flutters away."

"I misremembered." After a silence he said slowly, "Espresso'll sing. He'll hand it them in clear. Not cause he's a real stool, but cause he talks too fluent. So it's odds the Gestapo'll be waitin' for the steamboat too. But one thing Espresso could misremember—that we c'n wave the steamboat off 'n she'll sail on 'n come back tomorrer. 'F we c'n make the signal-box before she makes the estuary—"

"What signal-box?"

Fractionally, Jukie hesitated. Then he said, "You seen the flag-staff on the cliffs between Lodden Point 'n Great Bells Head? Well, for warnin', we run the jack up. Like it's a great teenage rag week. We'll circle 'n come to it fr'm the Yetland Cove side."

"That'll cut it a bit fine. If only we could go through Culverstone. Someone was bonkers when they plonked the vicarage slap across the road like that."

"Yeh. But she", Jukie patted the steering-wheel, "c'n do twenny 'n a ton without pushing. I reckon it's a go."

"Where will you hide her? Or else they'll know we've come back."

"Not her—she'll go over Great Bells with my very sincere regret. 'N they'll mebbe congratulate themselves I drowned with her. No—it's me I gotta hide. On'y where?"

Patrick bit the ball of his thumb again. He knew one place Jukie could hide in safety and he did not want to offer it in the least: he could not think why he felt this absolute compulsion to do so. He said rather desperately, "Where's your usual hide-out?"

"You kiddin'?" said Jukie, his voice suddenly forlorn. "Nowhere as I c'n be sure nobody won't uncover to get themselves good with the Gestapo."

Patrick shoved his hands deep into his pockets. "I have a place."

"You have? Where?"

"At home. It's a secret room. The only thing is," he hesitated and then went on firmly, "I'm only taking you there blindfolded. Does that make you very insulted?"

"You comin' the acid-drop?" said Jukie with an odd little grin. "I'll swallow it. 'N where will you be?"

"With you, I suppose. Where else?"

"No, now lissen, Herbert. That'd be a rafty great waste. Where you want to be is out in the open, limpin' home in the light of dawn 'n wailin' to one 'n all how I shoved you outa the dray 'n went on to Liverpool. That way they'll all go tearin' off—"

Patrick felt as if someone had burst a paper-bag behind him. He heard himself say, "But I've done that."

"You have? How?"

"I wrote on a window at that garage."

Jukie looked at him. There was a long moment while he chose visibly between fury and an astonished respect. At last he said, "Herbert, I underestimated you. You are a really very ice-cool operator. So then it's simple. All you gotta do is say it again in person."

"No," said Patrick. "That I can't do."

"Can't? Onestercreep, why not? You done it once."

"But then I thought it was true."

"Now lissen Herbert. You showed me how I could flip. You're takin' me where I c'n keep my head down. All I'm askin' is you put the icin' on—"

"No."

"But for *why*? Like man, it's not *logical*. Lissen—the Gestapo'll be dead choked with you anyway once they graft you aided me. It won't make no diff'rence——"

"I know. I'm not saying one's all right and the other's all wrong."

"Then *why not*? Just cue me *why not*?"

"As if you didn't know. You practically said it yourself earlier on. Because I'm Anthony Merrick's son, so they'd believe me. So *now* what? I can get out all right. You care to go on and see how you make out on your tod?"

Jukie looked at him, heaved a deep sigh and let in the clutch. "You want to watch that temper, Herbert. 'N you know what? One day I'm going to take you home with me 'n introduce you to me grands. They'll take to you, Herbert. They really will."

He backed into a lane, turned the car, and accelerated on to the by-road. Then, suddenly, he braked.

"What now?" said Patrick, surprised.

Jukie looked back through the rear window. "Yeh, I thought so. See, there's a chat-box back the way we come——"

"What d'you want a telephone for?"

Jukie went on looking back. "Like man, Kinky still weights me. That I didn't do nuthin."

"Why should you worry? You think one goes out like a light."

"That's right, I do. But it niggles me he may be sufferin' torments jus' the same."

"But if there's nothing, how *can* anything be happening to him?"

"Cause I see it this way. I reckon it happens the way you believe. *I* believe there's nuthin, so f'r me it'll be zero. Kinky believed this other thing, so f'r him it'll be his way. That's what I reckon."

Do-it-yourself theology, delivered with a portentous air of private revelation, usually made Patrick want to giggle. This was one of the few occasions when he felt merely baffled. After a moment he said, "So what d'you want to do?"

"Priests 're like doctors, aren't they? You c'n rouse them any time?"

"I suppose so. If it's very urgent."

"It is urgent. I want to know if Kinky can't still have his conditional what-name."

"I suppose there's no harm in asking——"

"Yeh, well, I'd feel more comfortable in m'self——"

"—but if it's Father Hunt he'll probably tell you to have faith in the infinite mercy of God."

"I'd like it a touch less chancy for him 'n that. Get on then, Herbert. Dial some."

"*Me?* I thought you——"

"Me dial a pope-shouter? You kiddin'? This is your speciality, Herbert. Get chattin'."

Patrick looked at him. Then he said, most reluctantly, "Oh all right. If it'll make you feel any better. What's Kinky's real name?"

"Why d'you want to know that?"

"Because he can't be absolved as Kinky. At least, I don't think so."

Jukie hesitated; frowning, it seemed to Patrick, from forgetfulness rather than caution. "It's Bernard then. Bernard Livesey."

As he walked back up the hill to the telephone kiosk, it occurred to Patrick that unless he could say what he had to under the seal of the confessional it was going to be a mighty odd conversation. He searched the directory in the patch of moonlight splashing the interior and found that of the three entries under *Catholic Churches* none read *Colebridge—Our Lady Immaculate*: so they were outside their own district and whoever he spoke to would be a complete stranger. He was just making his greatly relieved choice between St. Joseph's, St. Theresa's and Our Lady of Fatima when a shadow darkened the page and Jukie was dragging at his elbow saying between gasps, "Come outa there."

"Why? What's happened?"

"Nuthin yet. I hope. Come *out*."

Patrick came. "What on earth's the matter? I was just—"

Jukie leaned against the door, his chest still heaving. "Yeh, Herbert. What was you just?"

"Looking up the number. What else?"

Jukie shut his eyes, drew a long breath and tried to command his breathing. "You've not spoken to no one yet?"

"Not even the operator."

"That's good. Leave it then."

"With pleasure. It was your idea."

"Yeh. I musta been simple. You'da put the Gestapo on our tail inside a minute. Like at the garage."

Patrick looked at him. Jukie was still gasping, his eyes shut with relief and exhaustion. He had probably, thought Patrick, broken the world record for the 150 yards uphill sprint: and after a pause he said mildly, "I wouldn't have, you know. I never even thought of it."

"You would have. When he asked the questions."

"I wasn't going to answer them unless he made it seal of the confessional stuff. Anyway, he might not have asked. The Gestapo side of it wouldn't be his affair."

Jukie opened his eyes and stood staring at nothing. Presently he said, "Mebbe you're cueing me right. But I see it dicey. C'm on, Herbert. We'll keep movin'."

Patrick shrugged his arm free and came. They had covered half the distance to the car when Jukie said, half-apologetically, "Like man, how I see it, while you're with me, you're *with* me. But once start talking to the zombies 'n you'd be with *them* again. You read me?"

"I'm not stupid. . . . I don't *think* it's true."

"Mebbe not. 'N then mebbe you'd find another garage window some place. 'N then they'd snare me same's 'f you meant to spill fr'm the first. See, Herbert?"

"I see. It must be very wearing, never being able to trust anyone completely."

"Yeh, 'tis so. I trusted me grands till they handed me over 'n after that I never trust no one. Mind Herbert, I don't expect no one to be so simple as to trust me neither. 'F the Gestapo was to lay me 'n chance to say they'd see me right 'f I sing, *man*, so they'd give me my ticket outa the country, strickly no return, I'd be singin' like it was grand opera 'n the full orchestra 'n himself wavin' the little stick." And then he caught his breath and the silence was sharp as an exclamation point.

They walked on. Overhead, thin cloud began to move across the moon. Patrick kept his eyes on the car with its doors open like blunt wings, hoping he looked as if he thought the phrase merely a figure of speech, while Jukie's eyes searched his face in a succession of tense, furtive glances. As they reached the car he said "About Kinky—d'you want me to ask Father Hunt about him once you're away?" and sensed the tension go out of Jukie like air from a punctured tyre.

"Yeh, I been thinking about that. It come to me another thing Kinky spoke on," said Jukie as they got into the car, slamming the doors on themselves. "He said before we passed his loot to his sister to lush a pope-shouter enough for saying a few billion masses for him. His sister wouldn't exactly not think on it, he said, but she was a chick as suffered if she had to lavish for anyone but her. He said as it was priced a crown a go—right?"

"It's five shillings if you can afford five shillings."

"Yeh, well, he c'n do that." Jukie pulled the wad of notes from his pocket, peeled one off and handed it to Patrick. "That enough?"

"No one could tell you that," said Patrick, regarding the five pound note he was holding.

"That so? 'S queer, but Kinky seemed to have it a deal more cut 'n dried than you do, Herbert." Jukie pocketed the wad, his eyes on Patrick. "Spill the pensive."

"That you're not being madly generous to Kinky with Kinky's loot."

"That's readin' it one way. Readin' it another, what's in my pockets is my total till I find me another livin'. You gotta be practical, Herbert. Now 'f you c'd tell me exactly how many'd get him clear, that'd be sumthin' else. But as I read it, I could hand you the whole issue 'n he could still be sufferin' or mebbe after all jus' one'll open him those pearly gates. So", Jukie flicked the note, "the lush-out stays at that. Read me?"

"I read you. . . . What about his sister?"

"That's a very very practical chick as don't need nobody doin' nuthin for her. She's cut diamond, Linda is. Kinky was us' sentimental for her, that's all. So don't try thinkin' any more ways to get the loot flippin' from me, cause here", Jukie tapped his pocket, "is where it's homed."

Patrick decided he'd said his piece. They were on the move again and the backward-sliding hedges were beginning to blur. Jukie asked for a cigarette: Patrick lit and handed him one. Forty minutes and sixty miles, four cigarettes and a long silence were behind them when all at once the car swerved. It ran on to the verge, lurched on a pile of gravel and stopped dead with the bonnet nosing a telegraph pole. Jukie choked on a word, his hands dropping from the wheel.

"What happened?" said Patrick, startled. It had come too suddenly for fear, but he could see how close the shave had been.

"I nodded off, that's what happened." Jukie passed his hand nervously over his face. "I been feelin' it driftin' over, but I thought I c'd last out."

"Then you'd better kip right now. How long can you take? I'll wake you when it's time."

"We've not got time. Drop the window, Herbert. That'll freshen me."

He rubbed his hands over his face again and backed on to the road. Air blew into the car, shredding the smoke and staleness. They had gone another five miles at a cautious sixty, Patrick alert for the first sign of eye-closing, when Jukie braked again. "Seems like I'll *have* to kip. I got me flashes."

"Got your *what*?"

"You don't get 'em ever?" Jukie gave him a sidelong, uneasy look. "I never have met anyone else as did. Not as I get 'em offen. Jus' occasional when I been overdoin' it or things is dicey."

"But what is it—are they?"

"It's like bright little lightnin's across me peepers 'n they get more 'n more 'n I can't exackly see past 'em. 'N it feels there oughta be a massive agony, 'n so there is, somewhere, on'y it never quite hits me."

"Sounds fab."

"Yeh, well, it's that it's disablin' is the trouble. I'll get us off the road while I can mos'ly see 'n then I'll get me head down on the back seat."

"How long does it last?"

"Half-'n-hour to come 'n half-'n-hour to stay 'n half-'n-hour to go, mos'ly. We'll just have to do a steady ton after 'n hit Great Bells straight instead of circlin'."

Coasting quietly, they came suddenly to a stretch of heath. Jukie, now peering shortsightedly, turned off the road, jolted the car over the uneven ground and stopped in the middle of a clump of trees. Smiling uncertainly, he switched off the head lights, climbed blindly over into the back of the car and stretched out on the seat, turning his back on Patrick. His voice came muffled. "This is going to be a real mean go. I don't see nuthin but bright lights as don't go with sweet music this present time. Mind 'n rouse me in an hour, Herbert?"

"Yes," said Patrick to Jukie's reflection in the mirror above the windscreen.

"'F we don't make the steamboat you parole you'll hide me?"

"I parole."

"It's the doin' twelve chills me. . . . Suppose they drop the H before I'm out? I'll of had nuthin either."

Patrick said, "Now you're being morbid again."

"Yeh well. . . . Y' know, I can't get clear in me mind whether I meant to do Kinky or not, jus' that very moment. Mind, there's time I've lissened to him mouthin' off 'n I've thought *Man, I'll be corpsin' you someday* but whether I thought it jus' that very minute. . . . How did it seem to you, Herbert?"

Patrick hesitated, glanced in the mirror, hesitated again and said, "I think you meant to."

"Yeh. So do I, Herbert, really verily." He shifted around, trying for a more comfortable position and said, as he lay still again, "Like man, that kinda makes a tidier proposition. It'd be dregsville knowin' it an accident 'f the Gestapo were fakin' it a purpose. . . . Up that window, Herbert. I know fresh air is very very wholesome, but there's a rafty great gale blowin' on me."

Patrick found the right button. He waited for Jukie to say something more, but Jukie was silent. Within seconds, his breathing became regular and audible as if he slept.

Patrick looked through the windscreen. The thin cloud had trailed away and the grass beyond the trees was tarnished with moonlight, but even as he looked a thicker layer of cloud moved beneath the moon and the landscape faded. The luminous clock face on the dashboard showed just after half past one. He heaved a long silent sigh and gazed unseeingly into the darkness. It would, he thought, feel remarkably odd to be back in everyday life; yet if all (from their present point of view) went well, the moment was fast approaching when Jukie would sail away and he, Patrick, would be left to explain to everyone how very very helpful he had been. He took a quick glance at this situation, was mildly appalled by what he saw, and walked his thoughts hurriedly away. All the same, for no good reason he could think of, he hoped Jukie would make it. Provided one didn't mistake him for a friend, he was a rather likeable character: or not likeable exactly, but—

A gust of wind nudged the windscreen and the branches above the car creaked. Jukie slept as if he would never wake. The clock face showed twenty-five to two. Fifty-five minutes before Jukie was to be woken—and suppose he still couldn't see to drive, what happened then? They were miles from home—

They were much nearer Mrs. Denny's cottage.

Yes, *indeed*! Empty till Friday, no neighbours, a shed where they could hide the car—. His thoughts halted: no—they—he—couldn't. To help Jukie with what he himself could offer was one thing: but not to involve other people in—. In murder.

The memory of Kinky lying on the gravel jumped at him. He tried to drag his thoughts away but, like large and disobedient dogs, they refused to budge. They said first *I saw a man this morning Who did not wish to die* and next, from last term's school play *Unhousell'd, disappointed, unanel'd; No reckoning made, but sent to my account With all my imperfections on my head*—

The branches creaked and rain speckled the windscreen. Only three more minutes gone, fifty-two to wait. So he might usefully, he thought, fumbling automatically in his pocket, say the fifteen decades of the rosary for the repose of Kinky's soul; and the same instant remembered he had left his rosary in Kinky's hand. *So*, he would have to count on his fingers. Better begin with the *De Profundis*.

His mind said obediently *De profundis clamavi ad te, Domine: Domine, exaudi vocem meam Fiant aures tuae intendentes, in vocem deprecationis meae. Si iniquitatis observaveris.* . . . The words left him: he went back to the beginning and this time got as far as *deprecationis meae*. He began again, only to find himself in the midst of a long speculation on how to feed and exercise Regina tomorrow if he were hiding with Jukie in the priest's room. He put Regina aside. *De profundis clamavi ad te, Domine: Domine exaudi.* . . . *De profundis clamavi ad te.* . . . *De profundis clamavi . . . clamavi . . .* the words clotted and he sat up straighter. *De profundis clamavi . . . ad te . . . Domine.* . . .

He half woke, not knowing he had been asleep, the Latin still heavy on his tongue, the air in the car becalmed with staleness and sleep. Though the wind had herded the clouds eastwards it was dark still, for the moon was down and the stars in their last brightness. Instinctively, he pushed the window button and the dawn wind blew in, a freshness of chilled grass and water. The Latin went away and his mind said clearly

> *Fair broke the day this morning*
> *Against the Dardanelles;*
> *The breeze blew soft, the morn's cheeks*
> *Were cold as cold sea-shells.*

Cold as cold sea-shells he repeated to himself, acknowledging its exactness. And then he thought *morn's cheeks?* and looked at the clock and it was ten past five.

Behind him, Jukie stirred slightly, sighing.

"*Jukie!*" said Patrick, loud and urgent, leaning far over the seat back and grabbing at his shoulder. "*Jukie! Wake up! Jukie!*"

Jukie rolled on to his back. "Yeh? Wha' is it? Who's that?"

"Me—Herbert. Jukie, wake *up*! It's after five. I've been asleep too. Can you see now?"

"See? yeh—yeh. Me flashes is gone." He yawned.

"Then come *on*. We've got to get going. It's *late*. Jukie, *hurry*."

"Late? How's it late? Wha' time is it?"

"It's a quarter past five."

"Quarter past five?" said Jukie, still hazy with sleep.

"Yes, I just told you, I went to sleep too. I don't believe there's time now———"

Suddenly Jukie was climbing over into the driving-seat. "Quarter past five! Why, you scabby judas! You never meant me to make it!"

"Of course I meant you to make it! I never meant to go to sleep. I don't know when it happened even."

"Don't give me that, you hairy sordid." The car was already bumping out from under the trees. "You knew what you were doing. You didn't give me the wakeful till you cued yourself it was gone time. I musta been paralysed in me mind to trust you."

Patrick began another protest, saw its uselessness and let it die. He had been on the point of offering Mrs. Denny's cottage, but Jukie's profile, rigid with rage and concentration, dissuaded him. The car lurched over the grass, the speedometer needle swinging between sixty and eighty, and then they were on the main road. The tyres gripped, the speedometer needle rose; and for the first time since the previous evening they began to encounter traffic: at regular-seeming intervals they were meeting or passing the long-distance lorries.

One half of Patrick admired the skill and ruthlessness of Jukie's driving: the other half tensed itself for the inevitable crash as the speedometer needle wavered between a hundred and fifteen and a hundred and twenty and the tail lights of the lorries pricked the darkness ahead and were gone. Twice disaster closed with them, once on the brow of a hill where they met a lorry travelling, like themselves, on the crown of the road; and once at a hidden gateway through which a doctor's car came nosing faster than he would have risked in daytime. But the lorry swerved and the doctor braked: and the great white car rocketed steadily south past fields and woods lying idle and empty in the last of the dark.

A band of light showed along the horizon and a first scarlet segment of sun reddened the underbellies of the low-hanging clouds. The landmarks of their own countryside began to show themselves. Patrick wondered what Jukie meant to do. He would have liked to ask him: but the light grew and the road ran backwards and Jukie switched off the headlamps and the silence between them stayed unbroken.

They were into the home stretch: they had passed the crossroad which led to Mariot Chase and were heading down the switchback road which led only to the hump-backed bridge and Culverstone: Patrick thought, "So where's he making for now, Bell's Head or the estuary? This is *stupid—*"

They were up the last rise of the switchback road and over the crest and hurtling down towards the toys that were the hump-backed bridge and the village beyond. But the bridge was not its usual placid self: several match-box toy cars stood on either side, the outline of the parapet was altered and men stood and moved about and waited.

Patrick exclaimed—a curiously despairing sound. Jukie exclaimed too, furiously, and his foot stamped down on the accelerator.

"Jukie! Stop! We can't get through this way anyway!"

"Who says?"

"You know we can't! Why didn't you turn off at the crossroads? I said I'd hide you!"

"Like you woke me. I'd be simple."

A figure advanced from the group on the bridge, moved to the middle of the road and stood there, signalling them to stop. *Young Tom Catchpole*, thought Patrick, and waited for him to jump aside as they swept down towards him. But he didn't jump. He didn't budge. He went on standing there, waving them down. It was for the car to stop. *Now.*

"*Jukie, you have to stop! That's Tom!*"

But he knew as he spoke that no words would stop Jukie now and he never knew if he answered: he hit him hard on the back of the neck with the edge of his hand and, as Jukie fell forward, grabbed for the brake. *Stand in the trench Achilles, Flame-capp'd—*

But he could not reach it, for Jukie was in the way. He wrenched once at the steering-wheel and then the car took charge, flinging him sideways. It leapt a ditch, smashed through a hedge above a water meadow, somersaulted down a bank and, with a roaring noise of rending metal and breaking glass, charged, bonnet-foremost, into a tree.

The thin blue of the sky was islanded with unmoving clouds like stepping-stones. He must have been lying here a long time for the leaves on the branch-end to the extreme right of his field of vision had been fresh spring green when he had first seen them and now they were turning brown and blowing away in autumn; and now they were gone and the branch was bare and it was winter: and greyness was blowing over. Fog. Only it didn't smell like fog—

He began to be aware of a clamour of voices not very far away. Two or three different voices were shouting it was hopeless trying to get any closer, the heat was too fierce. Someone was being urged to come away, no one could live in that furnace, sir, they'd have been killed outright for sure anyway when the car struck the tree—

Would they? he wondered. Who would?

A face hung suddenly between his eyes and the sky—a scared, questioning face. It said something. It said it again before disappearing as abruptly as it had come; and in a slowly reviving part of his mind he knew that the face had been Peter's and that what he had said was *Patrick! Are you all right?* He could hear him now, shouting, "Mr. Merrick! Mr. *Merrick!* He's over here! It's all right! *He's over here!*"

Feet thudded towards him. A whole ring of faces showed suddenly against the sky: his father's, Peter's again, Tom Catchpole's, three or four unknowns under police caps. He looked up at them, wondering should he smile or something. His father's face said sharply, "Patrick! Are you hurt?"

Hurt? No, he didn't think he was hurt. Someone was down beside him, putting an arm under his shoulders to ease him up, while someone else said, "Better wait for the ambulance, sir. There may be internal injuries."

But, with Tom Catchpole's help, he was already sitting up and the world was coming into focus again. He said, half-surprised to hear his own voice, "I'm all right, I think, thanks," and his father's voice said, with the unnerved anger of un-bearable relief, "Then for goodness' sake stand up."

With Tom Catchpole's help he did so, feeling his feet sink slowly in the mud at the margin of the river. The reeds into which he had been flung lay smashed and broken from the impact. He walked forward on to dry ground, jerking bits of himself experimentally to prove he was still in good working order and his father, his voice still angry, told him to stop behaving as if he had St. Vitus's Dance: and then he saw the car.

He understood then what those earlier voices had been talking about. Flame and smoke still towered through the charred branches from the mass of distorted metal at the base of the trunk. He did not ask if Jukie too had been flung clear since it was sufficiently obvious he had not. But he stood staring at the wreckage with so stricken a face that when his father next spoke the anger had gone from his voice. He said, "Your jacket's soaking. Here—take it off and put my coat on."

They all went on up to the road.

He sat with the Inspector in one of the police cars and told him all he remembered. He couldn't tell whether the Inspector was surprised or not by Jukie's identification of the Boss Man with a top-ranking orchestral conductor; if he was, he wasn't letting on. He listened to the Inspector reading back what he had been told to make sure he had it right and watched through the car window the walk-about-and-look-busy-then-stand-and-talk activity which was all that was going on now. "Have I got everything there?" said the Inspector, finishing Patrick's statement.

Patrick nodded. Then he thought of Jukie's grands and, on the spur of the moment, offered the Inspector two pieces of fiction. One was that Jukie had turned back because he had decided to give himself up, the other was that Jukie had swerved the car in order to avoid P.C. Catchpole. The Inspector said non-committally, "I see. Of course, after what Mr. Trouncer told us we expected you to arrive in Liverpool some time during the night. But you say you slept for some hours in the car?"

Patrick blinked, wondering what all that meant, but glad the Inspector was happy with it. He said "Yes we did actually" and since that seemed to be all, climbed out on to the road. He saw their own car parked alongside the bridge and decided to go and sit in it. He hadn't been doing this for very long, watching the smoke bowling across the slow sparkling water, when Peter appeared, rather tentatively, in the car doorway. He said, "Do I join you? Or not?"

"Yes. Do. Come on in."

Peter sat down on one of the tip-up seats opposite, eyed Patrick for a moment and then said, "I may say you look a mite fragile. D'you want to hear yet what happened our side of the hill? Or not?"

"Natch," said Patrick, annoyed with himself for looking fragile but appreciating that Peter was heroically refraining from asking him to repeat his story immediately after telling it to the Inspector. "How d'you come to be here, anyway?"

"I'd rather tell all in proper order," said Peter expansively, and got down to bringing Patrick up-to-date on everything that had happened since they separated. He had just reached the bit where his mother had come out of the storeroom looking pretty peaked and saying it was all right, it wasn't Patrick, when Mr. Merrick looked in on them, saying, "Are you two bearing up? I don't think they'll keep us hanging about much longer. Then when they let us loose we'll drop

Peter and Lawrie off at Trennels, go home to breakfast and then back to Town. We can stop for luncheon on the way."

"Come and eat breakfast at Trennels," suggested Peter hospitably, but before the invitation could be either accepted or refused Patrick said, "Oh—no—look, Pa—"

"Well, what? I'd like your mother to see you really are in one piece as soon as possible."

"We can phone her. Look—Pa—this will not make you very highly chuffed—but Regina's back."

"*What?*"

"Regina. She's at home. It's all right, Pa, really. I'm not asking to have her in London. I have perfectly good plans for her future, but I need today at home to carry them out."

He gazed at his father with his exaggerated eye-batting expression of bland innocence. His father looked back at him with an expression which conveyed that at any other time he wouldn't have been won over so easily: as it was—"You can talk me round over breakfast," he said and went away again.

"That's settled," said Patrick with great satisfaction. "Go on, Pete. Your ma had just seen it was Kinky, not me."

"That his Thuggery name? Well, anyway, great relief felt by one and all—well, you know what I mean," said Peter, suddenly hearing how this sounded. "And then one of the cops we'd brought with us tottered in hauling Blue Bobblecap—Espresso?—actually, Michael Sabry if we're being formal. Anyway, Mike was in a right tizzy—trembling like a naspen and boo-hooing like Lawrie at her wettest—and Ma went maternal and he cried on her shoulder and the Inspector asked a question or two and all the beans came spilling."

"Jukie said they would."

"He was too right. When the Inspector asked Mike if he knew the Boss Man's name, Mike shrieked 'He said he'd knock me head in if I ever told—oh, me Da—me Da—' and had the panics again. And then a cop produced a cash-book he'd found and pointed something out and the Inspector looked quite pale and flabbergasted and said 'What *her*?' in a Doomsday utter and then he really turned the heat on Mike. Poor old Mike. He obviously didn't want to tell, but it was just like turning a kit-bag upside down. By the way, d'you know what Jukie's real name was?"

"Only his surname—Clark."

"*Cyril*," said Peter: but more smoke bowled across the river and he checked himself. "Well, anyway," he resumed, "when the Inspector reckoned he'd got all there was to get out of Mike he went and nattered on his car radio and then he rushed back and said he was pushing now, sharpish, and should he drop us at Trennels, and Ma said No, she'd stay with Mrs. Moxon and Olwen and Mike, so it was just Lawrie and me. And then, while we were on our way, there was a calling-all-cars to a shindy between four tearaways on Culverstone Bridge which (they thought) tied up with this case. So we steamed here."

Patrick had a sudden memory of Jukie's face as his motorcycle collapsed on the garage floor: the wreckers hadn't got far after all. He said flatly, "What was the scrap about?"

"It was a bit more lethal than that, actually. They'd gone quite a way, apparently, and then all of a twitter Yeller Feller got the panics or conscience-smit or whatever and said everybody back for Jukie. Which the others didn't fancy, natch, so he started back and they chased after him and he got as far as the bridge. And then they caught up with him and one bright custard had the stupendous notion of slewing across in front of him and that brought them all down."

"'Strewth! What a *fool*!"

"You may well say. One bike went into the river—that's what happened to the parapet—and Yeller Feller's and Red Ted's got knotted. So first they sorted Yeller Feller out, poor little nit, and then they had another right punch-up, mate, razors out, the *lot*, over the bike they had left. You've never *seen* such a shambles, just from blokes fighting. Real blood-and-gutsy. Lawrie got down on the floor of the car and didn't look, which was quite sensible really, being the way she is.

And then, of course, the cops started calling up ambulances and breakdown gangs and no one thought any more about taking us home. Which I was quite pleased about, natch. I wouldn't have fancied it much, being cut off at home, while you were still driving around with Jukie."

He paused, giving Patrick an opening if he wanted to take it, but Patrick only nodded so he went on with his story.

"Well *then* what happened—after the bods had been shovelled off the road—was a message from some man in a garage who said you'd been at his place, and the fair youth had said you were coming back, but there was also this message on the window pane. So they decided to take your word for it and got on to Liverpool and whistled up your father and he turned up about two hours ago. Looking a bit peaked, I'd say."

"Poor old pa. By the way, where *is* Lawrie?"

"Asleep, I expect. If you looked into the back of the Inspector's car she's probably still snoozing on the floor."

Patrick grinned. And then they were in the midst of one of those unexpected silences which occur when the narrator suddenly runs out of story.

"By the way," said Patrick after a while, "did Espresso—Mike—say *which* conductor was the Boss Man? I keep thinking of all the obvious ones like Malcolm Sargent and Adrian Boult and Basil Cameron but none of them——" He stopped. Peter's face was wearing an expression very similar to the one it had worn yesterday just before he'd announced that the second pigeon was a Scandaroon.

" 'None of them' is right," said Peter, very full of himself. "That was where they fooled Jukie—at least, actually, he fooled himself. You see, the person who really ran it was Mike's Da. He——"

"But—"

"No, let me tell. I know what you think, hearing it from Jukie. And having The Thuggery here did start as a sort of good works till Mike turned up. And then when he told his Da about Monks' Culvery, his Da, who is a very dodgy cove from all accounts, saw it as the opportunity of a lifetime. Because, you see, he comes from somewhere round the Persian Gulf and in the Middle East they're almost deader nuts on pigeon breeding than the Belgians are. I told you Scandaroons came from Syria, didn't I?"

"In terrific detail."

"Yes, and what's more, me boyo, there's a terrific trade in narcotics done in the Middle East, some legal, mostly otherwise. So Da knew all the right people. So he found out from Mike when Maudie would be in London, pigeon-fancying, and went round to her hotel and made his proposition."

"You mean M. Culver really is—was—*is* in it? Not just us thinking what a lark if she were?"

"Up to the neck as far as being a sleeping partner. She let the Dovecote be used and took her wodgy cut of the profits. Natch, she never went so far as to soil her hands with anything like actually tending Scandaroons or sending on drugs or any of that. But she did take wads and wads of lovely lolly—enough for rates and taxes and a nice little packet over for her own pigeons."

"But Jukie—*he* didn't seem to know any of this. He had a quite different story."

"That's right, he didn't. One of Maudie's conditions was that The Thuggery weren't to know she was in on it and that her rake-off was to be written down as pigeon sales. Mike knew, of course, but his Da had shaken him so rigid with threats of what would happen if he didn't keep his mouth shut that he obviously did. So when Da came down to inspect the Dovecote, Maudie kept right out of it, and the whole thing was apparently arranged between Da and Mike and Jukie. Only Jukie never actually knew it was *Da* who was coming. Mike was told to say 'a friend of me Da's with an interesting proposition' in case nothing came of it. And then when Jukie saw Da—you know Sir Hector Levenstein?"

"Of course."

"Well, they think his photograph was on the cover of the *Radio Times* that week. Start of the Proms or something. And

Da and Sir Hector really *are* very alike, so the Inspector said. It's the same type of face—you know—what's the word I want? The thing you mustn't be anti?"

The telepathy of friendship came to Patrick's aid. "Semitic."

"That's it. Hookish-nose, a bit swarthy and ruddy good-looking with it—anyway, it seems if you've seen Sir Hector you've seen Da. Which Jukie did, he thought, only vice versa. And apparently he was sufficiently shattered for Da to think Sir Hector a good cover. It made such a much more impressive-sounding gang, you see, than just Da and Maudie. So Mike was told to build on the idea and make out that Da was just a henchman, passing on the Boss Man's orders through Mike—and Da took massive good care, of course, that he and Jukie never met again, either as Da or Sir Hector."

"I don't think I shall ever take to crime," said Patrick, looking slightly bemused. "It all sounds much too complicated for a simple hick like me. . . . Tell me—*was* there this cottage in Ireland that Jukie thought he was making for?"

"Oh yes, that was there. It belongs to Maudie. And Mike obviously thought that if Jukie did get there he'd be safe because his Da found Jukie very useful. He thought he'd probably try to get him away to South America and they'd start again from there. They're still looking for Da, I think. But of course, no one but Da and Mike knew Maudie ought to be warned when the Scandaroon was brought down, and Mike didn't dare because of what Da had said about having his guts for garters, and Da, it seems, didn't trouble himself. So the Yard picked Maudie up coming away from the pigeon club dinner. Makes yer fink, doesn't it?"

Patrick agreed. It did. He had often thought he'd like a very nasty accident to happen to Miss Maud Culver and now it had. And it was true, as Peter had implied, that one felt more spine-chilled than pleased.

Peter sighed deeply for no particular reason and looked out of the window at the diminishing drifts of smoke on the surface of the river. And then he remembered something else. In a sudden trough of embarrassment he nerved himself to mention it. "Oh—look—Patrick—there's just one other thing——"

"Uh-huh?"

"You know—I mean—I don't know how it happened, but you know we found that—you know—your thing—your rosary—in Black Check's hand?"

"Did you now," said Patrick, teasing and unhelpful.

"Well—Ma thought, if you'd given it to him it must be—you know—because he was a Catholic too."

"Your ma can use her loaf."

"You are a nit," said Peter, scarlet-faced, but beginning to recover his poise a little. "Well, *anyway*, she thought she'd better get on to your parish priest just in case it was something he ought to know about. *I* said I didn't see what use it was by that time, but she wouldn't listen, *natch*."

"Natch. So?"

"*So* she rang him up—Father Hunt, I think she said his name was—"

"Yes, go on."

"Well, he was a bit stunned to begin with, apparently, never having seen Black Check at Mass or anything, but then he came to and said everyone was entitled to the benefit of the doubt and came buzzing over. And I don't know what happened then—I wasn't there, natch—but Ma stayed." Peter hesitated. "I think she was rather—moved, if you know what I mean. Anyway, I thought you'd probably like to know."

"Yes. So I would. Thanks very much."

"And I have your rosary here," said Peter, handing it over with the huge relieved sigh of *mission accomplished*.

"Thanks," said Patrick again, pocketing it and watching his friend return rapidly to normal. As he did so, he felt something else in his pocket—something he had quite forgotten and which was now no longer important. Even the police weren't likely to want it now. He pulled out the harness and capsule he had taken from Jukie.

"Souvenir?" he said, handing it to Peter. "Fair exchange no robbery?"

"'*Strewth!*" said Peter. "You really did get one? Why, you clever little man, you. Tell me how it's done—"

And then, as they grinned at one another, they both saw, coming across the road, the welcome sight of Mr. Merrick, with a yawning Lawrie in tow. They were on their way home.